"What ar

Susanna yelped, jerking ___ slung a shower of water ___ ___ ___ long wet hair. She scrunched the thick toweling closer, hastily covering as much of her as possible. "Get out of here!"

Her husband leaned against the door frame, biting back a grin. It shone like devilment in his eyes as his gaze traveled the length of her. "Pardon the intrusion," he said, so insincerely she wished she had something to throw at him.

Fortunately for him, she had nothing near enough but the bar of soap on the ledge. She *was* tempted. "Get out of here *immediately!*"

One shoulder shrugged. "You've seen me in the natural state. Turnabout's fair, eh?" He paused while he looked his fill.

Susanna shivered. Her teeth chattered. She was not that cold at the moment. But she *was* furious…!

Praise for LYN STONE's recent titles

The Highland Wife
"...laced with lovable characters, witty dialogue,
humor and poignancy, this is a tale to savor."
—*Romantic Times*

Bride of Trouville
"I could not stop reading this one....
Don't miss this winner!"
—*Affaire de Coeur*

The Knight's Bride
"Stone has done herself proud with this
delightful story...a cast of endearing characters
and a fresh, innovative plot."
—*Publishers Weekly*

LYN STONE

THE SCOT

HARLEQUIN®

TORONTO • NEW YORK • LONDON
AMSTERDAM • PARIS • SYDNEY • HAMBURG
STOCKHOLM • ATHENS • TOKYO • MILAN • MADRID
PRAGUE • WARSAW • BUDAPEST • AUCKLAND

ISBN 0-373-29243-0

THE SCOT

Please address questions and book requests to:
Harlequin Reader Service
U.S.: 3010 Walden Ave., P.O. Box 1325, Buffalo, NY 14269
Canadian: P.O. Box 609, Fort Erie, Ont. L2A 5X3

This book is in memory of my father, Harlan Perkins, who allowed me to make my own decisions, congratulated me when they were right and never said, "I told you so" when they were wrong.

Chapter One

Edinburgh, 1856

James Garrow slowly rotated his second tankard of ale with a thumb and forefinger as he mentally tallied the British pounds he had accrued during the past fortnight. A mere fraction of what was needed to carry the remnant of his clan through until next summer, but still better than he had anticipated. Stonework didn't pay much, but with all the new construction, it was steady. His hard-won degrees in the study of architecture were doing him precious little good.

He glanced around, grimacing ruefully at his surroundings. The Hog and Truffle Inn, despite its earthy name, did furnish clean sheets, fairly decent meals and passable ale. His private room here would have fit neatly into his garderobe back home, but the loneliness of the city notwithstanding, he'd rather have a small space than share one with a stranger. God, he'd be glad to return to the Highlands. Before the first snow, he promised himself.

His ears perked as he heard a name mentioned at the table behind him. *Eastonby. The earl?* James slouched back in his chair so that he was a few inches nearer and listened to the muted conversation with interest.

"His girl's with him, I hear," a rough voice whispered.

"So much the better," another answered in kind, the accent soft and cultured.

"Cause an outcry the like of which you ain't never heard," the other warned. "Killin' a man's one thing, but—"

"You want the money?" came the silky question. "Then you do as I say. There'll be the woman." An enticement that drew a suggestive growl.

"We'll take 'im on the road to York, then?"

A deep-throated chuckle, then the almost inaudible confirmation. "As soon as he clears the city. And no one survives. Is that clear?"

The same voice, the well-spoken one, then gave the exact location of what James understood as a planned assassination and continued to discuss the details of what needed to be done.

Were the men bloody drunk to bandy plans such as this in a public room? He noted the rest of the clientele who were few in number, deep in their cups and sitting far enough away they could not possibly have overheard. He was not that close by himself, but his own hearing was such that folk generally marveled at it.

Since he had yet to see their faces, James wondered how he could manage without getting up, walking halfway around their table and alerting them to the fact that he had heard what they said.

Instead, he quietly sat up, then leaned forward on the table and slid off to the floor in a heap, raking his tankard in a wide arc as he fell.

As he'd expected, the men who had been speaking

jerked around to see what had caused the commotion. Cursing him and complaining loudly about the ale splash, they rose. James grinned up at them through half-closed eyes until he'd set their faces in his mind, then sighed loudly and feigned an unconscious stupor. The smaller of the two kicked him soundly in the leg, but he lay still. Then they stalked out of the pub, still bellyaching about being splattered.

He had recognized neither of them. When the door slammed behind them, James rolled to his side and made a show of struggling to his feet. Stumbling drunkenly out the back way as if to answer nature's call, he dropped the guise once outside and managed to reach the front of the inn just as the men separated. He kept to the shadows and followed the toff. Eastonby should be warned.

The next morning, James arose quite early, dressed in his best suit and set out for the palace, hoping the earl had not yet left, if indeed that was where he was staying. A peer would likely have a standing invitation there, James thought.

As it happened, the earl was not a guest in the palace, but James was able to verify that the man was still in the city.

After a good deal of trouble and a long walk through the city, James found himself impatiently waiting to be granted an audience with Eastonby at the Royal Arms Hotel.

He reminded himself repeatedly why saving an English earl who starved his tenants and neglected his estate was a worthwhile endeavor. But there was also a female at risk, he recalled. James couldn't leave without doing what he could to prevent her murder.

"This way," ordered a liveried employee who had let him upstairs to the third floor and knocked on the door.

When they were prompted to enter, James followed the man into a well-appointed sitting room where sat a distinguished gray-haired gentleman at a large writing desk blotting the signature on some sort of document. "Mr. Garrow, my lord," said the footman as he backed out the room. The earl continued what he was doing.

Through the doorway to another chamber of the suite, James spied a red-haired lass curled in a chair reading a book.

At first he thought her but a half-grown bairn since he saw the chair in profile. She sat crossways, her back against the one arm and her legs draped over the other, facing him. All he could see was her bowed head, with its bonny mass of fiery ringlets over the top of the open book which rested on her knees. Swinging idly from the snowy mass of petticoats were slender ankles and small stockinged feet. She wiggled her toes.

That must be the girl the men meant to kill and worse. She looked up from her page and James smiled at her. She frowned back, immediately hopped up, strode to the door and firmly shut it. She was no bairn, he realized, but a woman indeed. A bonny one at that, of some twenty years more or less.

The man at the desk seemed hardly more eager to acknowledge a guest than the lass had been. Since James had no more time to waste here, he took the initiative. "Are you Lord Eastonby, then?" he asked.

The man turned, put aside his pen, took an impatient breath and confirmed his identity. "I am. State your business. Mr. Garrow, is it?"

"Aye, laird of Galioch, which is hard by your place in the North."

"Drevers?" the earl asked.

"Aye, but that's not why I've come. I chanced to

o'erhear a threat to you last eve and took it upon myself to warn you.''

The earl's mouth twisted in a wry expression. ''And I am to reward you richly for this information, I suppose?''

James took a deep breath and tamped down his anger. Some people were born suspicious, he reckoned. He shouldn't cast any stones since he was none too trusting himself. ''Nay, I'll not require coin for doing what I think's right. There's a plan to waylay you at Solly's Copse outside the city and do away with you and who-ever's with you.'' He glanced meaningfully toward the door the lass had closed. ''They mentioned a woman.''

The earl's eyes widened in surprise. He shoved back his chair and stood, approaching James, searching his face as if to discover a lie. ''You are certain of this?''

''Aye. Two men conspired in it. One resides at Ship-man's Inn and goes by the name of Ensmore. Sounded educated to me, but the publican there didn't know his rank. I could only follow the one, so I don't know the other, but he's a common man, rough speakin'. And prone to meanness,'' James added, recalling the kick he had suffered. ''Do what you will with the warning. Good day.''

James turned to leave, his honor satisfied. He had al-ready missed two hours' work and needed to get back to the building site.

''Wait!'' the earl demanded.

''Hire a few outriders and arm yourself. You'll be fine,'' James assured him. ''Good luck.''

''Stop! You cannot simply march in here with an an-nouncement such as that and then leave!'' Eastonby de-clared.

''I can and must, sir. There's no call to detain me. I've said what I came to say.''

All of a sudden the earl became friendly, forced a smile and gestured to the chairs grouped near the fireplace. "Come now, I admit I was a trifle hasty to dismiss your information in such a fashion. Do forgive me if I insulted you. Allow me to offer you a drink at the very least, by way of thanks."

"Too early for liquor and I canna stomach tea," James declared, impatient to take his leave.

"I implore you," the earl coaxed. "Stay a while. I need to hear more about this."

Resigned to missing at least another hour wielding his chisel and files, James acceded to the earl's wishes and took a seat in one of the fine brocade chairs the man had indicated. He succinctly related every word he had heard at the inn's public room and what he had discovered about the man who made the plans.

The earl nodded, leaning forward and giving James his full and undivided attention. Again, but sincerely this time, he offered a reward. "Won't you accept something for your trouble last evening? You did go out of your way and most likely have saved my life as well as my child's. I truly owe you, Garrow."

"Nay, I said I'll take naught and I meant it." James glanced down at his own scarred and callused hands when he noted his host staring at them.

"You work hard for a living, I see," the man observed.

"True enough."

"If you do not mind my asking, what is it that you do?"

Since he asked kindly and seemed genuinely interested, James saw no cause to avoid the answer. It was honorable work. "I'm a stone carver."

"And also laird of this...Galioch, was it? You need the added income to maintain your estate?"

"Aye, I do that." He could see the earl's mind at work, wondering how to settle what he considered payment of a debt without offending. "You owe me nothing," James insisted, "but there is another matter I might as well take up now the chance presents itself. I wouldn't take it amiss if you saw to feeding your folk at Drevers. I confess this has been a wee drain on our resources at Galioch."

"My folk?" The earl frowned. "What do you mean, feed them? Mr. Colin, my steward there provides for these people."

James stood. "Aye, well, he collects their rents and the wool at shearing time, is all. Most of 'em have left the country, but there's a few won't give up what they've considered theirs for centuries. I canna let 'em starve. If you won't see to 'em, then I must. They're my neighbors, y'see. Many are good friends."

The consternation on the earl's face told James more than anything he could have said in his defense.

"I swear this is news to me, Garrow," he said, shaking his head as he motioned for James to sit again. "I've not been to Drevers since I first inherited when I was twenty. What else should I know? You seem an honest man and you've done me a great favor already. Please, be frank, and do me another."

"Well, your place is in sad repair. To be honest, mine's worse, but I do all I can to see my people have what they need. Yours, as well, but a bit of food's about the best I can manage these days."

Eastonby sighed loud and long. For a good while he said nothing, but looked James straight in the eye. "You are obviously a man of honor and compassion. You have the title, I presume?"

"Baron, fourteenth of the name. Granted by King

James. Named for him like all the eldest sons in my family."

"*Garrow,* you say. My father was acquainted with your grandfather, I believe," the earl commented. "Are you Catholic?"

James hesitated, shrugged, then admitted, "Not so's you'd notice."

Silence reigned for a moment. "Are you married?"

"Nay." He refused to confess the why of that. Not many women would welcome a home at Galioch or a husband gone half the year, laboring like a peasant to fill the larders. "Why do you ask?"

The earl smiled. "Garrow, I think you and I can strike a bargain that will benefit us both. Are you game to give a listen?"

James nodded. He thought he knew what Eastonby would propose and it made good sense to him. Being awarded the stewardship of the earl's estate in Colin's stead would certainly be preferable to the six months James had to spend working in Edinburgh each year. No one would regret the departure of Frank Colin, either. As for asking his marital status, the earl must want a family man to run the place now that his bachelor steward had not worked out. "What do you have in mind, sir?"

"I will deed Drevers to you in its entirety, Garrow, if you will marry my daughter, Susanna," the earl announced proudly as if he'd found the solution to peace in the world.

James asked the first thing that came to mind. "What's wrong with her?"

In the room adjacent, Susanna Childers listened, her ear pressed shamelessly to the door. At her father's words, she squeezed her eyes shut and gritted her teeth until they ached. She moved away from the door then, unwilling to listen further and hear the accounting of what Father considered her misdeeds.

She knew she had only herself to blame for landing in Edinburgh, but Father had no right to marry her off to a Highlander. The scandal in London would blow over like the ill wind it was and she could go home again. Eventually. But not if she were wed and buried in the bleak hills to the north with that lot of wild savages. She'd heard tales of how those people lived!

For a moment, she considered storming into the room and protesting so vehemently, the Scot would run for his very life. But before her hand reached the doorhandle, Susanna reconsidered. Such a display would only prove her father's accusations of impetuosity and arrogance. It would serve her much better if she approached him later and pleaded like a penitent, she supposed.

The very thought went against everything she stood for. Women should take an unyielding stand against men ruling their lives and treating them like possessions. Hadn't she preached that to anyone who'd listen?

However, saying as much in public had gotten her into this predicament in the first place. And last evening's game of cards hadn't helped her cause at all. She should never have bet with her father, much less wagered her freedom to choose her own future. Now she would either have to throw herself on his mercy and beg him to recant his offer of her hand, or she must honor the wager, make good on her loss and marry that man in the next room.

No question. She would beg for all she was worth. If he would only change his mind about this particular choice of husbands, she would promise Father he could choose any man in England for her. She would swear to accept that man with grace and dignity and keep her unruly mouth shut. Anything would be better than living in a dirt-floored bothy and eating oats and mutton every meal. God only knew what those people expected of their women, but it could hardly be anything she'd be willing to provide.

The door opened and she all but fell into the sitting room.

"Susanna," her father said, a note of censure in his voice, "join us if you will."

The Scot was biting his lips together, stifling a grin. His green eyes were alight with merriment. She wanted to throw a vase at his head. Instead, she straightened, raised her chin and stared him down.

"May I present my daughter, Lady Susanna Childers. Susanna, this is Baron James Garrow, laird of Galioch," her father intoned, aware she had listened at the door and already knew very well who the man was. The man knew it, too, and seemed to find it highly amusing.

"Charmed." Susanna only inclined her head instead of a formal curtsy. Probably a mistake, given her father's frown.

The Scot bowed gracefully. "Likewise."

Apparently someone along the way had taught him a few manners, Susanna decided. Not enough, however, to employ her customary title or to dress properly for a call. Or to observe the accepted hours for calling, for that matter. True, he had done them a great service by warning them of possible attack, so she supposed he could be forgiven for that breach of etiquette.

"Entertain our guest for a few moments, Susanna. I will return shortly."

"Father, wait!" She put out a hand to grasp his sleeve, but the look he gave her stopped the motion. She swallowed the urge to shout a refusal and stamp her foot, knowing how useless—not to mention humiliating—it would be to defy him publicly. That would seal her fate for certain. If she kept her wits, she might yet change his mind.

The door closed behind him. There was nothing for it but to play this out. She turned to the Scot. "So, are you enjoying your holiday in Edinburgh?"

"Holiday?" He smiled, a singularly bold expression that set her teeth on edge. Then he inclined his head and his gaze toward the bedroom door. "Is it your hearing that's faulty, lass, or was the door too thick?"

She held on to her look of bland innocence. "I fear I do not take your meaning, sir."

The man sighed, looking around the chamber and everywhere but at her. "Well, I'd wager my last groat you heard the whole conversation. Not that I'm blaming you for listening, mind. What I canna ken is why you havena thrown a fit about it." Then he settled that curious green gaze on her. "Are you that desperate to marry, then?"

Susanna could scarcely draw breath she was so angry. It absolutely stuck in her throat preventing speech.

He ignored her silent glare and continued, "I admit I could use a wife."

"You could *use* the estate my father offered you to take me off his hands!" she snapped. "Can you possibly understand how insulting this is? And how dangerous for me even to consider?"

"Dangerous?" His eyebrows flew up.

"Yes, dangerous! Do you think I'm not aware that when a woman marries, everything she owns or inherits or earns then belongs to her husband to do with as he alone decides? Why, he can even do with her *person* what he will! Why should I beggar myself and accept what amounts to enslavement?''

''Ah, Mrs. Wollstonecraft speaks, I see.''

Susanna's gaze flew to his. ''You have read her views?''

''Nay, but I've heard of 'em. I had no hand in making the laws she spoke about,'' he argued. '''Tis true enough, they are not fair, and I'm sorry for it, but—''

''How dare you pity me, you wretch!'' she warned, her chest now rising and falling so rapidly, she thought she might faint. She fisted her hands in her gown to keep from flying at him in a rage.

''Well, I do, lass,'' he admitted. ''I've great sympathy for any woman saddled with the choice you're facing.'' He stopped for a moment to think, then seemed to come to some decision. ''Runnin' a place the size of Drevers is no small thing. If we marry, I'll see to it your father puts the place in your name.''

Susanna scoffed. ''A precious lot of good that would do. You know a wife cannot possess her own property.''

''But you will. I promise I'll deed it back to you alone. I think it can be done. All I'm wantin' is the stewardship and a fair wage for my trouble. I've people to feed and you'll have the same responsibility if you agree to this.''

''Ha!'' She threw up her hands. ''What makes you think I would trust you? I do not even know you, sir!''

''Because I give you my word. Were I a slave to greed, I'd not be here, forfeiting this day's pay. And I'd be demandin' a reward, aye?''

Her skirts swished around her ankles as she began to pace. ''You're a madman! My father must be mad as well!''

The Scot laughed. ''Neither of us as mad as you, judging by the fire in your eyes. Bonny eyes, too, despite the fury in 'em.''

She halted directly in front of him, hands on hips. ''Why are you even considering marriage to me? Do you know what hell I could impose on your life, Garrow? Can you even imagine it?''

Gently, he answered, ''I've had a fair warning. Tell me, do you gamble?''

She blinked. ''Gamble?'' After that last ill-fated game of cards with her father, she would never touch another deck of cards as long as she lived. Or perhaps the Scot was speaking of the risk she'd be taking to marry him. ''Absolutely not! I leave nothing to chance,'' she declared heatedly.

''Then we'll suit,'' he said with a succinct nod.

When she opened her mouth to speak, he grasped her shoulders and kissed her soundly. Shock held her still long enough to feel the heady warmth and taste the sweet, coffee flavor as his tongue touched hers. For some strange reason, she lacked the will to raise her fists and do him an injury. No one had ever kissed her in such a way. And he wasn't stopping.

Quite stunned and cursing her overwhelmed senses, Susanna pulled back. He released her immediately.

Instead of the self-satisfied, lecherous grin she expected to see, he wore a look of what appeared to be humility. ''Marry me, Susanna Childers. I promise on my honor I will do all I can to provide you the freedom you wish. That any lass with your braw spirit deserves.''

Freedom. So he had divined what she wanted most.

Suddenly, she understood why he was offering the thing she most desired. ''It is *you*,'' she whispered, eyes narrowed as she observed him keenly. ''You are the one who is desperate!''

"Aye," he admitted softly, his smile wry. "'Tis true enough I am that." Then, on a practical note, he added, "You canna go back to London and your da won't be leaving you here alone. Did you hear? He says you've the choice of me or your cousin in York with all those bairns for you to mind. There, I much doubt you'll have any say in what you do. With me, there'll be none to answer to, save myself."

"York? No, I missed that part." She backed up to a chair and sat down to mull it over. "Botheration!" He was right about Cousin Matilda. She was a martinet and her four children were absolute hellions. Susanna looked up at the Scot again. But how could she live in the Highlands with nothing but strangers around her? How could she live with a man who could steal her senses with a simple kiss?

She exhaled in despair. But she really misliked those children of Matilda's and her cousin's husband was a leering old fool who chased the maids around like a randy schoolboy. She hardly fancied *his* probable attentions.

The Highlander just stood there, his hands clasped behind him, patiently awaiting her decision. "We would have a marriage in name only, of course," she informed him succinctly.

He slowly shook his head. "Nay, lass. I am not quite *that* desperate."

She swallowed hard, imagining what would be required of her. Though not precisely sure of the exact details, she knew it would not be pleasant. She had heard whispers. "But you would give me time...time to adjust. Time to know you?" She hated the pleading note in her voice.

"All the time you need," he promised, then qualified it, "within reason. I will be needin' heirs sooner or later, and so will you. Who'll take the earldom after your father if not your son? He told me you're nearin' twenty-five and I'm close on to thirty myself. Won't do to wait years, but there's no powerful rush to it.''

She rose from the chair, feeling at a disadvantage having to look up at him. Yet when she stood, she still had to do that. He was incredibly tall. And well made, she noticed, trying to assess him in rather the same way she would a horse to be purchased.

His features were pleasing, especially the dark-fringed green eyes and mobile mouth that seemed to smile quite readily. And kiss exquisitely, she recalled with reluctance. Someone had broken his nose, giving it a hawk like character. Yes, she had to admit that the Scot was handsome in a rough-cut sort of way.

His dark wavy hair could stand a trim. For certain, he needed someone to guide him in the purchase of clothing. That suit was atrocious, his tie crooked and his collar wrinkled.

He did not strike her as terribly intelligent. What man with any sense would risk marrying a woman whose father had listed her numerous shortcomings so willingly and seemed so eager to be rid of her? Well, at any rate, he appeared to be one male she could easily outwit. That was something in his favor, she supposed.

It was a well-known fact among women that children usually inherited intelligence from the mother and physical appearance from the father, so she needn't fear she'd bear ugly imbeciles when the time came. If it ever did. She would stall for as long as possible, of course.

Aside from that consideration, Susanna knew it was highly unlikely she would find a better bargain down the road in York. There was nothing for it but to take her chances. And pray.

"Very well, I accept your offer of marriage," she announced in her most businesslike voice. "However, there are conditions."

"Aye, there will be those," he agreed. "You go first with yours."

So surprised that he would allow this, Susanna had to think quickly. "Uh...well, I would require the time we mentioned before. You know, before we..." Her hands were fluttering. She clasped them together in front of her.

He nodded. "Already granted. Have you aught else, then?" he asked politely.

She bit her lips together. "Never impose your will upon me. Freedom to come and go as I please, no questions asked."

"Come and go where? There's not much traffic about the Highlands, lass. We'll be coming down here or to Glasgow once or twice each year, I suppose. Not wise to strike out on your own."

"Hmm. I am beginning to see why my father thinks this will be beneficial. What are your requirements of me?" she asked.

"No gambling. Loyalty to my people and yours. Faithfulness," he said seriously. "And that you be just in your decisions."

She waited a moment. When he did not add anything, she asked, "Is that all?"

"That's a fair bit when you think of it, lass."

"No more than I would have given without your listing. But I have one more thing I require, Lord Garrow."

"'Tis James," he informed her, then held out a hand, gesturing for her to make her further demand.

She did, fully expecting him to argue. "You must allow me to speak my mind in all matters to anyone, as I will, without censure, even if you do not agree."

His teasing smile took her off guard. "Censure? That means punishment, aye?"

"Aye, lad, it does that," she replied, returning his smile as she shamelessly mimicked his speech.

He shook his head and laughed, a merry sound that made her join him. It felt wonderful to laugh. It felt even better to know she would not have to beg her father for anything, or worry about his criticism, or bow to any man's wishes, ever again. This one, she could wrap around her finger and do as she pleased. She knew it. At last, she would be free of all the constrictions women had labored beneath for centuries and so, could encourage others.

Her father returned at that moment, sweeping into the room as if prepared to calm the hell broken loose in his absence. He stopped short, obviously puzzled by their gaiety. "What—what have you decided?" he demanded.

"Why, Father, was yer ear not to the door? Or has yer hearin' gone bad? Jamie and me are betrothed, doncha ken?"

The Scot laughed even harder as he slid one strong arm about her waist, drew her close and soundly planted a kiss on her temple. Susanna permitted it without protest. It wasn't so bad.

Even if greed for Drevers, desperation for employment, or simple lack of good sense were his motivation, Susanna reveled in the unusual feeling of being wanted. She boldly slipped her arm around him and hugged him back. She meant it for show at first, to taunt her father, but found it felt good to have an ally, even if the Scot was an unwitting one.

Yes, she could manage him with no trouble at all. Within a year, she would have him convinced they should live in London where she could resume her crusade. Her father would have no right to cut it short the next time, and her husband would not gainsay her once she plied her wiles upon him. She did *have* wiles, she was fairly certain of it.

Who would have thought her luck would reverse itself in such a strange and rapid fashion? There was solid proof her cause was righteous.

Chapter Two

James usually resisted change, but there was little to be said for the status quo in regard to his current situation. Taking a wife seemed, on the one hand, a reckless thing to do. He could barely support the souls in his care already. However, he doubted Eastonby would grant him the stewardship of Drevers unless he wed the lass.

Working that close to home, without the necessity of leaving for half the year, would surely benefit both himself and the clan. The people of Drevers would certainly be better off for it. He could not afford to question his own preferences when this would affect so many lives beyond his own.

To be honest, he had to admit the idea of the marriage did not exactly put him off. Something about Susanna Childers sparked a sense of anticipation and excitement James had thought dead and buried along with his boyhood. The lass would prove to be an adventure, that was for certain.

He was suddenly aware of his life having been driven by little more than an almost desperate need to meet his responsibilities. What was a wife but one more of those? And yet...

She'd be a handful to tame, this one, he thought with a grin. A glorious handful.

Other than his mother, women had never given him problems. There had been quite a few, admittedly more in his youth than recently, due to the constraints of time and funds to spend on pleasure. Even the most temperamental females he had encountered had usually responded to even-handed reason or, barring that, ready affection.

No cause to believe a wife would react any differently than the rest. He liked women and they seemed to realize that. He also knew better than to love them. He'd made sure they understood that, too.

He had loved his mother, of course. Yet he had remarked what love had done to him and to his father. That man had suffered like the damned in his efforts to please a wife who gauged success by possessions and how many people she could impress by showing them off. Ten years after their deaths, James and the entire clan were still reaping the results of his mother's love of wagering and her extravagant spending. And his, as well, he admitted.

The last four years of their lives, James himself had made a remarkable dent in the family fortune, gaining his useless education and traveling to acquire the polish of a worldly young noble like the ones his mother admired. He had foolishly believed that improving himself in such a way might gain him her approval, if not her love. Maybe she would point to him with pride one day, he'd thought at the time.

The guilt over that conceit and the cost of it ate at him constantly, even though he hadn't known at the time how dire the state of the family finances. Well, this marriage and his new position could go a long way in making up for that bit of foolishness.

"Are you an optimist?" Eastonby asked him as if reading his mind.

James rolled his eyes at the thought. "Hardly."

"Neither am I. But I do think you and Susanna will suit one another or I would not have suggested this. She needs a firm hand, but not a cruel one, Garrow. Most important, I want her out of the way of those trouble-makers in London. That Bodichon woman has nearly ru-ined our good name, using Susanna to spout all that non-sense about freeing women from their bondage or some such. The papers actually printed my daughter's name, can you feature that? One knows a proper female is never mentioned in print other than at her marriage and her death! Her mother would have been scandalized."

"Embarrassed you, did she?" James asked, feeling faintly angry at Eastonby and rather defensive of Su-sanna's courage in taking a firm stand, be it right or wrong. She didn't strike him as being one who was easily led. Susanna was a woman of conviction and he thought that spoke well of her.

"Not so much embarrassed as perplexed. And I have to admit, frightened for her. There are those in power who greatly resent a woman speaking out so publicly. Susanna is passionate when she takes up a cause, but she's also a bit naive."

In his opinion, James thought the lass should be com-mended. It was not every woman who would dare speak out against injustice no matter what consequences she might face. But he remained silent. Now was not the time to engage in any debates on the evils of society.

The earl's expression looked grim as he splashed an-other dollop of liquor into a fine crystal goblet. "More?"

James nodded and held out his glass. They were drink-ing brandy to seal their bargain while the lady rifled through her wardrobe in the next room to find something appropriate for a hasty wedding.

It was to take place that very afternoon, accomplished without banns or fanfare, by a Presbyterian minister who owed Eastonby a favor. Apparently, the earl also knew one of the magistrates who would backdate a license. That had been sent for, as had a ring from one of the city's well-known jewelers. Amazing what an exalted title could accomplish, not to mention wealth and the comradeship of former Oxford chums.

"I must remain in Edinburgh for at least another week," James told Eastonby. "I've a commitment to finish the portal of the building we're close to completing. Then I'll be free to take on your estate."

"*Your* estate now, my friend," the earl reminded him. "As for your stone carving, I must say that pride in your work is to be commended."

James huffed. "Pride, indeed. I'll not be paid for what I've done of that bas relief unless I finish it."

Eastonby smiled and raised his glass in salute. "Then do so. Before you know it, you will be bringing your children to Edinburgh so they may marvel at your handiwork."

The man was wrong, James thought. He was definitely an optimist if he was expecting grandchildren any time soon. Then again, life did have a way of springing surprises and the winters in Scotland were damned cold for sleeping alone.

James took his time as he sipped the smooth French brandy, fully appreciating the way it slid down his throat like liquid fire. Tamer than his whisky, even when aged to perfection, but the taste was just as fine. "You'll be leaving directly after the ceremony?" he asked.

The earl nodded. "Yes. I regret I cannot stay longer

and join you for a wedding supper. You and Susanna are welcome to stay here in these apartments until you leave Edinburgh, of course.''

"I'll be coming with you far as Solly's Copse," James announced, then polished off the brandy and set down the glass with a thunk.

Eastonby looked surprised. "Thank you for the thought, but that should not be necessary. I can handle matters.''

"You're family," James said simply, "or you will be by tonight. I'll ride along." When the earl would have protested again, James continued. "I've been thinking, if you hire a number of guards to ride with you, this assassin will stay his hand until he catches you unawares later on. If I go, concealed in your carriage, he and his man will carry through with their plan. We'll have 'em, then and there.''

"By jove, you're right! I never thought of that. But what of Susanna? She won't take kindly to her new husband haring off on guard duty while she languishes at the wedding supper alone.''

"Nonsense!" the lady in question piped up as she reentered the room. "Pour me a jot of that, would you?" she instructed her father. "This *beloved* of mine must do what he feels is necessary to save your skin, Father. Will this dress do?" She twirled around.

"Don't be impertinent, Suz," the earl growled, deliberately and firmly stoppering the brandy decanter.

"Me?" Her wide-eyed look of innocence tickled James. She was a sly minx. "Why, I am the very soul of *pertinence*. Tell him, *darling*.''

Susanna had been peppering every address to him with endearments, likely trying to stoke her father's guilt for giving her away. One could hardly blame her for it.

"She's right, sir," James said dutifully. "Pertinent in this instance anyway. I must go with you. Otherwise, we'd both be wonderin' for weeks whether you'd made it home to London alive." He turned his attention to her. "And that blue gown is right becomin' to you, Suz. Matches your bonny blue eyes."

"Do *not* call me Suz," she hissed with a brief glare at her father, probably for making James aware of the nickname. "I despise it." With a jerk, she straightened a sleeve that didn't need it, then tugged up her gloves.

He just smiled. *Suz* suited her to the letter, short, sweet and soft. Her lips as she said it, pursed just right as if beckoning his kiss. He might never call her anything else.

Reason was not the thing to put this woman to rights, he decided. Nay, he would need to use affection. No doubt with the right words in the right places, he could turn her up sweet within a fortnight, just in time for their homecoming.

Susanna wished for her mother. In the three years since Anya Childers had died, Susanna had harbored an anger that very nearly obliterated all of the happy memories she had of her. Today's events had forced them out of hiding.

Now, at the moment of pledging her future to a stranger, Susanna imagined her mother beaming happily about it. Strange, when the vicissitudes of marriage had been the very thing that caused her death. Repeated attempts to produce a son in order to please her husband had drained the life right out of her. Two miscarriages and a stillbirth. She might have survived that had it not been for all of the other obligations forced upon her as countess of Eastonby.

A woman's lot, her mother would have said in that

soft voice of hers, smiling even then as if she accepted and didn't mind what fate had decreed for her. Susanna had promised herself at the funeral that such a destiny would never be hers. And yet, here she was, bound to answer *I will* before a clergyman who might be the one to speak over her own dead body in a few years.

One thing for certain, wherever she went, Susanna meant to continue her crusade to encourage women to speak up and be heard, to take care of themselves and take charge of their lives. She was not giving in, not giving up. This marriage could be used to her benefit. No woman worth her salt sat around waiting for things to happen to her. She made them happen.

"...love, honor and obey..."

The minister's words broke through her thoughts like a sharp stick thrust into a beehive. She gritted her teeth to keep her fury from flying out and stinging everyone there. They were all men, of course—her father, the Scot, the reverend and another stranger who just happened to be present when a witness was needed—and would shoo away her attacks as merely bothersome.

A large hand encased her own and she allowed it. His was exceedingly warm and hers felt cold in the absence of her gloves. If men could use women for comfort, why not the other way around? Susanna knew the justification made no sense in this instance, but the whole day seemed to have taken on a strangeness that defied logic anyway.

The remainder of the ceremony passed in a blur—even the placing of the ring on her finger.

"I now pronounce you man and wife. What God has joined together, let no man put asunder...." The voice droned on.

Asunder? God, she felt asunder at the moment. Her heart nearly stopped, then thudded so fast she thought she might faint when two large, very warm hands rose to grasp her neck. For an instant, she feared he would choke her for her rebellious thoughts.

The Scot's long fingers invaded the curls at her nape. His palms covered the pulsing veins at the sides of her neck. His thumbs caressed her chin. And his mouth drew nearer and nearer.

Susanna blinked her eyes shut just as his lips fastened on hers. Her mouth must have been open. She should have closed it. This was highly improper, his open mouth upon hers, his tongue touching hers. Good heavens, she could taste him! And he was tasting her, as if she were a comfit he wished to savor and not eat up too quickly.

Horrified at how her curiosity prompted her to linger over such a thing, Susanna pushed away, staring up at him to see if he would insist on a resumption of the kiss. She didn't wish he would. She *didn't!*

Obviously, he didn't either, she noted as he released her and dropped his hands to his sides. "Well then, wife, we've been wed and blessed. You look right fashed."

"Fashed?" she mumbled, unable to get her mind around the word.

Her father quickly embraced her, eliminating the need for her to reply to the Scot. "So, my little girl is married! I wish you all that is happy, sweetheart. I am certain you shall have it."

Susanna managed to thank him, if not sincerely, at least politely. She had made up her mind earlier not to give him the satisfaction of knowing he had upset her by throwing her to the wolves. The leader of a pack of them, in fact.

She could deal with the Scotsman, she reminded herself. Hadn't she been quite confident of that after he had made his promises to her? This was her choice. *He* was her choice.

When Susanna looked at him around her father's shoulder, she fully expected to see gloating superiority or some evidence of expression that he had tricked her into agreeing to this. Instead, he appeared almost deferential, as if pleasing her was his one goal in life.

She was not fool enough to believe that was so, but bit by bit, her courage and confidence returned. It only seemed to flag when the Scot touched her. Or pinned her with that steady gaze of his. "I will become used to it," she told herself aloud.

"Of course you will!" her father assured her. "I fear you haven't had too much in the way of happiness these past few years, but now—"

"That's not what I meant," she declared, pulling out of his arms and turning away. But she dared not explain what she did mean. "Are we going back to the hotel immediately? I'm famished."

"Of course," the Scot said, taking her by the arm, encouraging her to lean on him. She surrendered to it for now. Her knees were not functioning nearly as well as she would have liked.

Collapsing in the aisle of the church would hardly signify her ability to stand on her own two feet. As for that inability, Susanna was certain it was only a momentary lapse.

"I *am* hungry," she muttered, more or less to reassure herself. Surely that accounted for the temporary weakness she was feeling.

"Your slightest wish is my command," the man declared gently as he patted the hand she had locked on his forearm. "Today and always," he added, sounding quite sincere.

His words and the tone behind them reinforced his benevolent expression and shored her up as nothing else could have. She drew in a huge breath and released it with a sigh of relief. Yes, he would be putty in her hands.

That fact reestablished, Susanna decided she might as well start them off on the right foot. "That kiss was highly inappropriate," she whispered. "From now on, you should refrain from shocking everyone with such displays."

He seemed to take the criticism well, though she noted his lips working to suppress any expression. Then he nodded and acquiesced quite admirably. "My apologies, wife. Seems I was carried clean away by your beauty and the moment."

A blatant lie, but Susanna gave him points for attempting good manners. She might make a gentleman of him one of these days.

"Forgiven. Just see that it does not happen again," she told him firmly.

"Aye. Public kissin' might set people to talking behind their fans and we wouldna be wantin' that, now would we?"

Had that been a reference to her difficulties in London? Was this—this buffoon making sport of her troubles?

Before she could summon up a scathing reply, they had reached the coach that had brought them to the church. Later, she promised herself, later she would take him to task for that insolence. If he had meant it that way. Had he? Surely he would not dare.

Susanna let him hand her into the coach. The inside lanterns were lit, casting a warm glow over the interior.

The Scot's wide shoulders filled the space beside her, his left one pressed against her right. Though his suit seemed a trifle snug and could have stood a pressing, she noted now that it was of the finest wool and had obviously been tailored for him. Most men with his height would find that necessary, she supposed.

There was no hint of macassar oil in his hair or any of the parfums gentlemen usually wore to disguise unpleasant odors. Yet he had none of those. Rather, he smelled of fresh air, a unique heathery essence that reminded her of her childhood summers, when she had played upon the meadows in the Cotswolds. His scent intrigued her.

This close, she could see the pores of his fine-grained skin. Its color seemed a bit sun-darkened and partially shadowed now by the need for an evening shave.

Susanna was still contemplating his firm jaw and chin when her father entered the coach. He took the seat opposite, rocking the conveyance with his weight, appearing terribly pleased with himself for arranging all this. She turned her full attention on him and forced a smile. After all, wedding the Scot would probably turn out to be the best thing that could have happened to her, considering the options available.

And she had made this her choice, the first of many choices that would lead to her success. She planned to be the very first totally independent wife in Britain. She would set a fine example for others.

What better place to begin her work than in the outer provinces where she could more easily prove her theory on a small scale? Once those women in the Highlands realized their power to order their own lives, others would notice. Yes, it should progress as a word-of-mouth campaign. Much more effective than trying to convey her message to hundreds at once in some meeting hall.

She looked up at her new husband, the man who would provide her with the opportunity. Amazing how unmalleable he looked at the moment, but looks could be so deceiving. No doubt she was the very picture of wifely submission in his eyes.

He leaned forward and quickly brushed his lips across her brow before she had a chance to avoid it. "Thank you," he said simply.

Susanna smiled in spite of herself. "You're quite welcome," she responded automatically. One did have to observe the amenities on these occasions and he had been rather sweet and agreeable about the whole affair.

She settled back to enjoy the brief ride back to the hotel, satisfied that she had acquitted herself quite well, neatly avoided disaster and secured a way to live life to the fullest as she saw fit. This gentle bear of a man and the ring he had put on her finger would provide the validity a single woman would never possess when encouraging women to struggle against universal male domination.

I wish you could have stood your ground, too, Mother. You were simply born too soon to be a part of this. Susanna sent the silent message heavenward where she imagined Anya Childers looking down on her with pride.

James watched the play of emotions on his wife's face with interest. Her thoughts must be skittering hither and yon like a handful of birdshot dropped on the floor.

He wished he could get inside that head of hers. Just as well he couldn't, he supposed. Some of those thoughts might not be so flattering to himself. He'd have to fix that in due time, but not tonight.

"We shall see you to the Royal Arms, Suz, then James and I must leave," her father was saying as if he'd read James's mind. "It is almost dark now and we should take to the road as scheduled."

"Aye," James agreed. Though he would like to stay and sup with Susanna, he had to fulfill his obligation to help Eastonby. The man was his father by marriage now and James's responsibility as surely as were the wife beside him and the good folk of Galioch and Drevers.

Susanna's soft, slender fingers grasped his arm, pulling the wool fabric of his sleeve taut. She looked from the earl to him and back again. "Why can't you simply take a ship, or go by train?"

"Because I have business inland on the way home. And thwarting these fellows would only delay the inevitable."

"Please, both of you, I want you to promise—"

"Be calm, lass." James assured her, patting the small cold hand that wore the wedding ring. "We'll be going armed to the teeth and I confess I'm a fair shot."

"As am I," Eastonby bragged, his chest expanding beneath his satin striped waistcoat.

The earl fished a fancy gold watch from one of the pockets, snapped open the front and glanced down at it. "Just now half past six, my dear. Your husband should be returning to you well before nine."

James noted the instant of panic that flashed in her eyes. "When—when will *you* be back in Scotland?" she asked her father. Did she know how very like a brave, wee bairn she sounded? The poor lass feared abandonment to a stranger in a place strange to her.

"He'll be returnin' soon, aye, sir?" James asked.

"In a month or less, I expect," the earl said with a smile. "But I shall wait until spring to visit you in the Highlands."

Susanna's face fell, but James noted with pride how rapidly she managed to recover and hide her disappointment and apprehension.

"Well, then. We shall be happy to welcome you when-ever you find the time," she said politely.

"Dinna worry, lass," James told her gently, wishing he could alleviate her fears. "We'll keep you so busy, there'll be no time to greet for home."

She blinked and stared up at him as if he were Auld Clootie in disguise.

James sighed. He'd have to convince her she hadn't wound up with the devil himself and was headed for hell. Considering his eagerness to have her and the state of the properties where they'd be going to live, he might have a wee bit of a struggle with that.

Chapter Three

Susanna wished she could beg her father not to return to London this evening. They'd had their differences, of course. Well, that was an understatement of gigantic proportions, she admitted. They'd had confrontations that stopped just short of violence, if the truth were known. But she loved him and would feel like dying herself if anything tragic happened to him. Pride stood in the way of her cautioning him fervently, however. His pride as well as her own.

Nevertheless, she couldn't quite allow him to go, knowing the danger involved, and say nothing. The carriage had stopped in front of their hotel and the Scot had climbed out to help her down. Before leaving her seat, she cleared her throat and spoke to her father. "You will take care on your journey, I trust."

He smiled brightly. "Of course. And your husband will ensure nothing untoward happens, so you mustn't worry."

She searched his face in the light of the coach lamp, hoping for something besides the surface expression he wore. Some softening in his noble, imposing manner. Some sincere wish that she survive this marriage and some small indication that he would miss her. When she didn't find that, she sighed impatiently and busied herself with arranging her skirts for a decorous exit.

The Scot—Garrow or James, she must remember to call him one or the other—stood waiting, his large hand offered to assist her. She took it, placed her foot upon the steps he'd let down and alighted.

"Suz, darling, we are in rather a rush to be off," her father called, having slid over to the nearest side of the coach, his head out the window. "Won't you be taking sweet leave of your husband before we go?"

Sweet leave? She shot him a glare over her shoulder. He wanted sweet leave did he? She experienced the wicked urge to shock her father to the marrow of his bones. Well, thanks to the Scot, she now knew how. A kiss to seal a union in a church was appropriate and perfectly acceptable, however...

She turned abruptly to face her new spouse, grasped his wrinkled cravat in one hand, stood on her toes and pulled his face down to meet hers. With her other hand, she clutched the back of his neck and planted her mouth on his.

As forcefully as she could, she ground her lips against his, opening her own, insinuating her tongue into his mouth as he had done to her. Yes, this should do it, a wild and passionate kiss under the bright street lamps directly in front of the Royal Arms Hotel. Scandalizing enough, surely!

Suddenly the Scot's arms clasped her to him so firmly her feet left the street. Before she knew it, he'd wrested away every jot of power she exerted and took complete control of the kiss. Angling his head, he all but devoured her whole, stealing breath and thought and freedom of movement. She didn't *care. Oh, my.*

On and on it went, her body plastered so tightly against his, the stays of her corset bit into her ribs and her breasts ached from the pressure of his stone-hewn chest. She breathed through her nose and the wild heathery scent of his skin filled her. His groan of pleasure vibrated through her body as if it had come from her. She returned it without thinking. Her head swam in dizzying circles, lights flashed behind her eyes. Fainting had *never* felt this good before.

Then his lips were parting from hers. *No,* she wanted to cry. Not yet. She wasn't finished. Still holding to his neckcloth after his grip on her loosened, Susanna drew him back, kissing him more gently this time, testing, tasting, playing tongue to tongue, subtly changing position the better to feel, to gather in the sensations she craved like air.

Where his hands gripped her sides, her stays dug into her like steel rods, that pain the only thing saving her from total immersion into mind-drugging euphoria. It was then she began to notice the almost desperate flexing of those strong agile fingers, the almost audible thunder of his heartbeat against her hand that was buried in his shirt-front. A heady thrill of power overtook her. *She* did this to him, obviously affecting his composure as much or more than he did hers. What a marvelous revelation of newfound capabilities. What a wonder!

Susanna smiled against his mouth, abruptly let him go and pushed away. When she lifted her lashes to look up at him, he appeared quite stunned. His hands unclenched from her waist and retreated. Her own body pulsed with feeling, sang with desire, but she tamped it down as best she could.

She took a deep breath, then tossed the gaping earl a

triumphant nod. "There. All done. Do have a pleasant trip, Father."

Again she glanced up at the Scot and quickly smoothed out the fabric she'd so recently clutched in her fist. "And you, *dear heart,* may ride as far south as you care to. Farewell, then."

Swinging the beaded reticule that hung from her wrist, Susanna lifted her skirts daintily with her free hand and marched briskly inside the hotel past the slack-jawed doorman.

James watched a groom bring a saddled mount for the return trip to the city and attach its long lead rope to the back of the coach. The delay proved fortunate since James had to wait a wee while before he could comfortably climb back into the coach.

He ought to turn that cheeky lassie over his knee and give her bonny backside a sound drubbing at the first opportunity. Unfortunately, that wasn't the uppermost wish in his heart at the moment.

There wasn't the slightest hope that she'd give any encore performances of that kiss in private. If he thought there was a chance at all, he'd not be riding out with her da right now. The assassins down the road would have to bloody well wait a while.

She'd be a willful handful, that one, James thought, his eyes now trained on the third floor window where he hoped she would appear. Exasperated with himself for mooning like an untried lad with the first steelie beneath his kilt, James shook his head, scoffed and tore his gaze from the hotel back to the coach.

When he did manage to reenter the conveyance, he immediately noticed the earl's consternation. It might be politic to ease the father's mind about the daughter's future welfare after the shocking display the lass had provided out there in the street, but James wasn't inclined to discuss it now. Not in his present condition. That aside, he wasn't altogether sure he could promise anything with regard to Susanna.

"You won't beat her, will you?" the earl asked. "Even when you think she deserves it?"

James hesitated. He'd given her his word on that already and he doubted it would make a difference anyway. "Nay, I'll not and that's the end of it."

But he thought to himself she could have used a swat or two when she was a bairn. Might have made life easier for her later on. And for him now that she was his. *His.* Well, he wouldn't be dwelling on that until he could do something about it.

He changed the subject. "We'd best be making some sort of plan. The weapons? I have none, save a blade." He patted the scabbard strapped just above his ankle. No self-respecting Scot felt dressed without his *sghian dhub,* though the knife was of little use against a firearm.

The earl fumbled around beneath the seat, opening a compartment with a small hinged door. He withdrew two pistols and handed one, butt first, to James. "Here. These should do. Webley revolvers. Five shots each. Coachman's loaded them for us. You say you can shoot?"

James examined the newfangled gun, unlike any he'd ever seen or used. "I've a good eye and my aim's true enough, but you must show me how to work the thing."

They spent the next quarter hour discussing the assembly and operation of the repeating percussion revolver. Fascinated, James wished they had time to stop and get in a few practice shots before he was required to defend the earl's life with this. The only pistol he'd ever fired was his father's old brass flintlock, which he had not even thought to bring with him.

"You will keep one of these as a gift, of course," the earl told him. "When you oust that steward of mine from Drevers, you might have need of it."

James agreed, cocking and releasing the hammer, getting used to the feel of the weapon and sighting out the window, though he could see little for a target other than the silhouettes of trees in the distance. The moon was on the rise, full and soon to be bright enough to cast shadows, he figured.

Several miles before they reached Solly's Copse where they expected the attack to occur, James doused the inside lamps. "So our eyes will adjust," he explained. "No use in making ourselves lighted targets, eh?"

"Quite right. I should have considered that. It's been some time since my army days, though even then the danger lay right in front of you, out in the open. No need for this sort of thing."

The earl wasn't the only one who'd never faced trouble such as this, James thought. Oh, he'd tangled in fistfights more times than he could count, got caught up in a few where blades came into it, but he'd never been obliged to dodge a ball or a bullet. "First time for everything," he muttered.

They fell silent as they reached the short stretch of road that led through a section of fairly dense woods. The trees had been cut back enough to allow two coaches to pass one another if need be, but many of the towering oaks had spread their branches in a canopy that blocked out much of the moonlight. The coachman slowed the team to a near walk because of the lack of visibility.

James felt the hairs on the back of his neck rise with a prickling sensation. He could smell the danger closing in, feel it in his bones. Ears attuned to every sound, he cursed the noise made by sixteen clopping hooves on the road. If only he could have ridden up top, but there was no room to hide there among the baggage. Two men in the driver's box would signal they were expecting trouble.

The only advantage he and Eastonby had tonight would be surprise when the attackers realized they had two armed men well prepared to defend themselves inside the coach rather than a complacent, unarmed noble and his defenseless daughter.

A shout to halt rang out. One of the horses screamed and the coach stopped, rocking with the motion of the restless, stamping team. Someone had grabbed the leaders. If there were only the two men, at least one was busy.

"Now!" James rasped. He flung open the door and leaped out, rolling directly into the cover of the trees as a shot zinged past his ear.

He glanced up and saw that the coachman had ducked down out of sight below the seat as instructed. The earl was at the back of the coach, attempting to get around to the far side.

Suddenly the night erupted with the sound, smell and flashes of rapid gunfire. A figure dashed for the door to the coach and yanked it open. James aimed and fired. The man yelled, cursed and grabbed his right shoulder, even as he whirled and shot repeatedly into the trees where James crouched. One bullet whizzed by his head and thunked into a tree trunk just behind him. Another dinged against his boot.

Flat on the ground now, James aimed again, this time for the man's leg. If they could take him alive, they might find out who was behind this. Just as he pulled the trigger, something stung his hand. He watched the man grasp his chest and crumple to the ground. "Damn." Something had fouled his aim. He flexed his hand.

Then he scrambled up, left his cover and raced around the coach to find the earl. He was on one knee beside the rear wheel drawing a bead on a shadow tearing off through the trees. The shot obviously missed the mark. James threw up his pistol and simply pointed it, firing three times in rapid succession. The body crashed into the brush and lay still.

Suddenly a horse broke through the trees behind them, the rider twisted in the saddle, shooting as he rode away. James braced his gun hand with the other, took steady aim and fired, only to hear an empty click.

The earl was busy reloading, cursing the dark and his own clumsiness while the rider disappeared in the distance. Hoofbeats faded and the night fell still.

"'Tis over now, sir," James told him and handed the earl his pistol. "But you might as well take your time and reload 'em both."

He felt curiously light-headed and needed to sit down, but he didn't think he could make it back inside the coach. Suddenly his legs buckled beneath him and he had no choice in the matter.

"James? What's wrong, son?"

He lay on his back in the dirt, resting. The earl's voice sounded far away, which was odd, he thought. Only a moment ago, he'd been nearby. And the moon was gone now. Dark as pitch, the sky.

His hands and face felt wet. Warm as it was, a bit of rain would be good. Clear the air of stench and smoke. Then pain hit from all directions at once. Not rain, he realized suddenly. It was blood. His. Blood in his eyes and on his hands.

"I'm shot!" he exclaimed with a short laugh of utter disbelief. "Th' bloody bastards got me."

Chapter Four

Susanna snuggled deep beneath the downy soft covers and reveled in the touch of the man who held her. His hand was pale and graceful, skimming over her body like a whisper-thin scarf, leaving pleasure in its path. "Mmm," she crooned and arched into his gentle caresses.

She frowned when he suddenly grasped her shoulder too firmly and shook it relentlessly.

"Please, wake, my lady! I'm sent to fetch you! Hurry!"

Susanna's eyes flew open and she bolted upright in the bed, staring in surprise at a young, unfamiliar, red-faced maid instead of the fashionably pale lover of her dream.

"It—it's the earl come back," the maid stammered. "He—he says tell you come quick!"

Father had returned? Something must have gone horribly wrong. Susanna threw back the covers, slipped out of bed and raced into the sitting room. But he wasn't there.

The maid rushed past her, pointing to the other bedroom. "In there, my lady. He's been shot! Twice!"

"Mercy, no!" Susanna cried and broke into a run. Just

inside his doorway, she ran smack into him. He appeared whole and unbloodied as far as she could tell. She ran her hands over his chest. "Oh, Father! Thank goodness! The girl told me—"

He held her by the shoulders and shook her gently. "Suz, James is wounded. He saved my life. Now we must do all we can to save his."

She jerked her gaze from her father to the huge tester bed with its ornately carved posts and snowy linens. On it lay the Scot, hands clasped on his chest, stretched out like a corpse.

The back of one hand bore a small bloody gouge. Dark red stained his trousers well above his knee and a copious amount of blood, now dried, marred his high wide brow and the left side of his face. His eyes were closed and he lay motionless except for the almost imperceptible rise and fall of his chest.

Susanna crept around her father and went to the bedside. Tentatively, she lifted the unruly waves off his forehead and saw the deep ugly furrow that still seeped. "Oh, Father, it looks awful!"

"That's not too serious, I think," he said, now beside her as they observed. "That leg wound could be, however. The doctor's on his way. We should get the boy undressed and wash away some of this blood."

Susanna nodded once as she backed away. "I'll send in someone with a basin of water and cloths. Shall I call up a footman to assist?"

Her father turned and frowned at her. "He's your husband, Suz. Won't you help look after him?"

"But I've never…I'm really not…" Helpless to continue, she held out her hands and shrugged.

"Stuff and nonsense, Suz. You're a grown woman and married now, not some miss-ish little do-nothing. Besides, you preach strength and independence for women, so get yourself over here and help me get his clothes off.''

He shouted over his shoulder to the gawking maid. ''You, girl! Bring me that ewer of water and the towel, then go wait by the door to show the doctor in when he comes!''

Susanna stood wringing her hands, uncertain what to do.

''Here, Suz,'' her father ordered, ''you get his shirt off. I'll take care of the trousers.''

A bit relieved she'd been offered the upper half instead of the lower, Susanna began with trembling fingers to unbutton the wrinkled linen shirt as far as she could. There was no way to remove it other than over his head. Once committed to the task, she had to figure a way. With all the strength she could muster, she grasped the sides of the open placket and ripped the garment straight down the front.

When she parted it to pull it off his arms, she saw that he wore no under vest. Her father wore those. She remembered hemming them for him when she was learning to sew. Perhaps Scots did not fancy them, or else this man could not afford to have them made or buy one.

She tried not to notice the wide expanse of his bare chest, the mat of dark-brown hair that curled between his...well, whatever the male equivalent of those things were called. She had never before seen a man without a shirt.

Exasperated with herself, Susanna scoffed at her misplaced fascination. Gamely, she tugged the sleeves off his massive arms, trying not to dwell on the power that lay within those muscles. There. She had done it.

Gingerly, she reached out to touch him in the place where his heart must be.

Her father issued a sound of dismay and without thinking, Susanna swiveled to see what he'd found.

"Good heavens!" she gasped, her hands flying to her mouth.

"Yes, it's worse than I feared."

"Worse?" Susanna croaked, wide-eyed.

"The bullet's still in there."

"Oh. The wound." She shook her head to clear it of the shocking sight that had captured her attention. Blinking several times, she trained her gaze on the ragged red bullet hole halfway between the knee and the...other place.

"Check his pulse," her father ordered.

Susanna gladly turned to their patient's neck. For a long moment, she was uncertain whether the pounding pulse at her fingertips was his or her own. She had discovered his, she decided, feeling the regularly spaced thumping. Hers was racing much faster and at a much more irregular rate. "Steady," she managed to say.

"Good. Ah, I hear someone. Must be the doctor."

A tall, thin man entered carrying a black case in one hand. "Well now, what have we here? Stand away and let me see."

"He's been shot twice," her father told the physician. "Once in the head and once in the leg. The bullet's still lodged in the thigh, I believe."

The doctor looked up from the patient. "Two pounds sterling whether he survives this or not. Agreed?"

"He *will* survive or you'll have no use for two pounds," the earl said with a quiet, threatening tone Susanna had never heard him use. "What is your name, sir?"

"McNally," the skinny physician croaked. His black

eyes had widened and his face had paled. "I'm no surgeon," he explained. "I cannot guarantee—"

"Then take your damned leeches and get the hell out of here," the earl snapped.

The man left so quickly, Susanna barely had time to wonder what they would do now.

Her father took hold of her elbow, bared as it was by her billowing short-sleeved nightrail. "Suz, I can do this, but I'll need your assistance. Go ahead and cast up your accounts now if your stomach feels weak. And if you faint once we start in on him, I'll beat you when you come 'round."

"Father!" she exclaimed, unable to recognize the man she had known all her years.

"Hush and listen to me," he commanded, pulling out the pocketknife he always carried and examining it. "You send that maid down to the kitchens for boiling water and a large bottle of whisky. Also fetch me your curling iron."

"My what?"

"Do as I say while I build up the fire."

"I could call a footman to—"

"Hang the footmen. This is up to us, girl. By the time we get a surgeon awake, into his clothes and up here, this poor fellow could die. His leg's still bleeding and I daren't stop that until we get out the bullet. Now go!" He gave her a gentle shove.

A quarter hour later, Susanna joined her father at the bedside again, having done all the tasks he'd set for her. She'd also rushed into a shirtwaist and skirt, cinching her middle with a soft leather belt since she had no time to don her corset. Her face flamed every time she thought how she had darted around in her nightclothes for anyone to see. What must Father think of her?

She watched as he poured whisky over her curling tongs and set the business end of them in the coals. His strange set of surgery tools lay in a pan of hot water, awaiting their baptism in blood. There was the trusty pocketknife he had used long ago to whittle wooden toy animals for her amusement. Also, he had commandeered her sewing scissors, needles and a spool of black thread. Probably the most useful were the small tongs from the kitchen.

"Clean the wound, please," he instructed her.

Susanna took a soft cloth, dipped it into the hot water and bathed the portion of exposed limb. That's how she would think of it. Not the Scot's leg, but a disembodied limb. Not part a living, feeling human being. Thank heavens he was insensate.

But would he stay that way once her father began?

"What might he do when you start to probe?"

"Hmm. You're right, Suz. We should tie him. We could call some of the staff to hold him down, but the fewer people in here, the better. Besides, I doubt they could keep him subdued, as large as he is."

Suddenly the Scot shifted, straightening the injured leg and holding it stiff. "Gi' me a dram and get on with it," he commanded in a tight voice.

"Oh, my God, he's awake!" Susanna cried. "Father, he's *awake!*"

The Scot eyed her, his deep green eyes flashing with pain and impatience. "And he has a thirst, lass. D'ye *mind?*"

Susanna looked to her father for permission.

"Go ahead. He'll bloody well need it."

Quickly, spilling the liquor over the edge of the glass, she hurried to offer him whisky. Sliding her free arm beneath his neck, she lifted his head enough for him to drink. He gulped down three good-size swallows and clamped his lips shut.

"More," she coaxed. "Drink until you fall asleep."

"Nay," he argued, turning his head away from her effort to force it on him. "Trust me, you dinna want me drunk. I might hurt one of you. This much'll take the edge off."

"Hold my hand, then," she pleaded.

He grunted a short laugh. "And break your fingers? Find somethin' leather to bite on, aye?"

"Aye!" she gasped, her gaze darting around, unable to find a thing.

He calmly reached out and tugged at her belt until it came free. With morbid fascination, she watched as he laid it beside him, folded it one-handed and put it between his strong white teeth. Then he stretched out his powerful arms, gripped both edges of the mattress, looked at her father and nodded.

"Come lie across his feet to steady him," her father suggested.

Then she looked at the Scot for his permission. He smiled behind the folded belt and winked as if to reassure her he wouldn't kick.

"You'll be fine," she assured him, her voice breathless with the need to give him what comfort she could. "Father's done this countless times, I'm certain. Why, in no time you will—"

"Suz! Get to the foot of the bed, would you? And cease the prattle. He knows damn well I'll do all I can."

She jumped at the reprimand, then scampered up on the bed. As tightly as possible, she gripped the Scot's ankles in her hands and lay over them to anchor him firmly to the mattress.

In any other circumstance, she would have protested,

but there was nothing she could do but excuse him when he wriggled the toes of his right foot against her breast. After all, the man was half-foxed and in terrible pain.

Just how terrible, she could only imagine in those next few moments as his legs stiffened. She heard the intermittent clink of the makeshift instruments as her father dropped them back into the metal pan. There were several grunts that might have come from either man. She had turned her face away, unable to watch what was happening.

Her father left the bedside for a moment. She heard his footsteps. Shortly thereafter came a sizzling sound, the scent of burned flesh and a groan. The hard muscles locked in her grip and those lying beneath her relaxed.

"He's out. You can get up now, Suz," her father said, his voice little more than a whisper.

She collapsed for a minute, only then realizing that she had been as fraught with tension as the patient himself. Her stomach roiled.

"Get up, Suz. You'll need to sew that head wound before he wakes again."

She couldn't. She simply could not.

"But I have to," she muttered to herself. If the Scot could bear up under what he had without complaint, then who was she to cavil at such a simple ordeal? Bracing herself and calling up her fortitude, Susanna slipped off the bed backward, landed on her stockinged feet and went to thread her needle.

Surprisingly, she managed quite well and was feeling rather smug when her father led her into the sitting room and offered her a bracing bit of brandy.

"I have to leave, Suz. You'll be on your own to look after him."

She choked, coughed and fought for breath while he

patted her soundly on the back. "Wh-why must you?" she sputtered.

He crouched on the floor beside where she was sitting and took her hands in his. "Because someone wants me dead and if I stay, that could put you and James in danger."

"No! Suppose they follow you and—"

"You mustn't worry." He was shaking his head and smiling at her. "You see, I'm sailing after all. They'll know I've gone, but not *how.* Once I reach London, I'll hire the protection I need and a Bow Street man to find out who is responsible for this."

"Father, I am so afraid for you after tonight's shooting."

"Two of the men are dead. The one who escaped will need time to hire more help and find out where I've gone."

He squeezed her hands. "And you, my sweet girl, will be safer without me around. Still, I want you to promise me that you will head for the Highlands as soon as James is able to travel by coach. No one can touch you here at the Royal, so stay inside until you go. When you are ready to leave, do so with as little fanfare as possible. James will know how to arrange that. I'm leaving him well armed. Trust me, there's none better to protect you."

She sniffed. "He does seem rather proficient at stopping bullets."

The earl chuckled. "He's a large target, I grant you, but he's also a bang-up shot. I am leaving you in the best of hands."

Susanna knew she couldn't dissuade him. "Go then and Godspeed."

He released her hands and stood. "I shall wire you the minute I arrive."

"Assuming they have the telegraph where I'm going."

"Yes, assuming that. If not, I will get a message to you. Return one to me to let me know how James is getting on. Mind you keep an eye on him. Expect some fever, but I'm sure he'll be fine."

"You have done that before, haven't you?" she asked, inclining her head toward the bedroom where he had just performed surgery.

"A time or two in the wars," he admitted, "long before you were born."

Susanna jumped up then and threw her arms around him. "Please, please take great care. I no longer care that you gave me away to him. I still love you, Father."

He dropped a long kiss on top of her tousled hair. "And I love you, Suz. I promise you'll see the wisdom in this one day."

She doubted there was any wisdom in it at all, but that was the least of her worries right now. She had a husband in the next room who might die if she proved a poor nurse. And a father who might die if he made a misstep and trusted the wrong person.

James woke with a start. Rain pounded against the windows as incessantly as pain lashed his leg and head. His throat felt so dry, he knew he'd have trouble speaking. "Water," he groaned, wishing he could throw himself out that window.

No one answered. He turned his head on the pillow, not an easy feat. It felt as if it might roll right off onto the floor. His lass was curled in a very uncomfortable-looking chair not three feet from the bed.

"Suz," he croaked. Still she didn't move. She was asleep. For some reason that made him angry. The least she could do was wake up and watch him die.

He called to her again, louder this time. "Susanna!"

Her eyes flew open as she scrambled up from the chair, the act lacking her usual grace. "Hm? Oh!" she cried. Without pause, she reached for the basin on the table beside the bed.

James watched her hands plunge into the water and frantically wring out a large cloth. She slapped it on his bare chest and moved it side to side.

"Damn me!" he cried while icy tendrils streaked out from the site of impact. "I'm not a floor that needs scrubbin'!"

She backed off, leaving the rag where it was. Tears leaked from her reddened eyes and her fisted hands covered her mouth. "You are awake," she mumbled, adding a sniff.

"And freezing, thanks be to you!" He shivered, grabbing with one hand at the covers which lay twisted round his waist and flinging the cold soggy cloth off himself with the other. It landed on the floor with a plop. "Where's your da?"

"Gone," she said, releasing a deep shuddery breath and running a trembling hand through her hair. She looked a fright.

James narrowed his eyes and observed her a bit more carefully. Her simple skirt and shirtwaist were splotched with dark spots and looked as if they'd been wadded up somewhere for days before she donned them. The pale translucence of her skin troubled him. He'd seen statues with more color. "Poor lass, what's happened to you then?" He reached out one hand to her.

She stared at it, but moved no closer. "You…I thought you might die," she whispered, her gaze darting to the lower end of the bed.

James smiled up at her. "Ah. You've been worried."

Her nod was jerky and she wavered a bit, unsteady on her feet.

"Well, my head's fair screaming and the leg's paining me some, but I'll live. Help me up?"

"No! Wait!" she cried, rushing to the bedside again, bending over him and pressing both palms against his shoulders.

Not much need since he'd already discovered the agony of trying to rise. And the impossibility of it. His breath rushed in and out. He held it for an instant, trying to still his panic. He felt incredibly sick.

"I...I canna move my legs," he rasped, determined not to scream the words. Susanna had thrown herself across his body to hold him down and he couldn't see whether his legs were even there under the covers. Had a surgeon amputated? He had read once that pain could be felt long after limbs had been taken off.

Susanna raised herself a bit from her restraining position and looked him in the eye. "Be calm. Please be calm. If you thrash about you might hurt yourself worse than you already are."

He bit his lips, feeling the dryness. Everywhere she touched him prickled with pain, his skin overly sensitized by the fever. "I won't be thrashin', lass. My legs..." He searched her eyes, praying he could take the news with courage.

"Oh. I forgot. You could not get up even if you tried." She brushed a hand over his forehead. She seemed a bit steadier now and even offered him a saucy smile.

"Good God, woman, are you heartless? Where's your pity?"

She got up, pushing off him with a purpose. "Oh, spare me the dramatics, will you? I shall untie your ankles if you promise not to—"

"You *tied* me to the bloody bed?" he shouted, his arms flailing as he tried to sit up. God in heaven, he wished he'd not promised her da he wouldn't beat her!

She had paused now, her arms folded tightly across her chest. "You keep a civil tongue in that head of yours, sir, or I shall call a footman to bind your arms as well. And your *mouth!*" she warned him with a glare. "Now that you are lucid, there is no excuse for cursing!"

The curses he kept to himself in that instant would have curled her hair.

"There now," she said, nodding. "You see the importance of behaving yourself and shall be rewarded." In moments, she had loosened the strips of linen that bound his ankles to the bedposts.

James breathed easier now, overwhelmingly relieved to see the columns of both legs right where they should be there beneath the blankets. He couldn't seem to take his eyes off the welcome sight. One thigh was mounded over with what must be the bandages covering his wound. Gingerly, he tested his ability to move it. Bless God, it worked to some extent. It ached, but the pain was not piercing so long as he kept it still.

His head hurt much worse, as though it would explode. He reached up and explored his brow, feeling a sticking plaster.

"Either a bullet grazed it or you scraped it on a low hanging branch," Susanna told him. "I stitched it myself."

He heard the pride in her voice at the accomplishment. "Congratulations," he snapped, busy raising the covers to have a closer look at the condition of his lower appendages. All was in order. And bare as the day he was born. He shot her a glance and saw her blush.

"Get that footman you spoke of. I need assistance."

"I am here," she informed him primly. "What do you need?"

James felt himself heat under her glare. And it wasn't the fever. "Just get him in here! Now!"

She turned and trudged toward the door muttering. "I believe I liked you better when you were insensate."

"How long was I out?" he asked. "Did I miss a day?"

"Three," she answered succinctly, then disappeared into the other room.

Three days? She had tended him for that long? That must be why she appeared rather frazzled. He'd been a trial to her, James thought with a sigh. For three days she had nursed him dutifully and he'd rewarded her diligence and wifely care with sniping remarks and accusations. He would have to make it up to her somehow.

Before she returned, James had relegated his little wife to the status of sainthood and promised himself he would do all in his power to deserve such a woman. Had any man ever been so lucky? He didn't think so.

The paragon swept in, her energies apparently renewed and the aforementioned footman in tow. She smiled at the servant. "Here is Thomas Snively who has been a godsend to us these past few days. I suppose you don't remember him at all?"

"No, I suppose not." James muttered, regarding the handsome, strapping fellow dressed in the fine hotel livery of dark wine trimmed in silver. "Snively."

"Good morning, sir," the man said. "We're most happy to see you are better today. How may I assist you?"

Why was Susanna smiling so adoringly? Snively was obviously English, another mark against him, second only to his appearance. James felt the brutal stab of jealousy, a relatively unknown emotion for him and damned uncomfortable. He glared at Susanna, immediately reassessing her status as angel of mercy. "You may go now."

Her lips pursed, the smile wiped away as if it had never existed. Of course, she was no longer looking at Snively. "I shall not be dismissed in such curt fashion!" she declared.

James closed his eyes and said softly through his gritted teeth, "Then I implore you, lady. Would you kindly vacate this chamber in order to spare yourself embarrassment?"

"Very well, since you put it so nicely." She picked up her skirts and swept gracefully—and hurriedly—out of the room.

James heaved a huge sigh of relief and glanced up at Snively who looked vastly amused. "I make it policy never to strike a man bearing no threat, Thomas Snively, but I will have that smirk off your puckish face."

"Yes, sir." The smile sobered instantly.

"And your eyes off my wife," James added.

"She's an eyeful, I grant," Snively said with a wry inclination of his head. He rocked on the balls of his feet. "But I have one as lovely at home who would slay me if I poached. Not that I'm inclined. Now should you like to test that leg or shall I fetch a bedpan?"

James groaned. "I've made a right jackass of myself, aye?"

"That you have," agreed Snively as he approached and offered his arm. "But we'll set you to rights soon enough. Ever been shot before?"

"No." They continued to chat as Snively lent his support, seeming quite the expert at directing James in how to manage the damaged leg. In no time at all, he was standing, resting a moment or two at Thomas's order, to recover from the dizziness of being upright after three days in bed.

Once he was back in bed, the dressings on his leg had been changed and the pain had subsided a bit, Thomas nodded. "This afternoon, I shall fetch you crutches. I expect you'll be quite mobile in a few days' time, though I shouldn't attempt travel for at least a fortnight."

"You sound like a doctor," James accused.

"Guilty as charged. That is, I hope to be one day. I read medicine at University for six months of the year. The other six I work to finance my studies."

James was impressed. "I wish you luck then. Believe me, I ken how difficult that must be."

"I know you do. Lady Susanna told me about your work here in the city and why you do it. Most nobles would simply run up debts and let the devil take the hindmost."

James ignored that. He knew it was true. "I need to send word to my employer. He'll want to find a replacement."

"Done, sir. Your lady asked me to discover your former address and settle matters with your landlord, so I did."

"My tools and things? Where are they?"

"Here, of course. Everything but your clothing is crated and stored safely. I took it upon myself to ask the innkeep where you had been working and went to the construction site. Mr. Greaves sent his regrets that you were injured and produced a letter of recommendation and a cheque for the balance of your pay for the work accomplished. He bade me tell you that he will be hard-pressed to find another so skilled, but for you not to worry."

For a moment, James was so overwhelmed he couldn't

speak. Then he shook his head. "'Tis good of you to go to so much trouble—"

Snively backed to the door. "No trouble at all, sir. It is common knowledge now, what you did for the earl. He has been quite generous to us during his visits to Edinburgh and is a particular favorite of the Royal Arms staff. I was glad to do whatever I could for you. You will let me know if there is anything else you need?"

James nodded. He felt humbled and not a little chagrined. He wished he were a wealthy man like Earl Eastonby so he could reward Thomas Snively properly. He found he didn't much like being beholden, yet he would dislike it even more if he had to ask Susanna for funds. "I'll owe you, Mr. Snively," he said.

"It's Tom, sir. And I shall hold you to the debt if you don't mind. For starters, you might write a letter of commendation on my behalf to the concierge. I'm due a raise in pay and that might clinch it."

"Good as done, Tom," James promised. He trusted a man who understood obligation and the need to repay a good deed. "I want to thank you, too, for getting me through three days of fever."

The footman threw back his head and laughed. "That was no fever, sir. A bit perhaps, but not enough to lay you low."

"Nay?" James rubbed his aching head with the fingers of one hand. He realized then that the wound itself was barely sore, but the devil's own cymbals were still clanging rhythmically inside his skull. "Then why do you think I was out for the count?"

Thomas explained. "Had I discovered before last evening that her ladyship was pouring liquor down your throat with an invalid-feeder to kill your pain, I would have dissuaded her sooner. If you'll pardon the expression, sir, you've been drunk as a lord for three days."

Chapter Five

"Susanna!"

She had just seen Thomas Snively out of the suite with an order for their evening meal and was about to rejoin the patient. The angry bellow from his room made her jump clear off the floor.

He must be still perturbed about the restraints. With an eye-rolling sigh, she trudged across the sitting room, snatching up the half-empty bottle of Scotch whisky as she went. She should have ordered more. This would hardly last through the night.

Her hair was falling down around her face, the chignon sagging to her nape in back. She hadn't found time to give it a wash or more than a hasty brushing since before her wedding. Though she had left the room when Thomas had come to see to his needs every few hours, she had been afraid to stay away longer than absolutely necessary. Her father had made it very clear that her husband was her responsibility. And if the man died she would never be able to forgive herself.

She blew a frizzled strand out of one eye, took a deep breath and pushed the door open. "Yes? What is it?"

She could clearly see he was fuming about something.

He blinked slowly, hard, and his teeth were clenched, just as they had been when he had ordered her from the room. Susanna knew she should gather her patience and consider the fact that he was wounded and likely in great pain. But whatever nurturing instincts she possessed were worn exceedingly thin at the moment.

"What the devil do you think you're doing with that?" he growled, pointing at the bottle she dangled at her side.

She held it up and looked at the clear, amber liquid that had provided relief from his troubles, that had granted him sleep, that dulled the edges of a man's consciousness or eradicated it completely.

Obviously it had cured the worst of his ills. At the moment he certainly appeared hearty enough to give her a rousing set down. Damned if she would stand for that after all she had done for him.

Suddenly the three days she had just spent with her husband took their toll. With a determined movement of her free hand, she pulled out the cork with a pop, put the bottle to her mouth and drank as much as she could stand without stopping. Unable to breathe for the burning in her throat and chest, she plunked the whisky on the table by his bed and stalked out.

"Wait!" he called. "Where—"

She didn't wait to hear the rest of his question. Instead, she marched directly to her bedroom and into the bathing chamber. The water would be cold, of course, sitting there unused after having been brought up by the maids the day before yesterday.

Susanna stripped off her blouse and skirt, kicked off her shoes and tore at her stockings. She tossed her clothing this way and that, then climbed into the large tub and sat down with a splash.

Even the liquor-induced languor didn't prevent her screech. God in heaven, it was freezing!

She dunked her head under the water, raking the few hairpins out with her fingers. Not since she'd fallen in the mud when she was six had she ever felt this dirty, this unkempt, this ugly. Beggars on the street were cleaner than she was. On the ledge beside the tub she found soap, sweet-scented chamomile, her favorite. In moments, she was covered head to toe in lather and scrubbing herself to a fare thee well.

She could hear him calling her again, sounding almost frantic, but she refused to hurry. If he was well enough to stand for a few moments, he was well enough to remain alone for a few more. Anyone who could yell that loudly was surely in no danger of expiring.

"Ungrateful wretch," she mumbled as she pushed suds out of the way so she could dunk her hair in clearer water to rinse it. Only when she felt clean did she abandon her icy bath and climb out. She wished for a maid to hold a warmed towel for her, but that was a thing of the past. Father had refused to hire one when they came here and she doubted she would have another where she was going.

"Independent woman?" he had questioned in that imperial earl voice of his. "Let us see how independent you really are." He had not even brought his valet with him, probably to illustrate to her that men were of stronger constitution and better able to do for themselves.

To be fair, his valet Barnes was unable to make the trip, old and feeble as he was. And Minette, her own personal maid, had taken a position with Lady Bloom immediately after Susanna's fall from societal grace.

"I could not care less," she muttered. "Tending oneself is a hundred times simpler than tending that Scot."

"Is it now?"

Susanna yelped, jerking her head around so fast she slung a shower of water out of her long wet hair. "What are you doing?" She scrunched the thick toweling closer, hastily covering as much of her as possible. "Get out of here!"

He leaned against the door frame, biting back a grin. It shone like devilment in his eyes as his gaze traveled the length of her. "Pardon the intrusion," he said, so insincerely, she wished she had something to throw at him.

Fortunately for him, she had nothing near enough but the bar of soap on the ledge. Even that might have knocked him off his feet and she *was* tempted. "Get out of this room *immediately!*"

One shoulder shrugged. "You've seen me in the natural state. Turnabout's fair, eh?" He paused while he looked his fill.

Susanna shivered. Her teeth chattered. She was not that cold at the moment. But she was furious.

He braced himself more carefully, taking his weight off his bad leg. "I was worried," he said, sounding a bit more serious. "You seemed upset."

"I? *I* seemed upset?"

"Swillin' that whisky like you were, aye."

Susanna reined in her anger, warned herself that cold reason was more effective and schooled her voice to a whisper. "Please. Go back to your bed. I'll be in as soon as I've dressed."

He nodded, inhaled audibly and turned on his good foot. She watched as he made his torturous way out of sight.

She stood immobile for some time trying to decide what had really prompted the Scot to endure the pain he must have experienced in coming across the suite to her. He could not have known she would be unclothed, so she didn't think his intent was prurient. He said he had been concerned about her imbibing the spirits.

Suddenly shivering uncontrollably, Susanna hurried to don clean linens. Again, she ignored the corset. Why hamper herself with stays when she would probably be bending and stretching, repairing whatever damage he had done to himself by overextending his strength? By the time she got to him he would likely have collapsed and bled all over everything. The very thought hastened her to the point of clumsiness.

She pushed her damp curls back over her shoulders and rushed to see what must be done. After all, he was her husband and her responsibility. Father would be proud that she had borne up so well under this task. Well, for the most part, she had.

The Scot had not suffered much, she'd seen to that. But she supposed Thomas Snively was right. It was time to decrease or cease altogether dosing the patient with spirits. Surely the pain was bearable now and he could sleep naturally. It was just that she could not bear to listen to his groans and watch him thrashing about, knowing the agony slicing through him. She had almost felt it herself.

When she entered his bedchamber, she stopped short just inside the doorway. He had returned to bed and was sitting up now, his back resting against the pillows, appearing little worse for his short walk. She released a breath of relief.

Apparently before he'd left the Scot, Thomas had dressed him in that nightshirt, one of several she had ordered purchased day before yesterday when she had found none in the baggage brought from his rooms. The garment was made of soft linen with flat tucks across the upper chest. He had turned up the sleeves over his forearms and left the neck placket unbuttoned.

His smile made her uncomfortable, for she had fully expected a grimace or at least a wan expression of suffering. Before she could comment on how hale he appeared, someone knocked on the outer door.

"That must be Thomas with supper." She went to answer it. Thomas had arrived with a large tray bearing silver salvers and tantalizing scents. "Bring it in, please," Susanna instructed. "Put it on the chair beside his bed."

"Shall I serve, my lady?" he asked as he strode through the sitting room.

"No, you may leave it and return in an hour or so."

"My lord," he said, greeting the Scot. "I've ordered the crutches for you. It shouldn't be long before they arrive."

"Thank you, Thomas. They will be most welcome."

Susanna marveled at the strength of his voice now, considering how he had sounded not an hour ago. And she noted his way with Thomas Snively. Friendly, yet authoritative. Like Father.

For the first time, it occurred to Susanna that the Scot might not be unused to governing people. Or perhaps he was but imitating the earl's demeanor. Or hers. Apparently, he could banish his Scots brogue at will, though he never bothered when he spoke to her. A lack of respect? A taunt?

Thomas bowed himself out and they were alone. Somehow it seemed vastly different, being secluded with him when he was not so much the invalid. In fact, he hardly appeared bothered at all by his injuries.

"I'm famished," he admitted, his avid gaze fastened on the tray. "Have you eaten?"

"No," she replied. She had taken very little food while tending him, worried as she was for his recovery. A slice of bread and meat here and there, the occasional piece of fruit. Mostly she had subsisted on pots of strong tea and the large complimentary box of bonbons the hotel had provided.

Only today after realizing he was well enough to quarrel had she noticed her hunger and ordered a full meal. Of course, he could not tolerate solid food as yet.

She drew up another chair to face the one holding the tray and began to uncover the dishes, setting the domed covers on the floor beside it.

He inhaled audibly. "Ach, roasted beef. And onions!"

"The soup is for you," she told him. "Good, Thomas has put it in a cup so I shall not have to spoon it for you. Here," she said, handing him the porcelain mug as she uncovered another dish.

"'Tis green," he muttered and handed it back.

She stared into the cup. "Of course it is green. It is pea soup. Drink it."

He refused to look at it again, much less take it from her. "I abhor green foods," he announced, rolling his *R*s.

Susanna stared at his haughty profile, debating whether she should take him to task over this. Or perhaps pour the soup over his head. After a beat of silence, she decided this battle was of too little consequence to engage upon. She ripped off a portion of the bread, dunked it into the beef gravy and laid it on a small plate. "If your stomach rebels, you've only yourself to blame."

He wolfed it down and licked his fingers. Appalling manners, Susanna thought as she picked up a knife to slice a bite of her beef.

The little plate appeared, empty. With a growl, she plunked down the bite she had cut for herself. "There."

"More," he ordered. "And some carrots and onions if you please."

Her movements jerky with impatience, she complied. "At least use a fork," she snapped, handing him hers.

He smiled at her, a singularly captivating expression that arrested her thoughts. In awe she watched the workings of his sensual lips and strong throat as he ate. Now oblivious to her regard and intent on the food, he polished off the portion in all haste and returned the plate with an expectant look.

"More?" she murmured and watched him nod.

Before she knew it, he had consumed the entire meal, leaving her only half of the small loaf of fresh bread and the now cold cup of pea soup. She detested pea soup.

Immediately, he slid from his pillows to a prone position, issued a sigh of repletion, closed his eyes and slept.

How young he appeared when sleeping, she thought, wishing she could brush that wavy lock of hair from his brow without waking him. How many times had she done that in the past few days? His skin was incredibly fine textured, smooth and slightly browned by his working in the summer sun.

Susanna peered at the small wound on his right hand, now almost healed. He had wonderful hands. They were nicked and rough, though beautifully shaped with their long, supple fingers and broad palms. An artist's hands, she now knew, wasted on chipping away at stones to create blocks for buildings or whatever masonry work he produced here in Edinburgh.

Thomas Snively had brought her the small marble sculpture found with her husband's tools. After seeing that one and only piece, Susanna instantly realized what an incredible gift James Garrow possessed. The sculpture was done by him, without a doubt, for there were rough plans for it drawn in his sketchbook and he had carved a square *G* on the bottom of the base.

Susanna, determined that he should be recognized for that genuinely remarkable work, had sent it with Thomas to the Le Coeur d'Ecosse Gallery on Halpern Street to have it evaluated. She had not heard a word about it since. Perhaps the manager, Monsieur Aubert, was still examining it or even showing it about to potential buyers in the city. Not that she would sell it or ever allow her husband to do. She had instructed Thomas to make that perfectly clear.

However, she figured that without her taking a hand in the matter, the Scot's extraordinary talent as a sculptor would never be realized.

Susanna found both his artwork and the hands that had created it fascinating. She had touched those hands whilst he slept, even rubbed them with scented castor cream to soften the rough calluses. Her errant thoughts would drift dangerously when she did that, so she'd had to discontinue it. Imagining those hands on her had seemed devilishly wicked even if he was her husband. Someday she would have to allow it. She had promised.

Was it anticipation that had her tingling so or was it apprehension?

Embarrassed and uncommonly shaky, Susanna rose and hurried from the room. She needed some time alone, away from him, to plan her strategy for the next little while.

The Scot would not be lying there unconscious for the rest of their time in Edinburgh. He would need to be dealt with and she feared it would take all her wiles to remain in control.

He had beguiled her right out of her supper without so much as a by your leave. Susanna wondered if she had overestimated herself. Or perhaps underestimated him.

James watched the door close and wondered whether he could silently make it behind the privacy screen and be sick before she returned. The meal he had forced on an empty stomach threatened to make a return trip. Sheer force of will kept it down.

He dearly hoped she would let him suffer alone while he battled the consequences of establishing the upper hand with Susanna. The woman was entirely too head-strong.

It wasn't that he misliked her for it, he told himself. She would need all of that assertiveness and more when she took over her estate. But he would still be wed to her and he had no intention of living under any woman's thumb.

All he needed to do was redirect that aggression and imperious nature of hers toward business matters and away from their marriage. He had the feeling that equal footing was about the best he could hope for unless he was stern with her.

Whenever he had thought about taking a wife, James had always imagined marrying a happy, docile creature who would be satisfied to have the ancient roof of Gal-ioch over her head and a few clanswomen to give her a hand with chores. His mythical bride would lavish affection on their bairns and perhaps have a bit left over for the ol' lairdie come an evening in bed. He had never in his wildest flight of fancy expected to warrant the daughter of an earl, especially one who regularly spouted—and truly believed—that a woman should take charge of everything around her like a general commanding troops.

In the respect that she tried to lord it over everybody, Susanna reminded him of his mother, which was no good thing for certain. He did not plan to spend the rest of his life struggling to please another female who had no room in her heart for acknowledging his efforts. Or perhaps no heart at all.

Susanna did have that, he conceded. He had seen her concern for her father, felt her anguish when the earl had left her here. Mostly, James believed, Susanna's superior attitude was built up of false courage she was trying very hard to make real.

He tried to imagine what it would be like to be at another's mercy all the time. First her father's, now his. How else could she behave without surrendering her will altogether? No point being too hard on the lass. She was only trying to survive and flourish in a difficult world, one that was not overly tolerant of the wishes of women.

Well, he hadn't made the rules that governed this world, and frequently ignored the ones in place. He could at least grant her the freedom to do as she wished with her father's estate. She could surely do no worse than the earl had done by his neglect and disinterest, even if she worked at it. A good manager of the place—by her own agreement, himself—could easily rectify any mistakes she made in the process. But personally, in their private life together, he knew he had best retain the final authority. It was a matter of self-preservation.

Thomas entered. "Ah, you're awake again, sir. I've come for the tray and brought your crutches."

"My eternal thanks," he said eyeing the things with anticipation. "God only knows what else I have to thank you for. Have I been that much trouble then?"

Thomas laughed. "No, not at all, sir. I rather liked the change from my usual duties and was glad to be assigned to your suite exclusively for the duration of your stay with us. Because of my medical training, her ladyship requested it on behalf of the earl. And yourself, of course."

"Did she now?" James tamped down the surge of jealousy. Thomas had already assured him he had nothing to worry about. Still...

"Shall I assist you in getting up?"

"Nay, I'll manage for myself. Is Suz...her ladyship abed yet?"

"No, sir. Shall I say that you request her presence?"

James shook his head. "Bid her good-night for me and tell her I wish her to sleep 'round the clock. We must prepare to leave soon and she'll be needing to catch up on her rest first."

"Oh, no, sir! With that leg as it is, I would suggest—"

"The day after tomorrow," James insisted. "I have business to attend and so does she."

Thomas picked up the tray. "As you wish." In a softer voice, he added, "She'll never agree to it, sir."

"We'll see about that," James said with a grin and realized he was actually looking forward to the inevitable confrontation.

"I am sure we will, sir. Would you care for a drink before you sleep? Some whisky perhaps?" Thomas asked, his expression schooled to perfect innocence.

James didn't dignify that impertinence with an answer. If he did, he might begin to give her keeping him drunk and helpless more thought than it deserved. Then he might entertain the notion that having been at her mercy these past three days could be fostering this bid for ultimate power over her.

That was not the case, of course. Husbands having the final say in a matter was simply the natural order of things. They would be leaving Edinburgh the day after tomorrow and that was that.

They stayed for five days after James awoke and began to recover. Susanna had finally run out of excuses that would delay their departure. The clothing she had brought from London was not warm enough for a Highland winter and she had to procure more woolens. They were to be delivered this afternoon. Difficulty in hiring the proper conveyance only purchased her two additional days. Her final resort, hinting at a peculiarly female indisposition should have gained her another week here, but James was wise to her tricks by the time she had thought to use it.

She supposed he really was well enough now to travel by coach without suffering a relapse. He had discarded the crutches and begun walking with a stout cane Thomas had purchased for him.

Obeying her father's directive to ensure her safety, Susanna did not venture outside the hotel. In fact, she never left the suite. Everything they needed, Thomas Snively arranged to have delivered or went to fetch it himself.

To be honest, she was mortally bored with the hotel and being confined to three rooms with the Scot. He kept her on edge, as if she were traversing a high wire like a performer in the circus. Her balance was precarious and becoming more so.

At times, he could be entertaining, she admitted. He would not play cards with her. He seemed to have an aversion to them for some reason. He did agree to an occasional game of chess. She allowed him to win, but only because he crowed so proudly and all but beat his chest like a gorilla. It amused her to indulge his pride. She could have checked him at any time if she had put her mind to it.

Putting her mind to anything at all while around him was proving an ordeal. He filled their rooms with such presence, he was impossible to ignore.

"Are you ready, then?" he asked brightly, emerging from his room dressed for travel.

Her breath caught at the sight of him. Heretofore, she had only seen him wearing the impossibly wrinkled suit of clothes he had worn that day she married him or one of the nightshirts and long robes she had sent out for when he was invalided. Now he might have posed for a fashion plate. Gentleman traveler extraordinaire.

The snowy collar with its jet foulard highlighted the duskiness of his skin. The dark-brown suit she had ordered for him fit exceptionally well and his boots were polished to such a high shine they appeared new.

He propped on his cane with one hand and with his other tapped his gloves against his good leg in a gesture that seemed to signify impatience. He must be bored with this place as well.

"A bonny blue frock," he told her, raising one eyebrow and smiling at her. "New?"

She shook her head, wishing she had paid closer attention to her attire. The sturdy slate-blue gabardine had simply been the most practical choice for a traveling costume. It was also the only thing that matched her favorite bonnet which was comfortably lightweight and framed her face with simple tucks of ecru lace.

"I saved my best to wear upon our arrival. First impressions, you know." She adjusted her bonnet and attempted to tie the taffeta bow to one side of her chin. Her fingers were clumsy because he watched her so intently.

"Wait," he said, taking up his cane and limping toward her. She felt the urge to turn and run. Something about the look in his eyes as his gaze locked with hers. Did he mean to kiss her? He had not attempted anything of that sort since he had left her to ride out with her father. The memory of it struck her with the force of a blow to the midsection.

"Allow me," he said softly.

Susanna froze as he laid his cane and gloves on the arm of the settee and raised his hands to her head. The tug on her ribbons while he tied them for her did nothing to break the spell he had cast.

"So proud," he whispered, slowly trailing one finger down the side of her face.

"Pride is a sin, sir. You accuse me?" Her lips barely moved as she spoke. She wanted his against them, wished for it, waited for it.

He shook his head, an almost infinitesimal move. "The sin is mine. 'Tis I who am proud. Of you."

Oh, dear. Oh, she was not used to this tenderness, a thing missing completely in her life since her mother's death. He had discovered her weakness without any effort at all. She had little defense against it. However, she must use what scrap she did possess.

Brushing his touch aside, she grasped his face in her hands, stood on her toes and kissed him fully on the mouth. His swift intake of breath admitted his surprise.

Susanna hurriedly applied the lessons he had taught her by example, stroking his lips with her tongue until he parted them in invitation. She accepted that and explored his mouth as thoroughly and hungrily as he had done to hers at the height of their last kiss.

His faint taste of coffee laced with whisky and sugar intrigued, begged fuller inspection. She reveled in it, cataloged it into memory, saved it forever as a joy to relive. All accomplished with only the slightest realization that she did so and with the greatest pleasure that she could.

Taking the lead was the only way she knew to thwart his seduction of her senses. She would seduce his first. Well on her way to doing that, Susanna realized she'd caught herself in the trap as well.

His fresh heathery scent redolent with spicy shaving soap clouded her brain while his groan of encouragement reverberated through her like a deep-throated lion's purr. Her head spun dangerously and stars blinked behind her eyes.

Her entire body hummed with need, even when she pressed as close as she could. His arms locked like a vise around her, his hands caressing her back, her neck, while he insinuated his lower half into the billow of her skirts.

Her heart thumped so loudly in her chest it frightened her. He released her suddenly, standing away, his chest a bellows working furiously as he glared at the door. ''Damn.'' The word echoed throughout the room.

With a hand to her chest, Susanna realized it was not her wayward heart knocking after all. Someone was at the door. Thomas. Come to take down their bags. She closed her eyes again and leaned against the settee for a moment to regain her balance.

It was time to go. For a brief moment, Susanna wished she had undertaken the seduction a bit earlier in the day. But she knew it was not yet time to relinquish her body to him. Not until she found a way to avoid losing her mind and will in the process. "Too soon," she muttered darkly.

"Damned right," he said, doggedly making his way across the carpet to answer the knock. "I think I'll cut his throat."

Susanna laughed in spite of herself. Relief coursed through her as desire gave way to it. She had been afraid—and almost wishful—that he would insist on staying another day and finishing what she had started.

They were embarking on a new life with this trip to the Highlands. She was torn between holding to the safe and familiar, the relative isolation and careful acquaintance they had maintained during his convalescence, and grasping at the coming adventure.

She felt much better about her marriage to him after her glimpse at his inner feelings provided by that wonderful sculpture he had produced. He did have a grasp of the struggle womankind endured. She knew that now.

Oh, God! The sculpture! She had completely forgotten to send Thomas after it and she could not leave it here. Then again, if she delayed their leaving to see to that, she would be obliged to explain why. Until she knew whether she was right or wrong about her husband's exceptional talent, it might be best to remain silent. That way he would not have to suffer disappointment if she were wrong. And if proved right—as she surely would be—then he would have a wonderful surprise.

If he asked after the sculpture, she would tell him what she had done, but if not, there was no reason to admit anything. The next time they were in town, she would go to the gallery herself and find out what Monsieur Aubert thought of the piece.

Until then, she would go along with Garrow and content herself with the task of surviving life as a Highland baroness. But she would do more than survive, she promised herself. She would prevail in her quest. Her husband would soon see that she was a wife to be reckoned with, a woman with a mission, a force all her own.

And better than that, she would make him like it.

Chapter Six

Shortly before dawn they boarded the private traveling coach in the back alleyway of the Royal Arms. The timing of their departure, lack of fanfare and modest rented vehicle were all chosen in the event someone was watching the hotel. James had taken every care possible that their leaving would go unremarked, but he knew, too, that absolute secrecy was impossible.

The man who'd attempted to murder the earl had also planned the daughter's demise. That thought chilled him to his soul.

Susanna's father had telegraphed just that morning of his safe arrival in London and declared there had been no further incidents. James figured it was only a matter of time. The man who wanted Eastonby dead had sounded quite determined. No doubt about the dedication of the first effort. James flexed his leg in memory of it.

Thomas had arranged for two trusted men to act as outriders and the driver had been selected for his extraordinary ability to get the most out of his teams. Speed might be necessary. The entire party, save for Susanna herself, left Edinburgh well armed and as prepared for attack as he could make them.

The well-sprung coach creaked and rattled over the cobblestones in the early morning darkness as they negotiated the way out of the city. The driver set a leisurely pace so as not to draw attention.

"Four days of this?" Susanna asked, obviously not with anticipation. "We could have gone by rail in half that."

He shrugged. "This way we can stop when we like." And be more aware if any enemies approached and not be trapped within a rail car, he thought to himself. "There's no direct route and the tracks only go partway. Besides, it's damned uncomfortable. This is best, trust me."

"I wonder if we shouldn't have sailed. We could have put in at the Firth of Moray. Galioch and Drevers are near there, you said?"

"Aye, twenty miles or so, but this is how we must go. Both the roads and inns are fair and we're in no great hurry for all that."

He saw no reason to explain why he would never again take ship, even if he had to slog through muddy roads on foot.

They fell into comfortable silence for a while, sitting side by side facing the front. The interior of the coach remained dark though the sky outside the windows had begun to lighten a bit. He turned to watch her profile as she looked out the window and wondered what she was thinking. Was she dreading their arrival in the north? What had she heard about the Highlanders and their ways? Judging by her reaction to their first meeting, much of it must not be good.

As the days passed, they halted only long enough to switch teams, eat hurried meals and answer the call of nature at the post houses along the way. The experienced driver had timed their travel so that they reached adequate, if humble, inns along the way. As was customary, Susanna had separate accommodations while James slept in the common room with the other men.

En route Susanna alternately slept and worked at her knitting which she kept in a tapestry bag on the opposite seat. She'd declared she was making a shawl. It was growing into a bed covering, he thought to himself.

James mostly left her to it. He had asked polite questions about her childhood. She answered in monosyllables. He certainly had no wish to relay the tales of his own youth even if she had asked him.

Talk of politics interested her, but he knew little of the current affairs in London and she knew virtually nothing about those in Scotland. They exchanged information about what they did know on both topics. It took less than an hour to educate one another and they were back to staring out opposite windows.

He wanted to kiss her again but it did not seem feasible with the coach bouncing over the ruts. Cracking her teeth against his would hardly endear him to her.

Ever present was the closeness of her right leg to his left, separated only by the layers of her skirts and his trousers. Excellent conductors of heat, he found to his dismay. That soul-scorching kiss immediately before they had left the suite haunted him continually. Things had changed with that.

Gone was the relative easiness of their games of chess. At least while at the hotel, they had been able to retreat to their respective rooms when things grew tense. Now they were two strangers stranded together in the small island of the coach with nothing in common but escalating desire. And he wasn't absolutely certain she shared even that.

On the third day, they were still a good five miles from their last night's destination. His leg pained him something fierce, but he said nothing since they would soon be there. The moment he thought it, the coach slowed.

"Why are we stopping?" she asked, peering out the window. "There's no town here. Not even a village."

James heard the fear in her voice. "I don't know." He reached beneath the seat and brought out the repeater the earl had given him.

One of the outriders approached the window. James opened it.

"Sir, we've a leader goin' lame. Likely picked up a rock. You want to get out and stretch your legs while John sees to it?"

James opened the door and stepped down, surveying the landscape on all sides. Visibility was still good, but night would be falling within the half hour.

"Should be safe enough," he said to Susanna. The guard rode off to scout the perimeter of the clearing.

She already had one foot out the door so James lifted her out and set her on her feet. Her waist felt incredibly small beneath his hands. And stiff.

"Why do you insist on wearin' that contraption? How do you breathe?"

"Not very deeply," she said with a short laugh. "Most of my clothing will not fit properly without it. I do despise the fashion."

He glanced at her middle. "Most women wouldn't admit in a man's presence that such things exist."

"A corset is a corset. And I'm not most women," she said with a saucy inclination of her head. She reached up and brushed several stray curls off her brow. He liked that she dispensed with her bonnet most of the time.

"Barring further delays, we'll be arrivin' at Galioch this time tomorrow," he informed her.

She frowned. "Not Drevers? Why? From what you've told me it is newer and probably in more habitable condition."

"Aye, but first I'll have to oust that steward of yours. Unless I plan to shoot him outright, I'd better rest a bit first."

She shrugged. "Galioch it is then." Together they walked to the head of the coach and on to where John Whip knelt to ply his hoof gouge to dislodge a rock. Their second outrider, still mounted, held the horse's head.

"How bad does it look?" James asked.

"Not bad, sir. We'll be on our way shortly. Have to take it slow, though. She'll be a mite tender."

"Is there an inn closer than Kingussie?"

"Aye, sir. One at Drumgas, a few miles ahead, but it's scarce more than a barn." The driver lowered the hoof and stood.

"If they have food, beds and teams, let's make for it."

He glanced around them at the deepening twilight. Traveling in the dark was not the best of ideas. He thought again of the night when the attack on the earl had occurred. Up ahead he could see a similar configuration of trees.

Susanna twisted and turned on the narrow rope bed. The mattress, stuffed with heather, prickled her skin right through her clothes. She had not undressed except to remove her jacket, her stays and her shoes. The room held four beds, all occupied with other women. Two were the wives of soldiers who were traveling to meet their husbands when they sailed into Aberdeen. The other was a single woman of dubious occupation. She snored to high heaven and smelled of stale cheap perfume.

Susanna resolved not to complain. Her Scot had the worst of it, she figured. He slept in the public room with the other men where there were no beds at all. She worried about his wound. He had favored that leg more than usual since last evening. God grant he escaped an infection. To lose the leg after nearly recovering would be tragic indeed, but stranger things had happened.

Morning brought little relief. They were on the road once more for their last day of travel. "At this point, I do not care what Galioch is like so long as we can abandon this coach," she declared.

James laughed, but it sounded forced, maybe even a touch bitter. Was that because his home truly was a heap of stones with no comfort or was he suffering from his wound?

"You were limping worse today. That bandage of yours should be changed," she remarked.

"'Tis just the muscles protesting."

Susanna's gaze fixed out the window. "Look there. Something is afire." A huge black column of smoke rose in the distance as they approached a curve in the road.

"Kingussie," he muttered as he leaned across her to see.

"Where we were to stay the night?" she asked.

"Aye." He said nothing more until the coach halted on the road outside the town.

One of their outriders approached from that direction and drew up beside the coach. "The inn's burned to the ground, sir, and the two buildings that flank it." The rider shared a meaningful look with him before continuing.

"See what you can find out. Have Collum ride closer

to the coach.'' James sat back after giving the order. He appeared extremely worried.

"What are you thinking?" Susanna asked, but knew the answer before he gave it. "Was the fire set on purpose?"

"It could be coincidence," he said, but sounded in no way convinced of it.

"Who knew we were to pass the night in Kingussie?"

"That and our choice of the best inn would be logical assumptions, given our destination," James admitted. "And where else would we be going in the North but to Galioch and Drevers?"

"But we left in secret!" she argued.

He shrugged, sat back and released a sigh as he drew out and checked his pistol. "Not a secret from everyone. Some staff at the hotel knew we were leaving. How d'you think we got the basket of victuals prepared? And the coach is hired in your name if anyone cared to ask. There were the lads who loaded our bags, the hostler's hired help. Any number of sources impossible to control unless we had sneaked out in cover of darkness and stole mounts to ride. A simple matter to check our whereabouts for someone determined enough. And I think he is."

"He? But who?"

James shook his head, staring out the window as if expecting trouble any moment. "I wish I knew."

They rode straight through the town without stopping, passing too near the smoldering remains of the inn. Susanna shuddered when she saw the place that might have provided their final night of life if not for that pebble lodged in the horse's hoof. She was infinitely glad they need not spend another night on the road.

"What if he follows us to Galioch?" she asked in a whisper.

"I think we can count on it," James replied. "And that will be his great mistake. I know every man jack who lives within a day's distance of either place. That's when I'll get him." He spun the cylinder on his pistol and smiled at her.

"If he doesn't get you first," Susanna said with a shiver of dread and foreboding.

The memory of James lying on her father's bed, pale as death and bleeding, returned to haunt her. But it wasn't truly James this person had intended to kill, she realized. Along with her father, *she* had been the original target. James had put himself in harm's way. Whoever it was had no real quarrel with him.

The coach traveled faster than in the previous days, she noticed, and did not stop until early afternoon. Susanna noticed the driver had turned off the main road. The village where they halted was certainly away from the beaten path and quite humble.

James assisted her out of the coach and into what appeared to be a private home, though there was a sign hanging over the door proclaiming it a public house, the Gorse Dew. Susanna smiled. The dirt floor boasted a fresh covering of straw and the lanterns lighting the small room looked very old and quaint. So did the proprietor. He placed a hollow horn to one ear as he took the order for their drinks and food. The knobby legs supporting his short, portly frame were bare beneath his kilted plaid.

James seemed to pay little attention to the strange attire. In an unusual occurrence, the outrider he had sent to glean information about the fire joined them at table.

He wasted no time on social niceties, but leaned forward over the table and got right to the issue. "Sir, there were a young whip showed up at the inn last evening with his…'' The man's gaze flew to Susanna and back to James.

"Well, with his *what?*" she prompted. Men could be so thick-headed at times.

She watched him blush. "His, uh, light o' love, ma'am." He mumbled a brief apology for introducing such a subject, then continued. "Seems the lad's heir to Ambrose. Didn't want it bandied about he was, uh, seein' this girl. They took one of the two private upstairs chambers."

"They weren't killed!" Susanna exclaimed.

"No ma'am. The fire did start on the upper floor. Everyone below managed to get out safe. The young lord tossed his uh…companion…out the window when the fire blocked their escape by the door. There were men below waiting to break her fall, so she wasn't hurt bad. The puir lad snapped his leg when he landed, but he'll mend." He stopped to clear his throat. "See, the two of 'em arrived in a coach, not unlike your own, and according to the publican, paid well and gave no names. They went up to bed straightaway. The owner says another bloke came in asking questions about the couple, what they looked like, where they come from and such. He found out little, but I guess he thought it was enough. Three hours later, this fire breaks out above stairs." He shrugged, palms up, as if to invite their conclusion.

"The secrecy surrounding their arrival might have led him to believe they were us," James said, voicing her thoughts exactly. "And the fire was deliberately set because we were thought to be there."

"Aye, sir, I'd say so."

"Good work. Thank you, Quarles," James said. He pulled several folded pound notes from his pocket and slid them toward the rider. The man tucked the reward away, nodded and politely excused himself.

Their meal of stew and brown bread arrived and they ate hurriedly and in silence. James seemed lost in thought and Susanna was still too shocked by events to advance any theories about what they should do. She did know she would be infinitely glad to be home and off the road. *Home*, she called it, knowing nothing about the place that soon would be just that to her.

When they were on their way again, she ventured a few questions, trying to lead up to a description of the place without seeming apprehensive. "Have the Garrows always lived at Galioch?" she asked him.

"Nay, only since the king granted it to us after Charlie's Year."

"That would be Charles Stewart."

"Aye, who else?" The distraction she'd provided actually elicited a grin from him. "You're wantin' a history then?" he asked.

"Aye," she mimicked with a smile. "Are ye outlaws all?"

"Close enough," he admitted. "The Garrows go back to the 14th Century, the first bein' Alexander Stewart, a bastard of Robert, the Second Bruce. Alexander was also known as the Wolf Of Badenoch, called so for his wickedness, I expect. We know he took full advantage of his royal connection to avoid punishment for his antics. As libertines went, he was famous."

"Infamous, I would say."

He laughed. "He corrupted a priest's wife so they say, then he burned down a cathedral and was excommunicated."

"Nice fellow," she remarked dryly. "So that's how your family escaped being Jacobites?"

"Nay. He was reinstated when he expressed his remorse."

"So how did you become…not Catholic? What are you, by the way?" Susanna was dismayed to realize she had no notion what religion she had married into.

"Reluctant Presbyterian," he admitted and promptly skirted the topic. "Our name in Gaelic is Macgarraidh, which means Son of Wild and Wicked Man, referring of course to Alexander's way of life. We Anglicized the name sometime before, or more probably during, the '45."

"Culloden," she reiterated, recalling the history of the battle resulting in the death of the clans as Scotland knew them, the outlawing of their ways and customs. Poverty. Famine.

"Aye. One of the sons—courageous favorite and beloved of the clan—fought for Charlie and died on the field, claymore in hand, but another stayed home and swore to England. Hedged the bet, so to speak. It was not uncommon. And with our close ties to the royal Stewarts, the only thing that saved us."

"So he kept Galioch?"

"Only by the skin of his teeth. Before we were granted the castle and lands in the Highlands, the family was of Moray. The old Wolf's Castle is there, now but a pile of rubble."

"Interesting. You might have been homeless or worse. At least Galioch's not in ruin."

"Damned close," he replied, his lips firming and his gaze sliding away from hers. "I hope you're not expecting much, Suz."

She did not bother to protest the nickname. Susanna feared she might be called worse before she won the regard of his people. He had said nothing about hatred for the English prevailing after their living through a century of defeat, but how could it help but thrive in the Highlands, regardless of his wily ancestor's public declaration of supporting the English cause? There must be bad feelings even today.

With a murderer at her back and social hostility ahead of her, Susanna decided that becoming a real wife to James Garrow was the least of her worries. Maybe she should surrender to intimacy with him to ensure that he wouldn't toss her to the wolves.

No, though it would be no sin and almost certainly no great sacrifice, she could not do so yet. Not with a man who was, for all practical purposes, still little more than a stranger.

"I'll protect you, lass," he told her as he reached for her gloved hand and held it in his. Did the man read minds? "You're under the Garrow plaid now for good and all," he added.

She thought of the old publican in the Gorse Dew and the dirty woolen kilt he wore belted round his considerable girth. She supposed there were worse plaids to be associated with than Garrow's.

"Do you ever wear the kilt?" she asked.

He offered her a smile that wolfish ancestor of his would surely have coveted. "Aye, I do. They're all the rage now since your queen approves."

"My queen?" she asked pointedly. "To whom do *you* bow, Garrow, if not her royal majesty?"

He looked out the window, squinting at the distant hills. "No one yet," he replied.

Chapter Seven

With the last of the evening sun's rays striking the stone face of it, Galioch looked fair enough from a distance. Closer to, the faults would be all too obvious.

The crumbled remnants of the wall were hardly recognizable for what they were, but that was an old injury to the place, wrought centuries ago shortly after the advent of gunpowder. Now it merely served as a picturesque stone fence and was mostly disguised by brambles, vines and trash trees. Nay, it was the keep itself that fostered pity in those who had known it in its glory.

James tried to see it through the eyes of his wife as they approached it on the winding road through the hills and glens. Susanna would be used to a grand estate in the country with carefully tended gardens, also a fancy town house in Grosvenor Square, and maybe additional accommodations in one of the resort towns. Here she would have to make do with weedy, overgrown grounds and a drafty old place that was lucky to still have a few beds in it. He had sold everything worth selling.

He awaited her appraisal, determined not to apologize for his home. At least his people were fed, healthy and not living in squalor in the surrounding cottages.

"Charming," she said in that bright breathless way she had when she lied and tried to sound sincere.

James smiled at her attempt at politeness and simply said, "Thank you."

"The supplies I ordered shipped should arrive soon," she told him. "Then we shall begin repairs." She must have seen the roof.

"Supplies? What supplies?" He frowned, trying to recall whether they had discussed any such thing while he was drunk.

"Building materials, seed for planting, fabrics for clothing and the like," she replied offhandedly. "Oh, look! Someone is running down to meet us. Do you suppose he knows it is you arriving?"

James, not in the least distracted from her announcement about supplies, ignored her question and asked one of his own. "Who gave you leave to ship things here?"

She tugged at her glove and refused to look at him. "You did, of course. After all your mumbling about Galioch while in your fevered state—"

"Fevered state? I was foxed! And that's your doin', not mine. If I said—"

"I realized there was much to be done here," she continued as if he hadn't spoken. "More than at Drevers, I dare say. So I sent Thomas to arrange for what was probably needed."

"Probably needed!" He scoffed. "And how did you think I'd pay for what you had sent?" he asked, mentally tallying the small amount he had left from Thomas's cashing in of his wages from the construction site. It was doubtful there was enough left for the bare minimum of winter food stores, much less what she would have delivered here.

She granted him a glance. "It is already paid for. They would not agree to ship it otherwise."

"Damn you, I can care for my own, Susanna! How dare you—"

"I do dare. This is a trait of mine you must learn to live with, Garrow. You *were* warned."

"Then I'll accept no wages for my position at Drevers when I assume it," he declared.

"Pride goeth before a—"

"Fall," he snapped, completing her warning. "Aye, I know, but I've already fallen about as far as a man can without diggin' a hole beneath him. Pride's all I've got left and you'd take that as well!"

She placed a hand on his arm and he shook it off angrily.

"Garrow...James, I only meant to help."

"Aye, well, you did, I expect. And I'll be thankin' you for it no doubt, but it rankles to be dependin' on a lass's fortune if you see what I mean."

"You might not believe it, but truly I do. Imagine yourself a *lass,* Garrow, and what it would be like to have to ask a man for everything you get, from the food you eat to pennies for the ribbons. You don't imagine that I earned all of that money I spent on your supplies? No, it came from my father. As a woman of my class, I have no source of income whatsoever. If I took a paid position as governess or companion—my only options other than marriage, I might add—I should still be at the mercy of some man holding the purse strings. And might be forced to participate in something scandalously wicked with him in order to ensure that I was paid for my honest work. You're no better than I to find yourself obliged to accept the largesse of others."

James stared at her, seeing she was serious. Her plight

as a woman had nothing in common with his. Nothing! And yet...

"Later I might think on that. For now, spare me a minute to fume, would you?"

He crossed his arms over his chest and glared straight ahead, doing just that. Out of the corner of his eye, he noticed her bite back a smile. She'd had her way; why shouldn't she smile?

"Discounting pride, if you'd asked me, I could've talked 'em down on the price of the goods," he told her. "God knows I've had the practice."

She nodded. "I concede that. There probably will be more things needed than what I've purchased. You'll see to those."

"Thank you, your highness, for granting me leave."

"You're quite welcome," she said. "Now who is that man dashing toward us at such a pace. He looks fit to collapse."

"'Tis Orvie."

"The poor thing's hardly in condition to run headlong in such a way. Is he mad?"

"Some say so," James admitted.

"Truly mad?" she demanded, her worried expression shifting to one of fear.

"A bit daft, not dangerous." He lifted his cane, knocked on the ceiling of the coach and turned to Susanna when it came to a halt at his signal. "He'll be wantin' a ride. I hope you don't mind."

Before she could answer, Orvie appeared at the window. "Jamie! Where've ye been?"

"The city, Orvie. Edinburgh." He opened the door from the inside and beckoned. "Come inside, then. I'll give you a hand up." He grasped the huge hand and gave a firm tug. Orvie filled the coach, rocking it as he settled himself in the seat opposite them.

James knocked for the coach to resume its winding path up the road home. "Orvie, this is my wife, Lady Susanna."

"You got bairns?" he asked, offering her but the briefest of glances.

Susanna took a deep, audible breath of what was most likely shock. "No, none," she answered.

"Jamie likes bairns," he announced. "We've two dozen now. That'd be...uh...twenty and six. Aye, Jamie?"

"Twenty and four," James said, correcting him.

"Margie had twins," Orvie argued.

"Then twenty-six is right. *Very* good."

Orvie was a great lummox of a lad, almost as tall as James himself and half again as broad. His clumsy gait, stooped stature and layers of ill-fitting clothes gave him the look of a fat man, though he was only stoutly built. His body had aged three decades now, but his mind remained less than seven years old, the agreed upon age of reason in this day and time.

"What did ye bring me, Jamie?" he asked, his soft, childlike voice high pitched and eager.

James reached into his coat pocket and pulled out a smooth stone about half the size of his fist. He made his voice go deep, secretive, to pique Orvie's interest. "'Tis yers, laddie. A piece o' history, tha'. A stone from the gret vic'try o' Stirling Bridge where Wallace drubbed ol' Longshanks' laddies sae sound they ne'er halted till they gained Lunnon. 'Twas 1297, Orvie. Think on it, 1297, nigh six hundred years past."

"Och, a wonder, tha'!" Orvie's eyes rounded as he

took the rock between his fingers and released a great sigh. Suddenly he banged on the door with his fist.

Obligingly, James tapped the ceiling again for the coach to stop. He turned the door's handle and opened it, then watched as Orvie made an ungainly exit and took off down the road, huffing and running at a gallop, holding the stone out from him like some religious relic.

"Shame on you for such wicked deception," Susanna said, frowning at him as he turned to her. "You found that rock at our last stop, nowhere near Stirling Bridge. I saw you pick it up."

James shrugged off her criticism. "I know. Orvie's a mite hard to teach. I get in a short lesson wherever and whenever I'm able. We're working on history."

Her smile blossomed. "And he will repeat that story for everyone and thereby remember it." She bit her bottom lip and he could see tears in her eyes.

"Don't be feeling too sorry for Orvie, mind," he warned her. "He'll be taking advantage if you let him."

Her gloved hand pressed his arm in a gesture of what felt like admiration. "That is wonderful of you to make an effort to teach one of your people, especially one such as he."

"Oh, Orvie's not one of mine," James assured her. "He's one of *yours.*"

"From Drevers?"

"Aye."

"So he is actually *my* responsibility?" She looked daunted by the notion.

"Nay, I put it wrong. I only meant he was born at Drevers. But Orvie belongs to us all."

James was thankful for Susanna's compassion, but he knew how easy it was for anyone to be kind and caring of a simple lad like Orvie. But what would happen when she met the canny ones? Those would be her challenge. And since he would be the one to bring her among them, the task of seeing that she fit in here would be his as well.

Susanna felt much better about things after meeting the poor boy, Orvie, and seeing how her husband dealt with him. It was a feature of Garrow she would never have expected.

Well, that was not altogether true. He had shown kindness to her on occasion, though it was usually accompanied with a touch of amusement that invariably made her angry. Perhaps she had not given him the credit he was due. There seemed to be depths to the man that bore exploration, layers that she had not imagined.

Then she remembered the small statue that had spoken to her silently and yet so very eloquently about her husband's inner beliefs with regard to her cause. It was a thing they shared without his even knowing. He had a good heart beneath his bluster.

He had gotten past that pride of his quickly enough— or at least pretended to—when she had told him of the things she had ordered to make life more palatable here in the wilds. That had surprised her. He had been quite frank about admitting his petulance, then dismissed it without further remonstrance. What an enigma he was turning out to be when she had thought him quite uncomplicated. Still, she believed she could manage him well enough. So long as he didn't kiss her.

The thought of his doing so again continued to plague her.

All too soon, the coach halted again, this time directly in front of the gray stone edifice gracing Galioch Keep. The centuries old building itself was imposing, two joined towers, four stories high with slitted windows and a crenelated top. It was probably too small to warrant being called a castle, at least in this day and age.

Trees had been planted round it, which, for the sake of defense, would not have been there in days of old. It appeared that in the more recent past, someone had attempted to soften the harsh and daunting exterior with climbing ivy and shrubbery which had grown leggy and wild.

A riot of flowers bloomed here and there, dotting what used to be the bailey with splashes of color as foreign to this landscape as gorse would be in the midst of father's front lawn. As foreign as *she* would be here in this uncivilized place. But she would civilize it, she promised herself and smiled at the welcoming blossoms.

Garrow was already out of the coach now, had lowered the steps and was waiting for her to descend. He appeared somber as she reached for his hand.

"I bid you welcome to Galioch," he said very formally and with barely a trace of his brogue.

"Thank you," she replied, brushing down her skirts and straightening her bonnet. "Where is everyone?"

Though she had not expected a full retinue of liveried servants lined up to greet the master home, she had thought there would be a few people.

"Working, I hope. There's no reason for them to hang about here since there's nothing much at the keep to do. Word will go 'round soon enough. They'll come out of curiosity if nothing else. Orvie will broadcast the news I'm home." He shook his head as he led her to the main entrance. "But in showing off his giftie, he might not remember to tell them about you."

She laughed merrily. "Second fiddle to a rock! I've never had such a set down!"

He smiled at her. "I like your laughter, lass. Hold on to it."

Well, that sounded ominous, Susanna thought as he opened the huge oak-paneled door and stood aside for her to enter. She stepped over the threshold into another world. For a long time, she stood breathless, circling slowly, entranced by the primitive beauty of it all. "Oh, my...it is wonderful," she whispered. "Magnificent!"

"Magnificent?" He sounded disbelieving. He, too, looked around him as if he had never seen it before.

"Oh, *yes!*" The sibilance of her whisper seemed to echo about them in the grand hall. "It is so...old! Ancient, really! I love it already!"

He mumbled something that sounded like, "No accounting for taste." Then he took her arm and began to escort her through the cavernous stone chamber with its bare flagstone floors and half-timbered walls. She peered up, fascinated by the whitewashed plaster between the dark sturdy beams, the yellowed background enlivened by faded rose-and-green floral designs wrought by some long-dead artist.

The romance of it all nearly overwhelmed her. Her old nanny's fantastic tales of knights and ladies of olden times came to life in this place. Dragons and swords and silvery suits of armor danced through her mind.

In ghostly array, she saw a dais set there before the enormous fireplace at the far end of the hall. Long, narrow tables extending before it, all laden with white linen and huge roasts of lamb, fruits spilling from pewter platters, chased silver and carved wooden goblets and scooped-out manchets of bread to serve as trenchers.

There would be swords—huge claymores—crossed and gleaming above the heavy beam of a mantel. A device, of course, done in jeweled tones, its design that of Garrow's coat of arms. Or her family's. Perhaps both.

"A blank canvas," she murmured to herself. Someone had emptied this room so that she could fill it again with her own dreams. Oh, she hoped the rest of the keep was as unencumbered with late additions that would mock its ancient simplicity. She so wanted to restore Galioch to what it once must have been. Rather, how she pictured it as having been. "I do love it," she said again.

"Are you well, Suz?" he was asking her.

She shook off her fantasy for a moment, looked up at him and smiled her appreciation. "Oh, I am better than well, James."

"James, is it? There's a first."

Susanna felt her face heat with a blush and lowered her gaze. Suddenly she had seen him within the fantasy as a laird of yesteryear, wearing a flowing white shirt and draped in the colors of his patriarchal clan, a broadsword in his hand and geared up to do battle.

"This way's the kitchens if you want to see," he muttered in a cautious voice.

Susanna sighed and followed along. "You certainly know how to dash a mood."

Indeed, he hadn't done so at all, she soon realized. Everything about the tour of Galioch reinforced her need, her absolute craving, to make it hers in every way.

Until she met Hilda.

"You should be comfortable enough here," James was telling Susanna as he showed her his mother's chamber.

He heard Hilda stomping upstairs, coming upon them like a fury from hell.

"Gormless young snake, you wilna be puttin' yer fancy whores in yer mam's bed and tha's tha'!" Hilda shouted. "I'll no' have it!" Her fat finger shook dangerously close to his nose.

James wished to God he hadn't sold all the brandy in the cellars. The whisky was too damned new to drink and the only wine left had likely turned to vinegar.

"Hildy, calm yourself," he implored, grasping her offending hand, afraid his old governess was falling into an apoplectic fit, so red in the face she was. "Here's my wife, not a lightskirt. I'd never bring a—"

"Wife? Wha's tha' ye say? Yer marrit?" Her mouth fell open with surprise.

"Aye," James said with a smile meant to disarm her. "Meet Susanna. We were wed in Edinburgh."

Hilda's cheeks puffed out, pushing the wrinkles on them up under her narrowed eyes. "And who might yer people be, lass? Best not say Douglas." Her gaze darted to James's and stuck. "She ha' th' look of 'em."

James laughed away her fears. "Nay, Hildy. She's Earl Eastonby's daughter." He slipped an arm around Susanna's shoulders and drew her to his side. Whether for her protection or his, James didn't know.

"Och! God sev us, a *sassanach?*" Hilda beat one fist against her chest as if her heart was stopping. "Naaay," she moaned.

"Aye, but she—"

That was when the explosion occurred.

"You take your wicked, ungrateful, war-mongering hide out of my house!" Susanna had ordered, her voice starting dangerously soft and rising on every distinct syllable. She stood clear of him and flung out one hand toward the open doorway. "I'll have no lingering war under my roof, old woman! I never marched on Scotland to do you any grief and I will *not* be blamed for things that happened before my grandfathers were born, do you hear?''

James wasn't certain what he should have expected Susanna to do under such circumstances, but she shocked even him, not to mention the crotchety old woman.

Hilda gasped, speechless. She even staggered back a few steps, the first backing down James had ever seen her do.

But Susanna advanced. ''And as for your tone with the baron—your own laird—who has been working his fingers to nubs trying to put food on your table and clothes on your back, you owe him a profound apology for insolence. One accomplished on your misbegotten knees! So, do that immediately. Then get out and do not return here until you can keep a civil tongue in your head!''

Hilda fainted. James caught her before she hit the floor and carried her—sweating profusely with the effort, more because of her weight than his leg injury—to his mother's bed.

Susanna wrung her hands, leaning over Hilda. ''She isn't dead is she? Have I killed her?''

Now her voice was tiny, like a bairn knowing she'd done wrong and sorry for it.

''Nay,'' James assured her, his thumb and first two fingers pressed to Hilda's wrist. ''But I guess she could do with a bit of water to revive her.''

''I have something better,'' Susanna declared, grabbing up the drawstring purse attached to her wrist and rummaging inside it. She brought a small container out. ''Smelling salts.'' She opened it and stuck it directly under Hilda's nose.

The woman flew upright like a corpse come alive. Her language even singed his ears and he'd lived amongst sailors for a year.

James winced, grasped Susanna's arm and dragged her back out of reach. Hilda had scrambled off the bed quick as a lass of ten and stalked out of the room, slinging her arms wide along with epithets. Mixing Gaelic, English and profanity like saltpeter, charcoal and sulfur.

Another explosion in the making, James thought. She was stirring up ammunition and going for reinforcements.

He and Susanna had listened, dumbstruck, as the clatter of Hilda's hard-soled shoes grew faint on the winding stone stairs and they heard the eventual slam of the stout oak door.

Susanna recovered first. She blinked owlishly, released the breath she'd been holding in a prolonged huff and looked perfectly calm. "A bit temperamental, isn't she!"

James had been at a loss for words. God only knew what would happen next. If Orvie hadn't spread the news about the new wife, Hilda surely would. And it would be more in the nature of summoning the clan for war than for celebration. Damn.

He would have to put his foot down and demand they accept Susanna in the name of peace and order. Though he had asserted himself in the role before, he hated playing the ogre. So many of Galioch's people were old enough to have known him since he was born. Hilda had nursed him, coddled him and bandaged his hurts when he was a bairn. He knew how difficult it was for her and most of the others to see him as a grown man and ruling laird even though he was near thirty and had proved his mettle. But he would have to assert his authority now and maintain it.

No more of this hale-fellow-well-met Jamie Lad who joked about and permitted their teasing. He must establish Susanna as lady of this house and institute some kind of accord between them and her. Otherwise, he would have to remove her to Drevers and live there instead.

News traveled like thistledown in a fierce wind, however, and she might find no warmer welcome there than here.

Aye, he did need that drink. He left her in his mother's room, now hers since it was the only one besides his own that had any furnishings left. She had seemed strangely unmoved by the exchange with Hilda after it was over, as if it were no more than the usual introduction.

Was it the usual for her? His own first meeting with Susanna had been markedly hostile, he recalled. It had not taken all that long for them to come to an understanding, but he couldn't yet say she had completely gotten over her anger about the arranged marriage. Though she had claimed it was her choice to go through with it, they both knew what her options had been.

Her defense of him to Hilda came as a shock. How should he interpret that? Had she defended him personally or his station?

And he had thought he knew a lot about women. Ha. Maybe it was only wives that were this puzzling. He should talk to her before she faced the clan, he thought, but hardly knew what he would say. *Smile at them? Be yourself?* Maybe she was being herself. Maybe the smiles she'd had for him lately were an expression beyond what was natural for her.

Or maybe she was only a frightened young lass and that bravado was the only way she knew how to face her fears.

Slowly he got up and went down to the kitchens to see if he could find that vinegary wine. He needed some sort of bracing up before the inevitable confrontation. It should have occurred to him there might be one, after his choosing an Englishwoman like his father had done. Somehow, James had hoped his people would be more appreciative of the fact that he had married for their own benefit. But the clan would have its say, especially the womenfolk.

By his reckoning of the speed with which Hilda could run, tell her tale and fire up her wee army for the march on the keep, he had considerably less than an hour to prepare.

Chapter Eight

James waited for them outside the front door. Susanna, who had no inkling about the approaching furor, was still upstairs. Though he had advised her to rest, she'd set right in unpacking her trunk and his. He had brought up the wrapped remainder of the bread and cheese acquired at their last stop and had watered down a cup of the sorry wine for her.

Something had to be done about meals, he thought as he paced and waited. When Hilda and the rest arrived, he would give his orders and see they were followed to the letter. The place must be made habitable for Susanna. They'd kept it clean, but save for the two bedchambers, it stood as empty as the bloody coffers.

Until assured that she would not be made uncomfortable and unwelcome, he dared not leave her here while he went to settle matters at Drevers. Yet it might be even more dangerous to have her come with him. The steward there would almost surely kick up a fight about leaving. He knew Colin well enough to know the man considered the place his now after Eastonby's leaving it to his mercy for years.

He stopped pacing and scanned the horizon when he

heard the noise. They were striding with purpose from the cots that dotted the hills of heather and gorse, darting around fences that set off the planted keel gardens and wading through Margie's ragged flower beds.

Children and old alike, they came, showing an energy he had not observed in years. For an instant, he was almost glad that most were away working where the money was, just as he had been. Few were present betwixt the ages of sixteen and forty unless they were women with bairns to look after.

Were there rocks in those sacks some were swinging? There had better not be! Nay, he decided, they probably carried their meager belongings and would be on their way after giving him a piece of their collective mind. Was he running them off by bringing in an English-woman? They'd been none too fond of his mother and her circle of friends, that was for certain.

When they drew closer, he saw the smiles. Hilda's in particular, rare as it was. Gloating was she? Relishing this setdown she planned? His anger flared so high, he thought he might combust. They wanted a fuss over this, they'd damned sure get one!

"Jamie, lad!" cried old Bertram, picking up speed as he ran at him like a battering ram. Before James could decide what it meant, Bertie had grabbed him in a bear hug and near lifted him from the ground. The noise grew deafening and he could hardly get a deep breath with all the pounding on his back and bodies closing in around him.

He began to laugh, with relief at his own foolish worries and with them in the delight they were showing at his being home again. They carried him high now—Bertie, Will and Doug—mostly, jostling him on their stout shoulders and knocking his head on the door frame as they hauled him inside the hall.

Calling for the bride, they were, loud and lang. James could only hope she stayed put and would bar the door. When several of the more raucous bampots took off up the stairs to get her, James struggled to get free. But they were having none of it, dancing him around to Bobby's fiddle while Angus stood cranking up his pipes.

It looked to be a ceilidh in the making, not a rare occurrence whenever he returned, but more boisterous than usual. His gaze met Hilda's over the crowd that surrounded him. Her laughter had gone, replaced by a beatific smile. He returned it, hoping to God it meant what he thought it did. If not, he would have to banish her when this day's business was done.

Susanna's screams filtered through the carrying-on. They'd found her. No great feat. Getting her down to the hall might be, he thought, suddenly afraid they might drop her on the stairs. "Lemme doon, Will!" he shouted, tugging on the smithy's sparse hair. "My wife's afeared!"

That wrung hoots of laughter. "Would ye hear the ill-trickit braggin' th' noo? Scares her, he does! Wi' tha' wee sausage o yers?"

James pounded the smith's head. "I'll be havin' tha' sausage o' yers served up to ye bashit like neeps if ye don't mind m'order. Put me doon!"

They dropped him. He landed on his arse and might have broken something if someone hadn't grabbed his arms on the way down to break the fall. "Bastartin wags!" he bellowed and frowned up to see Susanna standing in the circle opened before him, her hair loose and flowing, a lopsided wreath of flowers hanging down over one eye.

A hush fell over the assembly. She raised a hand and snatched out one of the offending blooms, strode over to him and tucked it behind his ear. Then she straightened, threw back her head and laughed, snatching up Will's hand and motioning with the other to Bobby and his fiddle. Pandemonium erupted and the ceilidh was on.

By God, she'd won them over.

He got his feet under him and managed to stand, only to be swept into the circle of dancers and dragged along tripping over his feet until he recovered. His leg ached like the devil, but it was a good hurt.

James threw himself into the revelry with abandon, eyeing sacks each had tossed in a pile to one side of the door. Gifties, he realized, got up within the hour, treasures from their pitiful stashes of family trinkets and sadly depleted larders.

When exhaustion claimed him, he bowed out and went to sit on the huge raised hearth to rest.

Several of the women had laid a fire and were putting mutton on the spits to cook. Not whole legs or roasts, but the smaller portions that would have been carefully rationed out to each family for their week's supply.

He grasped the hand of the nearest and brought it to his lips. "My thanks, Margie. To all of you. There'll be plenty soon, I swear on it."

She grinned and pinched his nose. "Aye, Jamie. We ne'er doubt ye'll provide one way or t'other. Is she rich then, this wife of yers?"

He nodded and cast a glance toward Susanna, who looked to be having the time of her life with hair and skirts a-whirl, hands clapping and steps agile as she danced an eightsome reel.

"Richer than she knows at the moment."

He shook off the sentiment and smiled up at Margie.

"Twins for you this time, Orvie tells us. Jack'll be that glad."

She beamed as she took up the bowl she'd brought to stir up oats and water for the griddle. "Get yersel' busy now ye're marrit. I'm four ahead of ye."

He looked at Susanna again and smiled with anticipation. She'd thrown herself into their marriage celebration with a whole heart. Would she follow through with the rest of it?

Kenneth, his favorite cousin and master brewer, shoved a cup into his hand and plopped down beside him, grinning. "Green whisky, best there is!"

"And all we got," James muttered, taking a long draught of the biting brew. "Melt yer damned teeth," he gasped.

"And all yer troubles," Kenneth added, bouncing his cup off of James's. "Slaint."

They watched the revelry for a while, then James spoke. "We've a shipment of goods arriving up the firth. Might have beat us here. Go, come the morning, and see to it for me? It's paid for." He fished out a few bills and handed them over. "Rent some carts and beasts to pull 'em, however many's needed."

"Aye, glad to. Ye'll be right busy wi' yer wife these next days, I expect."

"Nay, I'm for Drevers to oust Mr. Colin. Eastonby gave the place to Susanna and I'm to manage it."

"Ach, God's smilin'. No more traipsin' off to Auld Reekie to cut rocks?"

"No more," James agreed.

It surprised him to realize he would miss it a bit, his carving. It satisfied some need deep within him to create something smooth and elegant out of mere rough-dressed stone. He looked around the hall, noticing as he never had before the roughness of this place. Maybe, if he put his mind to it, he could fashion something grander, something a bit smoother, out of this stack of rocks.

He took another healthy swallow of the unaged whisky, ignoring the burn in his throat and gullet.

Susanna had stopped dancing and was headed over to join him on the hearth. He watched her, admiring her graceful carriage, the flush of excitement on her smooth alabaster cheeks, the curves of her slender figure.

Maybe, James thought, if he put forth the best of his efforts, he could also carve out something wonderful in the way of a life. For the past few years now, his had been nothing but rough, cold and hard as the densest block of Italian granite.

The laird in James felt cautiously optimistic, the artist in him itched to begin, and the husband couldn't wait to take up the challenge.

Susanna returned his smile and sat down beside him.

"Did they give you a fright when they came to get you?" James asked her.

She laughed and pressed a hand to her chest. "I was terrified! Only when they stuck the flowers on my head did I realize they didn't mean to chop it off! They spoke very kindly, but I fear I could hardly understand a word they said. And I thought your brogue was thick. When you forget yourself, that is. Most of the time—"

When his eyebrows drew together and his smile dimmed, she rushed to explain. "Oh, not that I mind at all the way you…or they…speak. It's fine. Musical in a way. But some of the words, I've never even heard before."

"I speak Queen's English as well as you do, Susanna. It is my mother tongue. If my speech offends you, you must say so and I will change it to please you. As for the others," he said in the perfect manner of her own peers, "you must take them as they are. It seems they have accepted you well enough despite your unfamiliar vowels."

Instead of snapping back at his accusation, Susanna simply nodded and sighed. "I know. You misunderstood me entirely. I only meant that I wish to understand what they say. Instead, I find myself nodding and smiling or frowning, taking my cues from their expressions. Answering their questions is impossible."

"They've questioned you, have they?" he asked with a grin.

Susanna rolled her eyes. "Yes, and I might have agreed to milk their goats for all I know."

He laughed and slapped his knee. "That I'd pay to see!"

"I did understand Hilda this afternoon. She made herself quite clear. I won't apologize for what I said, James."

"Nor should you. Flyin' in her face as you did is what got you all this respect."

She looked up at him warily. "You think so?"

He leaned close and slid his arm around her, splaying his fingers at her waist. His lips drew close to her ear. "Aye, I know so, though I didn't expect at the time it would turn out that way. Began as you mean to go and I applaud you for it. You stood right up to her. Where was your fear then?"

"Hiding behind my anger? I can't really say." She drew away a few inches, aware of their being observed.

"Are you afraid of me, Suz?" he asked, his voice brushing across her senses like warm dark velvet.

She cleared her throat and sat straighter, tearing her

gaze from his lips. "Not at all, but you are being rather forward for the time and place, sir."

His soft rumble of laughter was almost her undoing. "*Sir*, is it now? My, we have a ways t'go, lass, if it's back to that."

"Sir, it must be," she hissed between her teeth. "Mind where we are if you will!"

"They'll be expecting me to haul you off up the stairs and have my wicked way with you when darkness falls. What then?"

She shifted nervously, unable to put the picture of that out of mind. "Then—then we pretend, I suppose. I won't put up a fuss if you urge me upstairs. But when they go away, I would prefer not—not doing as they might think we are doing." She sounded horribly prim, even to herself.

He removed his hand and shrugged. "As you wish." But the expression he wore in no way agreed with his concession to honor her wishes.

"I believe I am afraid of you, after all," she admitted.

His gaze slid over her and returned to meet hers. "Maybe you could hide it again behind something other than anger this time?"

His suggestion tugged a smile out of her in spite of herself. "Behind what?"

"I'll think on it and come up with something," he said. And that sounded much more like a promise than a concession.

"Meanwhile, shall we dance?" he asked. "Do you waltz?"

She was both surprised that *he* did and tempted that he asked her to. "Everyone knows that is a scurrilous and improper exercise, sir!"

He grinned and stood, offering his hand. "Do you not read history?"

She blinked up at him. "History is my passion, I'll have you know."

"Well then, you should be well aware, Scots are scurrilous people cursed to hell with impropriety. Every one of your chroniclers says it."

"So they do. I suppose we should live up to their expectations!" Susanna took his hand and rose from the hearth. Without so much as a signal from her husband, the fiddler ended the current reel abruptly and plied his bow to three-quarter time. She could have wept at the beauty of the lone violin as James swept her across the smooth flagstones to the strains of Strauss.

Susanna closed her eyes and followed his lead, imagining how many brides of yesteryear must have glided elegantly across this ancient floor on the arms of their handsome lairds. And here she was, following in their very footsteps.

The romance of it was enough to make her forget her ultimate mission here if she wasn't careful.

As he had predicted, after he had admired all the gifts, thanked the clan profusely, made the obligatory speech and toasts to his bride, the crowd made a huge to-do over rushing them off to bed. The revelers followed them all the way up to the door of his bedroom and made the token effort to accompany them inside.

James knew he had been wise to warn Susanna beforehand. Good as her word, she went willingly as he ushered her ahead of him. She blushed becomingly at their bawdy suggestions—though he hoped she didn't ken *all* of what they'd said—and even laughed with him after he closed the door.

He held up the half bottle of freshly brewed whisky and raised his brow in question.

"Oh, no!" she answered, shaking her head emphatically. "Not again! I lost my breath on the first swallow. Put it away!"

James had one more taste and set it aside on the mantelpiece. "They'll be cleaning the hall for a bit and then will go home. Meanwhile, you'd best stay with me."

When he saw her smile fade, he assured her, "Only for an hour or less. Won't you sit down?" He gestured toward the only chair in the room, a threadbare thing of comfort he had known would not sell for more than a few bob and so, had kept.

She sat gingerly on the edge of the seat, looking up at him with an unsettled expression, obviously trying to pretend the huge canopied bed on the other side of the room did not exist. "So. What—what shall we do? Have you a deck of cards or something?"

"No cards. We might have to resort to actual conversation."

"Oh. Well, I can't imagine why you would put it that way. After all, we have been conversing for over a week now."

"And have said very little to one another that really matters in the way of things."

She glanced about nervously and twisted her hands in her lap. "What shall we discuss? Drevers!" she exclaimed, latching on to an impersonal subject. "That matters, certainly."

James nudged the small footstool on the hearth to one side of the fireplace so that he could sit and lean back against the wall. He sat, stretched out his legs and crossed his ankles. Susanna tucked her feet back slightly so that they would not be so near his. "So it does. First thing tomorrow I plan to go there and get rid of Mr. Colin."

"High time, if all you say is true about the man. He will resist leaving."

James agreed. "Aye, but I'll leave him no choice about it."

She leaned forward, frowning, and almost reached out to him. "You will go armed. Have you another weapon besides the one Father gave you?"

"Aye."

"I shall take that one, then. Could I see it please? What sort is it?"

He laughed at the thought of her hefting the heavy old pistol. "Not a thing you'd be waving about in *my* vicinity. No reason for you to come, Susanna. Wait until I have—"

"Drevers is mine, you said. I shall be going with you, James. If you leave me here, I shall ride over alone."

"On what, astride one of the ewes? There's but one mount here."

"Then I shall walk. I will follow you," she insisted. "You're laughing, but what if Mr. Colin won't have your word on my father's wishes?"

"And he'd have yours, you think? I have the papers deeding Drevers to me. Speaking of that, I'll ride on into Beauly afterward and change that as I promised."

"I will ride pillion. Is the horse able to bear both of us?"

"Susanna…"

She threw up her hands and scoffed. "There's nothing that says Colin will be violent, is there? He won't be expecting us, so you have the element of surprise in your favor. We will simply tell the man to pack his things and leave immediately. He'll have no recourse!"

"I will not put you in danger, Suz!" He stood up and glared at her, thinking perhaps he could intimidate her the way he had done without trying or wanting to only minutes before.

She stood, too, planted her fists on her hips and glared back. "Suppose I would be in greater danger here! What if we were followed? What if that man who set the fire at the inn comes here?"

He gave up his attempt to back her down. "You are a stubborn woman, Susanna Garrow. And damned persistent!"

"Thank you," she said, raising her chin even further. "Now show me the weapon. Even if it's not necessary for me to carry it tomorrow, I should like to fire it. Mechanical things interest me."

"Do they now?" He shrugged off his anger since it was totally useless anyway and went to the clothes press to get the pistol.

"Ah," she cooed, her eyes widening at the sight of the old brass-mounted flintlock. She reached for it and held it braced against her wrist and arm while she ran a finger over the flat brass inlay that vined down the dark wooden stock. "Beautiful workmanship. How long have you had it?"

"It belonged to my grandfather. 'Tis actually a holster weapon, made before dueling pistols were created for that specific purpose."

"So it hasn't a twin?"

"One of a kind."

James opened the small box with the powder, ball and accoutrements. Setting that aside on the mantel, he proceeded to explain to her how the weapon worked. Their hands touched as he turned the gun this way and that to point out the features and pantomime how it was loaded, primed and fired. She seemed enthralled with the weapon, excited about handling it.

He was enthralled with *her* and excited, period.

"So heavy," she said, looking over her shoulder at him expectantly from beneath her fanlike lashes. He was standing behind her, his arms around her, his hands guiding hers. He caressed her trigger finger with his in a slow suggestive movement. She trembled. "Is it...accurate?"

"Not very," he murmured, leaning down to brush his lips across hers.

She made a small sound in her throat, then drew in a deep breath, pulled away from him and turned around. Both her hands locked around the pistol as she held it to her chest. "Um. You had best use this one and give me the other."

"Other what?"

She tore her gaze from his and held out the gun. "The Webley Father gave you. This one is too complicated and it would take too long for me to become familiar with it."

James had to shake his head to clear it. He turned away to place the weapon on the mantel beside the whisky bottle. "The earl allowed you to shoot?" he demanded just for something to say that didn't include another demand he had no business making.

"He thought I might enjoy hunting if I learned how."

"And did you?" He could not imagine her stalking about in the woods or fields after game.

"No," she admitted. "I could not bear killing anything, I think. Though I never really did, I saw it done. Grouse. Pheasants. Once, a deer." For a moment she remained silent as if recalling the occasions. "I suppose if there's no other way to obtain meat, hunting is acceptable, but to do so merely for sport..." She shook her head.

James thought now was not the time to engage in a debate about that. He had done both, hunted for the sport of it when younger and later on, to feed his people. "A steady diet of mutton quickly depletes the herd," he remarked.

"Oh, no need to justify that to me," she declared. "I quite understand."

She did no such thing, James knew. But he was very glad she had never gone hungry, had never wondered if her father's larder would empty out before he could afford to replenish it. He silently promised she never would have to worry about that.

Thus far, he had managed to keep food on the tables at Galioch and also provided what he could for those at Drevers. But he often experienced the fear that he would fail at it some day. So many in the Highlands had failed.

The thing that angered him was that Galioch's absence of plenty had nothing whatsoever to do with wars, the old clearances or anything outward imposed on it. It had been his family's fault, clear and simple. His parents had wasted everything and he, though unaware of it at the time, had helped them do it.

In the silence that followed, he heard no sounds from below. "It's safe enough to go to your room now," he told her.

"Yes," she agreed, apparently relieved. "You needn't come with me. I know the way."

"Good night, then," he said softly as he opened the door for her and watched her walk through. "Sleep well."

Disappointment left him in a sour mood. The whisky hadn't helped, either. James slowly undressed, checked his wound, which seemed to be healing despite all his activity, and climbed into bed.

Susanna's sweet scent lingered and should have kept him awake for hours, but when he awakened the next morning, he could not recall its doing that. In fact, it had provided dreams that haunted him throughout the night and lingered on awakening.

The woman was in his blood, deviling him something fierce. Prompting noble thoughts while tempting him to entertain some not so noble. Forget acting nobly. He had not even played at being a gentleman for so long he'd nearly forgotten how.

But he must look like one today. He browsed through the hanging garments in the humble clothes press that had replaced the cherry armoire and found the best suit he had kept after selling his father's clothes.

The black thigh-length frock coat and trousers were exceptionally well cut and styled, the dark waistcoat embroidered in emerald and black silk. He drew out a folded white shirt and fumbled in the drawer beneath the hanging clothes to find a starched collar. Did he still have decent cufflinks left?

Susanna and her father were the first who had ever expected him to act as a baron should, much less look like one. As a youth, James had run wild on the family estate, living a rough-and-tumble life he loved, encumbered only by the few hours a day spent with tutors.

At eleven he had run away to sea simply for the adventure of it. A huge mistake. He had come home broken, sorely regretting the loss of his childhood. After that, he had tried to adapt to adulthood, employing the nearest and dearest examples, his parents. Another grave error in judgment. Then he'd become a university student, one of many struggling to gain knowledge that would never be put to any practical use.

He'd traveled abroad after his last year of study, spending months in Pietrasanta, Italy, hardly the place for a gentleman of any substance to land. That happiest time of his life had been cut short by the accidental death of his parents and the necessity of his returning home.

Inheriting the title of baron had paled to insignificance when compared to the mountain of debts he had inherited. He had sold nearly everything to repay them and had nothing left over. Since that time, James had assumed the yoke of a workingman.

No, he was not nearly as noble as his title might indicate. Certainly nothing like Eastonby should want for his darling daughter. But there it was. He was married to her, for good or ill, and resolved to make it work.

With a snort, he extended his chin upward and attached his collar. That done, he donned the dark-green foulard and rummaged for a stickpin. "Hmph. Brass." He quickly polished it, wishing for the emerald on gold his father had worn with this.

He would never apologize for the way he had handled his debts. The experience of working had proved valuable in many respects. He was glad he had heard tell of numerous new construction projects taking place in Edinburgh. His dabbling in stone sculpture during his months in Italy had paid off. The fact that he had studied architecture helped, too. Had Edinburgh not been so far from home, or his worries about the clan not so intense, the specialized work he had been doing there would have been perfect for him.

But the fact remained: a baron was a baron and a stonecarver was a stonecarver. Rarely did the twain meet in one man. Probably never before.

He set the inexpensive links through the slots in his cuffs and straightened his sleeves with impatient tugs. It was accepted that poverty stricken barons marry money to retain their status as gentlemen. In theory, it seemed practical. In actuality, it stuck in his craw. But he would play the part as was expected.

Checking his appearance as well as he could without a proper mirror, James reached to the shelf where he had put the loaded revolver. It was too large to conceal at his waist so he slipped it into the pocket set into the side seam of his frock coat.

He continued thinking about his marriage because the subject troubled him. Susanna objected to his brogue. It proved damned hard to eliminate it now, after working these past few years next to others born with it, and spending his off months with only the locals for company. There were no gentry close to Galioch or Drevers, as Susanna would soon discover.

She was not yet ready to share his bed, that was the most difficult way in which he must oblige her. He had promised. Noble or not, he did have his honor to uphold.

Ready as he would ever be to take up the new role as Garrow, laird a'mighty, James raked a hand through his hair, noted the omission of hair tonic to slick it down, and groaned. He would never get the hang of being a gentleman again. He was not even sure he wanted to.

"On to conquer Drevers," he muttered and marched out to fetch his baroness. He couldn't very well have her stomping through the heather at the heels of his mare. Might as well drag out the old ponycart and see if the wheels were intact.

"There you are!" Susanna exclaimed, emerging from her room just as he exited his. She remarked on how fine he looked.

He didn't answer, but merely stood as if transfixed by her words. Was she underdressed? Susanna glanced down at her simple green marino. Over one shoulder and belted at the waist she wore the length of heavenly soft wool tartan one of the women had given her last evening as a wedding gift. "Is wearing this not appropriate?" she asked.

He shook his head a little and cleared his throat. "Nay, it's fine. The plaid becomes you well." He sounded ill at ease and she was not certain she believed him.

"I'll be another quarter hour or more seeing to the cart," he told her as he glanced down the stairs. "I smell coffee. Hildy will have been here, I expect. If you'd like to pour us a cup, I'll join you in the kitchens in a while."

He sounded incredibly different this morning. Distant. Formal. Terribly English. She widened her smile and nodded. "Excellent idea. I'll await you there then."

Susanna watched him until he disappeared around the curve in the stairs, then proceeded to go and collect what she would need to take with her. She thought it best to be prepared.

Chapter Nine

"Keep in mind that Colin's not the sort you would be used to," James warned Susanna. He saw by her quickly veiled look of amusement that neither was he. She must think it funny he would point out social differences that were all too obvious.

"What I mean is that he puts on airs," he explained.

"You have had dealings with him often?" Susanna asked, grasping her edge of the cart as the wheel hit a particularly rough patch on the path.

"I spoke to him several times about providing what he should. He was for me minding my own and leaving what he called his alone. Fact is, he's come to think on Drevers as his these past few years, and it has been just that for all practical purposes. His word's law. He cracks the whip and collects the rents."

"He is cruel?" Susanna asked.

James shrugged and tapped the mare's hindquarters gently with the tip of the whip to speed her a bit. "I would not have stood for having anyone hurt. He likely sensed that much. But he deprives them, so I guess you could say he's mean enough. Times where he's let them go hungry. Most who are able—and not more afraid of the unknown than the devil they know—have moved elsewhere. Some came to me or other landowners hereabout and some took ship. There are few left.''

"Then who maintains the estate?" she asked.

"All that's really needed are a few to tend the flocks and do menial jobs about the place. At shearing time, Colin hires. The herds look healthy from what I've seen and he should be getting prime wool off 'em. At first I figured it was Earl Eastonby who demanded big profits and ignored the needs of his people. Then I began to notice how high Colin was living. To tell the truth, I blamed them both until I spoke with your father. He told me Drevers was a huge drain, unable to support itself. Considering the resources Colin has to draw from, that shouldn't be true at all.''

She eyed him for a moment. "Unlike Galioch?"

James sighed. He would have to tell her. "I've had huge debts to settle these past few years. It's taken all I had and could make to pay off liens on Galioch in order to keep it. Once repairs are made—our next largest expense—and I've doubled the herds, I expect we'll begin to see a profit.''

"Heavens, how much did you owe?"

He ignored the question. "We were speakin' of Drevers.''

"Why didn't you write to Father about Mr. Colin?"

James clenched his teeth for a minute before answering. "I did. A Mr. Durston wrote and instructed me not so politely to keep my nose out of the earl's affairs.''

"He's Father's business partner! What has he to do with Drevers?''

"He identified himself as the earl's solicitor. I figured then that the earl didn't dirty his hands fooling with management and keeping track of accounts. God knows, he'd be having enough to do spending all his money, thought I.'' James shot her an apologetic look. ''To tell you the truth, I was loath to give him the benefit of the doubt when I first met him. He comes on harsh, your da.''

She made a face. ''Small wonder you didn't allow those men to do what they planned. If you had not warned Father, he would surely be dead now. I might, as well.''

''I don't hold with killing,'' James told her. ''There's times it's unavoidable, as with those men who attacked us that night, but to ambush someone is wrong in any light.''

''Father does care about those at Drevers, James. I promise you that. He has always been most conscientious about everyone in his employ. I'm certain he merely assumed Mr. Colin was doing what he was paid to do.''

''The earl's a fair man, I grant, but he ought to take heed, dealing with the likes of Colin. And that Durston fellow, too.''

''I've never thought Mr. Durston an unpleasant sort. He seems quite charming.''

James very nearly spat out the side of the cart before he caught himself. ''I'll let you read his letter to me, then see what you think.'' He clicked his tongue to the mare to hurry her along. They were topping the rise and would be at Drevers in a matter of minutes.

The manor house came into view. At least two centuries newer than Galioch, it was built of imported stone and enhanced with ornate carving around and above the doors and numerous windows. The roof was Welsh slate, precisely cut and shaped. Though the place stood but three stories high, James estimated it would contain at least forty rooms, even if some were quite large. Drevers was built entirely for show and not defense.

Susanna leaned forward, her hand at her brow to shade the sun from her eyes. "It is rather large, isn't it?"

"Compared to Galioch, aye. More spread out. Grander. Better furnished, that's for certain, unless Colin's beggared the place."

She straightened and looked at James, shocked. "He wouldn't dare!"

"Nay, I doubt he would," James said with a short laugh. "He'd have had a braw task explaining such if the earl showed up one day, aye?"

"Then the furnishings will be there, you think?"

"They had *better* be there or I'll haul the bugger off to the magistrate for outright theft. We'll probably have reason enough as it is once we see the accounts."

James drove the cart right up to the double front doors of Drevers and got out. He was assisting Susanna down when a lad of about twelve—one of the MacLain boys, James thought—came running to welcome them. "Seamus, is it?" James asked him.

The lad looked at him, then at Susanna, with bright-eyed curiosity, shifting sidewise to take the mare's bit in one hand. "Nay, I be Fergus, sar. Seamus is the elder."

"Well, you've grown then. Last I was here, Seamus had your post."

"He's gone, sar. Took t' the boats." The boy tied the mare to the ring of a hitching post nearby.

James sighed. Another forced away to earn a coin or two for the family.

Susanna nudged him and James remembered his manners. "Lady Susanna, meet Fergus MacLain."

She smiled at the lad. "How do you do, Mr. Mac-Lain."

Fergus's shoulders straightened at the address and he bobbed his head. "Verra well, m'lady. An' yersel'?"

James, anxious to get on with the business at hand, interrupted the pleasantries. "Where are Mr. Colin and Holmes?"

Fergus nodded toward the road. "Mr. Holmes rode awa' three or four days back, but Mr. Colin's inside. I daren't knock."

"Well, I dare!" Susanna said, stalking right up to the doors. Before James could stop her, she opened the portal and walked right in. "This is *my* house, after all!"

Well, she had a point. No reason to act the guest. He followed her inside and left the door standing open.

"Colin!" he shouted as he stepped around Susanna and stood in front of her. "Let me take care of this. 'Tis what you'll be paying me for, aye?" he said in a softer voice.

She didn't answer, but she did stay put.

One of the doors off the foyer opened and Colin appeared. He was a large man of forty years or thereabout. He wore a black suit of expensive worsted and his shoes were buffed to a shine in which you could see your face. He carried a sturdy cane, though he wasn't using it to walk with. That had to be the closest thing to a weapon on him, James thought. His clothes fit too snugly to be concealing a pistol. If he resorted to a fight, James knew he could take him down without much trouble, stout stick or no.

Colin did cut a fine figure and had a face women would likely consider handsome. The dark wavy hair and curled mustache showed no evidence of gray. Both were impeccably oiled and waxed. He could easily pass for a gent if one didn't know what a thieving blackguard he really was.

"Mr. Colin," James said by way of greeting. He hoped

this could be accomplished without a scene since Susanna had come, but he wasn't too optimistic, for all that.

The man looked surprised to see him. "What the devil are you doing here, Garrow?" He drew himself up to his full height, chin out and staring down his nose. "Begging a handout for that ragged huddle of crofters you claim?" He held the smooth ebony, gold-handled cane in one hand and tapped it in the opposite palm.

James smiled. He reached into his breast pocket and withdrew the new deed Eastonby had given him. "I've come to terminate your employment, Colin. You are to vacate Drevers within the hour. The place is ours now." He opened the document and held it up, facing Colin, though he was probably too far away to see anything but the large bold signature of the earl.

The man simply glared at it, then at him. "Forged, surely as you stand there. I've had no correspondence from Earl Eastonby to indicate any change in ownership. Take the woman and get out of here."

"The earl might not take kindly to your ordering his daughter off her own property."

Colin's gaze flew past James's shoulder to Susanna. James knew he shouldn't be enjoying this quite so much. Susanna remained silent, standing several feet behind him and he was thankful for her prudence. If things got rough, she could easily step back outside the door.

Colin sneered. "I'm not going anywhere. You want Drevers, you'll have to take it, Garrow."

James shrugged. "If you insist, I will. But mark well the cost to dignity beforehand," he said pleasantly. "Your toady Keifer Holmes is not around to pick up your pieces when I'm done. I'll bury them in the pig lot." He smiled.

Colin's composure was swinging by a slender thread.

He would either cut and run now or stand and fight. James didn't much care which. Since Susanna was here, he resisted a final push for the latter course.

Seething, obviously torn between fury and discretion, Colin replied, his teeth gritted and his color high, "I *will* kill you, Garrow." He glared past James at Susanna. "And you."

Maybe he didn't believe Susanna really was the heiress. To tell the truth, she did not much look the part today wearing her simple gown adorned with only a plaid. She could have been any lovely lass from hereabout, hired to play the part. James folded the deed and tucked it away. He cocked his head and nodded once. "Then you'll require that I remove you bodily?"

James heard a rustling noise behind him, though he sensed Susanna had not changed positions. He could hardly believe she'd maintained her silence and kept this still, but was glad for it all the same. Since matters were about to turn ugly, he needed to get her out of the way.

"This would be an excellent time to begin your tour of the house, my dear," he told her without turning. "Why not wait for me in the small parlor just there?" He inclined his head toward the room to their left without removing his gaze from his opponent.

Suddenly as that, Colin zipped his cane apart and steel flashed outward, catching the sunlight from the window on the wicked blade. He whipped it back and forth, smiling. James slid one hand into the side pocket of his frock coat for the repeater, knowing he had time to draw it out before Colin could possibly reach him with the sword.

A loud boom deafened him just as the gun cleared his pocket. The cane-sword flipped once and bounced on the floor tiles as Colin cried out, grasped his hand and sank to his knees.

Susanna rushed past James, scooped up the sword and moved back to her original position. She still held the smoking old flintlock in her other hand. He shook his head, hardly able to hear at all for the ringing in his ears.

James looked in disbelief from his wife to the man crouching on the floor. "Damn me, Suz, you shot him!"

Belatedly, he recalled the gun *he* was holding and leveled it on Colin. "Well, get up, man, and let's see the damage," James ordered. "I'll not be sending you on your way bleeding to death."

Colin got himself under control and rose to his feet. He glared past James at Susanna with hatred so absolute, James felt a shudder of foreboding run down his spine.

Without another word, Colin stalked past them and out of the house, clutching his wounded hand with the good one. James cast Susanna a worried look. She seemed perfectly composed, standing there near the door with the now useless pistol in one hand and the gleaming sword in the other. Amazons had less gumption.

"I was in no danger," he snapped, chagrin warring with his pride in her.

"You are quite welcome," she snapped back.

Thoroughly disconcerted, he left her in the entrance hall and trailed Colin out to the stables.

"Saddle him a mount," he ordered Fergus who had run on ahead, anticipating the order. "The mule will do."

"Consider that your severance," James told the ousted manager. "If you're wise, you'll head for parts unknown. The earl is none too pleased with your service here and neither am I. After examination of the accounts, there could be serious charges of embezzlement. And warn that snake of yours, Holmes, not to return here when next you see him. He'll be worm food if he does."

Colin said nothing. He dragged off his striped silk cravat and wrapped it around his hand. The wound did not look to be very serious, James decided. Just as well he wouldn't have to play surgeon before Colin could leave.

The man merely watched as the lad led the saddled old mule out of the stables and handed over the reins. Colin mounted without looking at James again, and rode away.

When he was out of sight, James turned to Fergus. "Mr. Colin has been replaced."

"By *yourself*, sar," Fergus said with a crooked toothed grin.

James laid a hand on the boy's slender shoulder. "Aye, lad. Things will be different now. While you're about telling the others, see Hamish and tell him I said to trail Mr. Colin and see where he goes. I'll be wantin' a report."

"Aye, sar." Fergus ran a few steps, then stopped and turned back, daring a question. "Th' leddy, sar? Are we to know aboot tha'?" He cleared his throat and glanced at the cots grouped down the lane.

The scamp had already known before they arrived, of course. How could he not when news traveled a hell of a lot faster than a pony cart? Last night's gathering at Galioch would hardly have been a secret to anyone but the Englishman in residence here.

That fact aside, James knew he'd be expected to make it official with the announcement, so he made it to Fergus. "Lady Susanna is the daughter of Earl Eastonby. She is the new owner of Drevers and she is my wife."

"Och!" the boy almost choked on the exclamation, and his eyes flew so wide with fake astonishment, James had to laugh at his overacting.

He shooed Fergus away with one hand. "Well, get on

with it, laddie. Let's be getting her a welcome together, aye?''

Not pleased with the way things had happened, but infinitely glad the task was over and done, James strode back to the manor to have a word with the bonny shootist he'd wed.

He shook his head in wonder and no little dismay. Did she need him at all, then? She was like to have made him a laughingstock with this day's work. Good thing he had a humorous turn of mind or he'd be taking her over his knee.

No doubt young Fergus had seen the entire event through the open doorway and would describe it in full to everyone within miles of Drevers.

After this, Susanna should have no problems with discipline, he'd wager. Nor any question whatsoever when it came to respect. He, on the other hand, might have a bit to live down, letting his wife settle up with Colin while he stood by with his hand in his pocket.

James looked down at the fancy pistol he was holding. He hadn't even had a chance to cock the damn thing. Slowly, he pocketed it again and walked back to the manor house. In all fairness, he'd have to give Susanna her due. She was a damned fine shot. Unless, of course, she'd been aiming for the man's head.

The thought made him laugh. Even if that were true, no one would ever believe it. She'd shot that sword right out of his hand, bold as you please. Whether she had meant to or not was beside the point. He couldn't very well quibble with success.

Susanna stood in the doorway, observing her husband. She fully expected a long, blustering speech of censure the instant he reentered the house. Used as she was to her father's frequent diatribes, that would scarcely bother her. What troubled her most was the fact that she was still shaking and could not seem to stop.

She dropped the sword and stared at the gun she held. Her thin, ostrichskin gloves and the narrow bands of lace edging her sleeves were ruined with black powder. It had really happened. She had truly done it.

Never before in her life had she fired a weapon at a person. She had not even been able to shoot a beast or a bird when her father had taken her hunting!

Now she had shot a man and had fully intended, in that instant, to shoot him dead. She rolled her eyes heavenward and thanked God for redirecting her aim. No matter how foully Colin had behaved, she had no right to take his life. But she had been so afraid. He could have run James through with that horrible sword.

She looked up to reassure herself again that he was all right. James stopped just outside the door, clasped his hands behind his back and rocked a time or two on the balls of his feet. When he looked at her, his eyes were narrowed.

"I have but one question, wife," he said, his voice ominously low pitched.

She raised her chin and one eyebrow, willing her knees to stop trembling. "And that would be?"

He raked his bottom lip with his fine white teeth and cocked his head to one side. "Will you be giving lessons in marksmanship now?"

She took a deep breath. Her head was spinning and beginning to ache. "If you insist."

His hearty laugh surprised her. "Damn me, Suz, I've never seen the like in all my days. You'll be a legend, y'know?"

She backed out of the doorway and he followed her

inside. "Do you think you could find me a tot of sherry in this place, Garrow?" she asked, handing him the old flintlock and putting her hand to her head. "Suddenly I feel rather done in."

Before she could protest, he had scooped her off her feet and was carrying her into one of the rooms. He deposited her on a long narrow sofa. "Are you well, hinny?" he asked, his voice now absent of anything other than concern.

"I—I think so."

"Nay, you're not." He sat beside her and pulled her close, pressing her head to his chest and resting his chin on it. "Please weep a bit, would you?"

She pulled back and glared. "Weep? Why ever should I?"

He smiled down at her. "Because I need something to do for you and you've left me nothing but to give you a little comfort."

Susanna frowned. "That is the most ridiculous thing I've ever heard. Why should I weep to make *you* feel better? Besides, I gave you something to do. Pour me a sherry!"

He sighed and sat back. "In a short while we'll have all the drinks we need, I expect. They'll be here soon now."

"They? Who?"

"Your folk. Tonight's like to be a repeat of our last."

She sat up straight and clutched his arm. "The people here? But I haven't even seen the house yet!" She stood and paced for a few seconds. "Do you suppose there's food to offer them? Surely Mr. Colin will have something put by. Where is the kitchen?"

James stood. Smiling now and looking satisfied with

himself, he reached for her hand. "Come, we'll find it together."

She saw now what he had done. He had recognized that she was that close to falling into a swoon like some miss-ish weakling, and had saved her from it with his teasing ways. Part of her thanked him, but another wished he had been sincere.

Yes, a great part of her wanted to be held, protected, coddled and petted. She would have to mind that flaw in herself. If she did not, she might as well abandon her cause altogether, because that was precisely what prevented women from becoming strong in today's society. Dependence. She loathed it.

Still, she took the hand he offered and got to her feet, noting how much steadier she was now. "Very well, let me see what Drevers holds and how I might make use of it."

They strode out of the room and down the corridor, stopping to identify which room was which along the way.

"I'll need to get to the magistrate and have the deed changed soon," he said.

"You are *not* leaving me here to face strangers alone!"

"They're your people now, Suz," he said, pushing open the door to the library and grunting a sound of pleasure at the sight of two walls filled with books.

"He might return," she murmured, almost shuddering at the thought of Colin's glare of promised retribution.

"Not likely after what you did, but I'll be staying close today in any case. And I'm having him followed just to be safe." He crossed to the desk where a cut glass decanter sat, picked it up and sniffed. "Aha! Brandy."

Susanna blew out a breath of relief that he planned to stay, even as she realized what that meant. She was depending upon him for support. How quickly a woman was seduced into such a state by perceiving herself weaker. "Not that I would be unable to manage on my own, you understand."

"No question about it," he agreed as he poured out a jot of the liquor and offered it to her. "But I'll stay. If nothing else, you could use a translator."

She laughed. "Yes, there's no telling what I might agree to with my nodding responses. You *must* begin instructing me soon before I get myself into trouble."

He sipped his portion of brandy, then quirked his mouth to one side and grunted. "Sae lang's yer aphaudin yer end o'it."

She blinked. "What?"

"So long as you uphold your end of it. You have to do your part. Pay heed," he explained as he motioned for her to sit at the desk in the large leather chair. When she had done so, he propped one hip on the edge of the desk and looked down at her.

"Why do you think I would not?" she asked. "I have very serious intentions of improving the lives of the people here. Especially the women. Poverty's not the worst of *their* problems."

"And how'd you be after knowing that? I wonder."

"As much as you pretend not to, I think you do understand. Rich or poor, women bear a common yoke the world over, James."

"Do they now? Everywhere?"

"Yes, they do. And I need to be able to speak to them and have them understand me clearly."

"Aye, but will you listen as well?" he asked.

"Of course I will."

He sighed. "Well, here's a first lesson then, in the *claik* as well as dealing with people, especially with the women of the Highlands. *Tsun's ussna wha tay seemt tae pe.*"

When she frowned in confusion, he repeated in English, "Things are not always what they seem to be."

Chapter Ten

The ceilidh had been one to remember, James thought as he rode the twenty-odd miles back from Beauly a week later. Not surprising the celebration had been one to end all. Drevers was that glad to have anyone other than Colin in charge. Her people would walk through fire for Susanna for that reason alone. Add to it that she had shot the man and sent him packing, and in their eyes, her name rivaled that of old Robert the Bruce. She had freed them, given them pride back and done it with a flair they greatly admired.

He had to admit she was something to be proud of, and he was. If only she didn't confound him to hell and gone he might even like her. Only every time he began to think they might eventually find some common ground, at least enough to substantiate this marriage of theirs, she would do something outrageous.

James shuddered to think what kind of children they might produce. If they possessed his temper and her impulsiveness, he predicted they would be gallows bait before they were half grown.

However, getting any sort of children by her was going to prove an impossibility if he couldn't somehow establish accord between them. At least for the time it would take to sire them.

At first, he'd thought she was merely skittish about the bedding. God knows, she was passionate enough that he could get around that problem eventually. But it now seemed there was more to it than that. He just had to figure out what that was.

He had given her time alone this past week to think about it while he was gone to see about bringing home the lads who were off working near the coast.

While doing that, he had also collected two wagons full of additional supplies in Beauly to augment what Susanna had ordered while in Edinburgh. Since these were mostly for Drevers, he had paid with a draft drawn on the bank in Edinburgh where the earl had set up an account for Susanna. In James's name, of course.

He had hated to use it, but there had been no choice. It was because of her that he'd had to give up his work in Edinburgh and come home where there was no money to be made. Everything destined for use at Galioch would be in lieu of what she had agreed to pay him for acting as steward at Drevers, he decided.

The solicitor he had visited in Beauly had refused to put the account or the deed to Drevers in Susanna's name, stating that James must be mad to even think of such a thing. He had assured James that he would get the same response from any legal source.

Instead, the man had suggested a will, granting Susanna the usual one-third of the monies and property and the remainder to any children that might be a result of their union. How was he supposed to explain that to a woman who already believed all men bent upon giving women no independence?

She already considered Drevers hers, and for all intents

and purposes, it was. But on paper, it was still his and likely to remain that way. But James had made her a promise and it was wrong not to keep it.

Consequently, he had written out a declaration of his own, dated after the will, granting her Drevers. How legal it was, he didn't know. He had always been under the impression that females in Scotland could own their own property. Apparently they had to be widowed or orphaned to do so, and then only until they were wed. This issue would require a light tread on his part, James knew.

He had also visited the post while he was there to save the rider a forty-mile round trip this week. There were letters from the earl addressed jointly to himself and Susanna, so he had not opened them yet. It was a small thing, really, to wait and read them in her presence, but he hoped it would signify he was not trying to play overlord.

So with the wagons in tow, the lads at the reins and his worries about his wife to keep him company, James plodded along, taking his time. And yet, he could hardly wait to see her again. Why that was, he could not imagine. Probably curiosity as to what she had turned upside down while he was away.

They reached Drevers very late that afternoon of the seventh day he had been gone. Fergus ran to meet them, his bare feet flying and his wee plaid flapping in the breeze. "Laird Jamie! Laird Jamie!" he cried, laughing as he ran. James reflected on how long it had been since he had heard happy laughter hereabout.

He reached down a hand and hoisted the lad up to ride behind him on the sturdy gelding. "Fergus! How's our lady?"

"Guid! She's a braw surprise for ye, sar!"

What now? James was afraid to ask. He squinted toward the manor house and saw lights in all the windows of the ballroom on the second floor. "We've company?" he asked the boy.

"Nay, only the womenfolk gathered. Leddy Suz is holdin' court."

"Court?"

"Aye. Ye'll see," Fergus said, his voice both cryptic and amused.

James halted. "Hop down. Go with the lads on to the storehouses, then you be after minding those ponies. They'll be that worn out, coming all this way, and must make a return within the week."

As soon as Fergus was well away from the hooves, James urged the gelding to a gallop and rode on ahead. He dismounted and entered the house quietly, both unwilling to disturb whatever meeting was in progress and also to find out what Susanna was about holding it.

He took the stairs with some stealth and stood outside the ballroom doors.

"And so, you need not bear a child every year if you do not wish to," she was saying. Preaching, rather. Her voice raised in authority. "Your health will fail you and there you will be. No one to tend the bairns you do have after you're laid in your graves."

"Lady, we've no say in when the good lord grants us bairns! 'Tis no thing to dither o'er. We has 'em as they cooms."

"No, Florrie. It need not be so! Your husband determines when you get with child. Abstention is the only answer, of course. If you practice abstention, you shall not conceive. Does everyone understand this? Surely you do." Susanna's voice sounded frustrated and she was very nearly pleading with them to ken what she said.

"Abstention?" one of the women cried, sounding outraged. "I'm no one fer allowin' strange goings on under my covers, Lady Susanna! And neither are these others. We be God-fearin' Christians bound to do the natural. And dinna be describin' how you do this *abstention* thing! We'd no' be wantin' ta hear suchlike!"

James clapped a hand over his mouth to stifle his laughter. He could not wait to see how she got out of this one. He was not about to march in there and explain for her. The women would be mortified if a man took a hand in such discussion. He shouldn't even be listening. But he did.

Susanna piped up, her voice rising with frustration. "No, wait! You did not understand me at all! Abstention simply means not doing…anything. Say no to your husband…at least for a while after you bear—"

"Och, see?" the other woman demanded. "I knew 'twas somethin' twisty, this thing! We'll no be denyin' our menfolk, Lady. There beint naught wrong wi' giving 'em bairns. I've six meself! Do I look like to die?"

The room erupted with laughter. If that was the woman James thought it was, he could see why. She probably outweighed him by two stone and was sturdy as a draft horse.

James had heard enough. He left the upstairs corridor and headed back downstairs. Tonight was not the time to take Susanna to task for trying to limit the population. If she thought she could direct the private lives of her tenants, they would set her straight in a hurry. Those females she was dealing with made their own rules. If their husbands couldn't order them what to do, Susanna didn't have a chance in hell of succeeding.

The sad thing was, she made a valid point. The number of infant deaths was discouraging. And even healthy women often did die during or shortly after giving birth.

Small wonder the idea of it frightened her. But if a woman chose to risk it…

But *were* they left with a choice? James suddenly saw very clearly Susanna's real concern and it was not concern for herself alone. It was also nothing to be taken lightly, he thought. Certainly not some flighty bit of rebellious nattering in public to make her feel important. This was serious.

Maybe she was trying to practice what she preached, saying no, setting an example. If that's what kept her out of his bed—instead of that she was afraid for herself or that she didn't know him well enough yet—then they needed to talk about it.

She wanted him and that was no idle boast on his part. He wanted her, too, and there was no earthly reason to *practice abstention,* as she put it. There were other ways. He had no doubt that every woman within fifty miles of here, except *her,* knew all about most of them and probably had a list longer than his own.

He reached the front door, turned and slammed it shut, making as much noise as possible. ''Susanna!'' he boomed, ''I've come home!''

That done, he stomped into the library and poured himself a drink. Idly, he lounged in the big leather chair and sipped as he listened to the cacophony of some two dozen women clattering down the stairs. He heard the mixed gabbling of Gaelic, Scots and English, but paid little heed to the words.

When she rushed in, all innocent smiles and red face, he stood. She came over to him somewhat hesitantly and held out her hands. He kissed her cheek, then briefly, her lips.

Her laugh when she tugged away sounded uneasy.

"Welcome home, James. I've a surprise for you! I hope you won't be angry."

He hoped so, too. "Ah, well. What have you done then?" He breathed deeply, enjoying the smell of roses that wafted from her. It mingled subtly with the scent of wildflowers arranged in several vases about the room. The library looked different, he noticed then. Homelike. Comfortable. Clean.

She had ducked her head, but now raised that defiant little chin. "I moved some things to Galioch. You don't mind, do you?" She bit her lips and looked apprehensive.

"Moved what?"

"Some of the furnishings from here," she explained. "There were too many extra pieces about and I really wanted to do something with Galioch. It is so gloriously old and wonderful, I simply couldn't help myself. We've done some painting there, too."

"Painting?" Horror grabbed his gut. She hadn't done the outside, had she? God, what color? He blinked to dispel the pink image that formed.

"We whitewashed the hall. And we added a bit of color to the murals there. Morag has a true talent for restoring things." She preened. "And I painted our devices myself. We'll need gold leaf, of course, to complete them properly."

Gold leaf? He could scarcely afford oats. He shook his head and ran a palm over his face, feeling the grime and sweat, not to mention the fatigue there.

"Would you like to come and see?"

"It's fair dark, Suz. Tomorrow's time enough. I need a bath. We'll speak when I've come back from the pond."

She grasped his arm as if to stop him though he'd not yet made a move to leave. "The pond? Surely you do not mean to bathe there! There's a perfectly good tub above stairs in your chamber. I shall have Kait prepare—''

"Kait?"

She smiled. "Kait McLemore. I've hired her as my maid. She asked if I needed someone, and I've no doubt she can use the money."

That seemed reasonable. "Fine, but you need not bother her now. I'm going to the pond."

"But—but that is highly improper, James. You would have to…well, undress yourself. In public." Her hand slid from his arm and he wanted it back there, despite the heat radiating from her palm right through his sleeve.

"It'll be dark as pitch by the time I get there," he argued. And, being spring-fed, the pond would be ice cold. The last thing he needed at the moment was a warm, scented bath. He always grew a bit randy when he indulged in one of those, maybe because he was usually in a place to satisfy that when he did succumb to the luxury.

He drew out the letters from her father. "Here. Read these while I'm gone. We can discuss them when I get back."

Without waiting for her next argument, he grabbed up his pack and headed outside. By the time he returned, he would not be so susceptible to that rosy scent of hers. Hopefully, he'd be frozen from the waist down so he wouldn't make an ass of himself by moving too soon on that seduction he planned.

Susanna tossed the letters on the desk and sat down in the chair James had vacated. She rested her chin on her hands, her elbows propped firmly on the desk, and sighed. Whatever was she to do with him? Bathing in the wilds like a savage.

No doubt he would be gauche enough to remove every garment he wore, even his unmentionables. Some eyeful for anyone, male or female, who happened to be out and about at this hour. Perhaps they all did so whenever they had a bath and would take little notice.

Her own imaginings ran rampant just thinking about what he was doing. If only she'd not seen all of him while he was abed recovering. Now she could not get the image of his overwhelming masculinity out of her head. The mere mention of his taking off his clothes had brought it forth and she couldn't seem to dismiss it.

His skin would look pale, most likely bluish in the dusk, with deep shadows carving out the recesses of his body. Waning light of evening would highlight the robust planes of his chest, his thick shoulders and arms and heavily muscled legs. When he rose from the waters of the pond, he would glisten like a rain wet statue in the moonlight. A nude statue like the Greek and Roman ones she had seen in the museum. If there was a moon tonight. She had the wildest urge to run outside and see. To run outside and see *him,* if only to convince herself that her mind exaggerated.

He was not precisely like those statues, she recalled with a slow exhalation of pent up breath. In one respect, he exceeded certain of their respective…attributes. She wiped the perspiration from her brow with a shaking hand.

"Damn me!" she cried aloud, slamming one palm down on the desk blotter as she borrowed his favorite curse. She shook her head so hard a hairpin flew and pinged against the globe of the lamp.

She gathered her scattered wits and lit the lamp against

the increasing darkness in the library, determined to put her mind to better use. Angrily, she snatched up one of her father's letters and opened it, almost slicing her finger on the ornate, swordlike letter opener.

There was little contained in it other than what they already knew from the telegraphed message they had received before leaving Edinburgh. More detail, of course. He went on about the hired Bow Street man who would investigate the attempt on his life. Not that her father expected to learn much since the attack had occurred in Scotland so many miles from London.

He wished her well in her marriage, much more eloquently than he had done personally, though even now he favored brevity.

Did he really care for her happiness or were these words and the few he had spoken before they parted merely for form's sake?

She had embarrassed and angered him dreadfully while espousing her cause in London. She could not dismiss the idea that if he truly loved her, he would have supported her in what she believed. But then, he had been one of the primary offenders she had called to task. He had driven her mother to an early grave. Susanna had not accused him directly, but she must have stirred his guilt, and he could not forgive her for it.

She laid the first letter aside and opened the other. As she read, her mouth dropped open and she frowned with consternation. Now here was news! James would not be best pleased and she knew it. To be truthful, neither was she, but she must put a good face on it or else he would totally ignore the precepts of hospitality and send the guests packing before they alighted at the front door.

Say what one would about the hospitality of Scots, she knew for a fact they were a closed society where outsiders were suspect. Especially English outsiders. *Sassan-achs.*

The war might be long over and their sound defeat recorded for all time, but she had yet to meet a Highlander who accepted that. She could see it in their eyes when they looked at her. Not hatred or personal dislike. Only thinly veiled mistrust and a staunch barrier against all but surface friendship. Even James.

She sighed again. Most especially James. Though kind and tolerant and even approving at times, he still kept a distance.

For all that, Susanna trusted him with her life. He would never allow anyone to hurt her, but that was due only to the promise he had made her father. And his own honor, she supposed. He had taken her as his wife and, English or not, considered her his. Heaven help any man who threatened what James Garrow claimed. She was property. The very idea made her angry enough to spit.

Susanna heard a distant door close and recognized the tread of his boots on the marble tiles of the foyer. Before he reached the library, she concealed her anger, admitting he hadn't really done anything to warrant it. However, when she raised her eyes to confront him with the news her father had written, both the anger and any words she might have uttered completely deserted her.

Droplets of water beaded the waves of his hair and dripped onto his bare chest and shoulder. He still wore the shadow of an evening beard. And little else other than his boots. Several yards of blue-and-green plaid were gathered round his waist, held in place by a wide leather belt. One end of the fabric was thrown carelessly over one bare shoulder and left to trail loosely in back.

He tossed his leather pack beside the door and strode

The Harlequin Reader Service® — Here's how it works:

Accepting your 2 free books and mystery gift places you under no obligation to buy anything. You may keep the books and gift and return the shipping statement marked "cancel." If you do not cancel, about a month later we'll send you 6 additional books and bill you just $4.47 each in the U.S., or $4.99 each in Canada, plus 25¢ shipping & handling per book and applicable taxes if any.* That's the complete price and — compared to cover prices of $5.25 each in the U.S. and $6.25 each in Canada — it's quite a bargain! You may cancel at any time, but if you choose to continue, every month we'll send you 6 more books, which you may either purchase at the discount price or return to us and cancel your subscription.

*Terms and prices subject to change without notice. Sales tax applicable in N.Y. Canadian residents will be charged applicable provincial taxes and GST. Credit or Debit balances in a customer's account(s) may be offset by any other outstanding balance owed by or to the customer

If offer card is missing write to: Harlequin Reader Service, 3010 Walden Ave., P.O. Box 1867, Buffalo NY 14240-1867

NO POSTAGE
NECESSARY
IF MAILED
IN THE
UNITED STATES

BUSINESS REPLY MAIL
FIRST-CLASS MAIL   PERMIT NO. 717-003   BUFFALO, NY

POSTAGE WILL BE PAID BY ADDRESSEE

HARLEQUIN READER SERVICE
3010 WALDEN AVE
PO BOX 1867
BUFFALO NY 14240-9952

Play the Romance Crossword Game

and get...
2 FREE BOOKS
and a
FREE GIFT...
YOURS to KEEP!

Scratch Here!

Yes! to reveal the hidden words.
Look below to see what you get.

I have scratched off the gold areas. Please send me my **2 FREE BOOKS** and **FREE GIFT** for which I qualify. I understand that I am under no obligation to purchase any books as explained on the back of this card.

349 HDL DRT3   **246 HDL DRUK**

FIRST NAME   LAST NAME

ADDRESS

APT.#   CITY

STATE/PROV.   ZIP/POSTAL CODE

Visit us online at
www.eHarlequin.com

ROMANCE	MYSTERY	NOVEL	GIFT
You get **2 FREE BOOKS** PLUS a **FREE GIFT!**	You get **2 FREE BOOKS!**	You get **1 FREE BOOK!**	You get a **FREE MYSTERY GIFT!**

forward to the desk like some fierce heathen conqueror come to claim his prize.

She pressed one palm against her chest to calm the rapid thudding of her heart before she fainted dead away.

"Well?" he asked, raising one dark eyebrow.

"You—you're wet," she stammered.

He shrugged and gathered a handful of the smooth woolen material draped over his shoulder and began to move it idly back and forth across his chest, then blotted at the hollow of his neck, causing the whole of the upper length to fall away, leaving him naked to the waist. And damp. Glistening. Her throat closed. She could hardly blink her eyes. And moving was out of the question.

"What news from London?" he asked.

By sheer force of will, Susanna tore her avid gaze away from him and focused on the letters, struggling to compose a cheerful speech about how delighted she was they would soon be entertaining. But she delayed too long, surely revealing that anything she said would be nothing short of pretense.

He leaned forward, his palms flat on the desk, and faced her. "Suz, what is it? Is aught wrong with your da?"

"No!" she exclaimed, surprised by the note of concern in his voice. "Father is well. It's only that…well…" Her gaze landed on the mat of dark curls that arrowed down the center of his body.

"Does my wearin' this upset you?" he asked, raising one hand to sling the errant length of plaid back in place to cover half the view. "Do you dislike my wearing of the plaid? I rarely do, but it seemed futile to put everything on again when I'm off to bed so soon."

Susanna bit her lips together for an instant and met his gaze. Then she shook her head emphatically.

"It *does* disturb you," he argued, sounding resigned and worse than disappointed. "I figured it might."

And it did, she thought. She had never felt quite this disturbed in her life. Well, perhaps that once after he had been shot and she had unwittingly spied what lay beneath that old-fashioned garment he was wearing tonight.

He removed his hand from the desk and straightened, looking very regal in his deshabille. "I'm a Scot, Susanna. For all I can sound English when it serves me, there's no use denying to yourself what I am and will always be. If my people refused to give up their plaids for the Butcher Cumberland, I sure as hell won't be giving mine up for you."

Susanna looked away and cleared her throat, uncertain how to explain her response to his native dress without revealing her all too frightening response to him in it.

With one finger, she pushed her father's second letter forward. "Then you had best put on a shirt with it in the days to come. We are about to have company."

"What? Who is the earl sending here and why?" James demanded.

She could almost cringe at the thought of Miranda's reaction to the fine laird and all his glory. That one could be cruelly cutting with her remarks when she chose.

And worse yet, she could turn as provocative as any courtesan. She had cut her teeth on clever London dandies out to capture themselves the daughter of a wealthy cit. Miranda had led them on, then left them bleeding in her wake, their self-esteem in shreds and their hearts broken beyond repair. And, too, there had been rumors of married gentlemen....

James would need protection.

Susanna marshaled all her strength of will and stood, putting on her bravest smile. "Not to worry, Garrow. I shall take care of matters here. You might want to go and see how things lie at Galioch this week while I entertain my friend and her cousin. No doubt her visit will bore you to tears.''

"Ashamed of me, Suz? Wishing me out of the way?''

"No and yes," she answered honestly. "Will you go?''

"Yes and no," he retorted, propping his hands on his hips in a defiant stance, all rugged male and in command. "Yes, I will go at sunrise tomorrow and see what you've done there, but no, I won't stay. Expect me back before noon. If you think for an instant I'll leave you here alone to greet anyone I don't know, you are dead wrong.''

It was no use. "Be warned, then. There's no danger to me in this visitor's arrival, but you had best keep a sharp eye out for your own welfare.''

He smirked. "And just who might this dire threat be?''

"Miranda Durston, daughter of my father's business partner.''

"I'm to fear a woman now? Your estimation of me seems to lower by the minute.''

She shook her head, knowing full well he would neither listen to nor heed any warning she issued. "You misunderstand. But then, you always do.''

"I beg your pardon!''

"Beg all you like," she snapped. No matter how she behaved or what she said or how she said it, he seemed to take things amiss every time. "If you will excuse me now, I think I shall retire.''

"By all means." He executed a mocking half bow, a curt gesture rife with condescension. She ignored it and swept past him without another glance, resolved to stop trying to please him in any way whatsoever.

Chapter Eleven

James left Drevers early, before Susanna awakened. How could he have gotten angry with her over nothing? They had so much that needed solving between them and he had delayed that in a fit of childish pique. Today he would do better, he promised himself.

For now, he wandered through the hall at Galioch, marveling at the changes Susanna had wrought with but a few furnishings and a bit of paint. It looked nothing like it had in years past.

His mother had been prone to overdo. The delicate and ornately carved pieces she had shipped from England had been out of character for a structure this primitive. Like some massive shire horse tricked out as a sequined circus pony. He wished to God she had charged sixpence admittance to everyone she enticed here to show it off. That might have paid for her fancies.

In her day, Galioch had been filled to overflowing with visitors they hardly knew, curious fellow nobles who mingled freely with the leeches, impoverished artists and poets she brought there. And Father had denied her nothing. He'd merely secluded himself and continued with his painting as if totally oblivious to the hotbed of pretension and faux culture teeming within Galioch's walls.

For James, those guests and their goings-on had provided an education within itself that influenced his personal ambition, his attitudes toward class structure and even his sexual habits.

He had certainly grasped the evils of overindulgence before he reached manhood. Despite the fact that those lessons had proved expensive and almost always disheartening, they still served him well. If not for the concentration of negative examples his mother had assembled, he might be just like those people today.

James could not imagine those creatures existing here now. Susanna had created a calm and almost elegant sedateness. Her tastes ran to simplicity and seemed in perfect accordance with his, though he could never have envisioned or accomplished these changes as well as she had done.

She had trestle tables set up, three of them. Where she obtained them, he had no notion, but they were now covered in coarse white linen and graced with baskets of wildflowers. On the mantel above the newly scrubbed fireplace sat a row of pewter mugs, draped round with strands of ivy. Above the ancient fireplace were two crossed swords, relics she had probably scavenged from the lofts at Drevers, he guessed, since he had never seen the weapons before. To either side of that arrangement were painted coats of arms, one belonging to his family, the other to hers.

He smiled at what he was certain she had done unintentionally, and that was to call attention to the existing conflict between them. At swords crossed. Like warring clans.

Still shaking his head at her ingenuity, James mounted

the curving stone stair to the bedrooms and entered his. The bed was still there, but with different hangings. She had left the comfortable chair, now obviously in an early stage of being recovered with the plaid fabric folded across the back of it.

He noticed other touches here and there that softened the chamber and made it feel welcoming: a plain white porcelain ewer and pitcher rested on a linen-draped table and a vase with simple lines contained poppies from the dooryard out back.

On one wall hung a large painting of pheasants in a handsome frame of natural wood. His father's work, one of the early ones James had not been able to sell. He was glad of that now because it seemed at home here in this room.

He smiled again at her thoughtfulness, wondering whether he had woefully misjudged her. She must have known how he would like this. It had been so long since anyone had bothered to please him in such a way, he hardly recognized it for what it was.

Eager to see what else she had accomplished, he went to her room.

A mistake. James halted in the doorway, hardly daring to enter. All around him were the trappings of femininity he recalled from his mother's day. Oh, they were not his mother's things, for he had sold all of hers long ago. Sold them first, actually, because those had been the most expensive possessions within Galioch.

Susanna obviously had appropriated these particular things from Drevers, as was her right, of course. But they reminded him all too vividly of the woman who had inhabited this room before her. A room he had never been allowed to enter unless summoned. A room that held nothing pleasant in the way of memories.

Without pausing to examine the changes and additions other than to mark colors, frills and flourishes that were all too familiar in nature, James turned on his heel and slammed the door shut behind him, closing off the sight of the place. The scent had been different. At least that was something. Roses.

Any pleasure he'd found here so far rapidly dissipated. It was time to return to Drevers anyhow. If the earl's estimation in his letter was correct, Susanna's guests should be arriving tomorrow or the next day. He cursed the timing of the visit, but understood the reason Eastonby thought it necessary to send his partner's daughter north.

Mr. Durston, who conducted Eastonby Enterprises and owned a considerable amount of the stock in it, had also been the victim of an attempt on his life. The two of them figured it must be the work of a competitor. There were many of those to choose from these days, shipping being what it was. It was a cutthroat business with fortunes to be made for the fittest, the most daring, the survivors.

James had few dealings with the shipping industry other than to ship his wool or make use of goods once delivered, but he certainly understood the nature of men vying for lucrative contracts and their willingness to obtain them at any cost.

The construction business was not unlike that. Though he'd never served in any managerial capacity in the company he had worked for, James was well aware of the ruthlessness cloaked in the gentlemanly pretense of civility. The owners or their representatives would shake the competition's hand and smile while they neatly sliced the jugular.

Someone was out to destroy Eastonby's company by

eliminating both its figurehead, the earl, and his partner cum manager, Durston. According to the earl, the perpetrator must also intend to dispose of any heirs to the business as well. That would be the daughters, Susanna and Miranda.

All the way back to Drevers, James ruminated on who might benefit most from such a move. However, he knew only a fraction of the names involved in shipping that would rival the importance of Eastonby's outfit. He would need more facts than he had now to figure that out, facts he could not hope to obtain unless he left the Highlands or employed someone else to investigate.

Since the earl had already hired someone, James concluded the best thing he could do was stay put and keep the women here where they would be least vulnerable. Any strangers hereabout would be reported immediately. The women would be safe.

Suddenly his horse reared, pawing the air while James struggled to keep his seat. It took some doing to settle the beast, but when he had, James scowled down at the large figure twisting his cap in his hands. "Damn me, Orvie! Give us a warning!"

The lad cowered at the sharp words, dropped to his knees and backed into the brush he had crawled out of. James cursed himself, then forced a grin to soften his rebuke. "What's got you scrambling through the bracken on all fours, Orvie? Hiding from somebody or making sport of me? Come out now. I'm no' angry."

James dismounted and began to gentle the gelding, knowing his soothing actions would be observed while Orvie came back out of the bushes and recovered his speech.

Again the cap twisted, only more frantically than before. Orvie's heavy body shifted rhythmically from one large foot to the other. "A witch's come, Jamie. Puttin' spells."

"A witch? The lads been having you on again, Orvie? How many times have I told you—"

"Nay, I seen her meself!" Orvie insisted, stumbling over his words in haste to tell the tale. "She gimme the evil eye more'n once and then flung out her hand at me. Aw sayin' things I didna ken. Will I die, Jamie?"

Ah. It must be that the guest, Miranda Durston, had arrived earlier than expected. And Orvie obviously had gotten in her way. With a weary sigh and a shake of his head, James stepped closer and placed a steadying hand on Orvie's broad shoulder. "Nay, lad, you'll not be dying." But Orvie would take more convincing than that, James realized.

He reached in his sporran and retrieved a silver penny, then took Orvie's hand and placed the coin in his callused palm. "This," James assured him, "is made of magic silver. It destroys all curses when it touches your skin. Ken that? All you do is take it out and rub it when a curse occurs, just so between your thumb and finger. Aye, that's it. The curse is gone now. Feel better?"

A great smile blossomed and Orvie ducked his head in thanks. "I feel guid. Magic?" He rubbed the penny for a moment, then placed it back in James's hand, closing the fingers over it and giving them a rough pat. "Ye'd best keep th' siller, Jamie. I'll no be goin' back there, but ye hafta. Leddy Suz is scared."

James tensed. Susanna, frightened? He recalled the warning she had given him last night about Miranda Durston. Was it possible the woman really did offer some sort of threat?

He shook off the concern for what it was. Poor Orvie had the wild imagination of a superstitious child. One

disgusted look from the visitor would have been enough
to set him off, thinking himself doomed. It stood to reason, Orvie would also worry about leaving James's wife
at Drevers with someone he feared was dangerous.

James tossed the penny into the air and deftly caught
it, magically weaving it in and out between his fingers
until Orvie laughed at the trick. Then he dropped it back
into his sporran and quickly remounted. ''Go along to
Hildy's now, Orvie. It's baking day and she'll be having
warm bannocks.''

Without waiting to see whether Orvie obeyed, James
kicked the gelding into a gallop and rode off to meet the
witch.

Fergus dashed out of the stables at a run and met James
near the front entrance. Unwilling to suffer another opinion of their guest before he met her and judged her for
himself, James tossed Fergus the reins and hurried inside.

He heard voices in the parlor. One of them male and
quite clearly uppercrust English.

Suddenly he wished he had not donned his plaid this
morning just to spite Susanna. He had already suffered
for it, riding bare-assed all the way to Galioch and back
again. Now he would likely embarrass her in front of
company.

He was not wearing his dress kilt with its form fitting
jacket and silver-trimmed sporran, but his old faded phil-
abeag, self pleated—and not too neatly at that, given he
was out of practice. He'd added a full-sleeved, open-
necked shirt, leather ghillies and wool leggings cross-tied
in the old manner. Comfortable when walking about, to
be sure, but not anywhere near proper attire for a baron
and laird.

If he'd had other clean clothing here at Drevers, he

would have gone up to change before joining them, but unless he rode all the way back to Galioch, they would have to take him as he was. His curiosity was greater at the moment than his reluctance to encounter disdain. Besides, it would serve Suz right for belittling his plaid last night.

He figured he might as well play the part to the hilt since he was dressed for it. To that end, he stepped into the doorway of the parlor and drew up to his full height, nearly filling the opening. Standing proudly, one hand on his hip, the other braced against the door frame, he awaited an introduction.

Susanna's swift intake of breath drew his attention away from the couple seated side by side on the settee.

"Ja—Garrow!" Her teacup bobbled in its dish as she tried to set it down and stand up at the same time. "I did not expect you back quite so soon!"

James thought she recovered quickly and hid her urge to kill him rather well.

"Won't you join us?" she asked, probably praying he would refuse.

James sauntered into the room, granted the guests a glance before looking pointedly at her for the introduction.

"Good morning, James. May I present Miss Miranda Durston and her cousin, Mr. Broderick Fowler." She gestured toward him. "This is my husband, Lord Garrow."

Fowler had stood when James first appeared, and Miranda did so now, extending her graceful, ungloved hand. She was a brown-eyed beauty, hair like midnight and skin like fresh cream. And an expression like the cat that just lapped it up. He disliked her instantly. He reached out, grasped the hand she offered and gave it a firm shake instead of the obviously expected kiss. Her eyes narrowed when he summarily dropped it and took Fowler's in a like manner, only a bit more crushing. "Welcome to Drevers," he said.

"So you are the infamous laird!" She raked him with a sin-dark gaze that made him all too aware of how little he was wearing.

"I am that," he admitted. "And you'd be the redoubtable lass from London come to while away time in the hinterlands of hell."

She toyed with the delicate gold necklace that graced her long, slender neck. "My, but you do roll those *R*'s of yours. How perfectly enchanting!"

He spared Susanna a teasing glance. "So I've been told."

Susanna blushed and frowned. Miranda laughed.

He had met Miranda Durston's kind before. Cold, hard and glittery as a diamond. One with deep flaws that made it worthless for anything other than grinding something. Preferably him, judging by the blatantly sexual look she offered.

"So, Lord Garrow," Fowler spoke up, "what must one do to wheedle a nip of that fine Scotch whisky we sell souls for in England?"

James turned his head and assessed the man more closely. "One must stay in England to wheedle for it. That's where it all goes."

Fowler laughed hesitantly, as if he couldn't be sure whether James was serious. "A bit of brandy, then?" he asked politely.

"Of course!" Susanna chirped and went about retrieving the bottle from the library. His lady, the soul of hospitality. James felt like swatting her backside as she passed him to leave the room. Why was it she could be so gracious to this popinjay and not to him?

The bloke's sartorial splendor did nothing to impress. If anything, it made James feel much better about what he, himself, was wearing. Fowler's clothing sported the latest cut, but the fabric was inferior, the waistcoat a rather gaudy blue, and his stickpin and links made of fake sapphires if James was not sorely mistaken.

Either he was a man of modest means set on being taken for one of wealth, or he simply had no taste and spent his ready for something other than his attire. No quality about the man whatsoever, James decided. And he did not like the way Fowler's gaze roved over Susanna. He wasn't jealous or anything so daft. It was simply the man's manners that piqued. A guest definitely should not ogle the hostess.

Fowler was fair-haired, though his locks were obviously darkened by the overabundance of hair tonic. The mustache curled upward at the pointed tips like cow horns. Though his features were regular and might even be considered attractive to women, James thought the chin weak and the gray eyes a bit piggy. *Fowler, the peacock.*

James almost let loose a smile when he recalled the fate of the peacocks that had strutted and screamed about Galioch for years on end. They had gone the way of all fowl the year that the drought made wild game scarce. Plucked, cooked and presented at table looking like plain old geese.

Susanna returned with a tray and set about dashing brandy in two snifters. She then poured for Miranda and herself from a squat bottle of madeira she had found somewhere.

Miranda tasted hers as if she contemplated buying the remainder with her last farthing. "Adequate," she pronounced. With a languid wave of one hand, she asked,

"Susanna, darling, what a shame you must fetch your own refreshments! Are there no decent servants to be had here?"

James sipped his brandy, eyeing Susanna over the edge of the glass, interested in what her response would be to that. Would she bemoan the fact that she had no bevy of staff to do her bidding? Hell, he'd been gone for a whole week. Maybe she did have by now, though he certainly hadn't tripped over any of them when he came in.

"I hired a cook and a maid-of-all-work to assist me now and then, but I really prefer doing most things for myself," Susanna answered with a smile. "It is one of the tenets of my belief that women should arrange their own fates, depend upon their own initiatives and not always rely upon others..." she declared, looking pointedly at him and then at Fowler, "...to take care of them."

Miranda laughed merrily, tossing her black curls and clasping her free hand to her overabundant bosom. "Oh, yes! I do recall your trotting out those ridiculous notions before you left Town." She leaned forward as if imparting a secret. "I suspect that is what got you into this fix, isn't it?"

"This *fix?*" Susanna repeated, her voice clipped and her face red. "I beg your pardon."

Very little begging to it as far as James could tell; sounded more like a demand. Suz at her most imperious.

Miranda realized her mistake. James almost laughed at the way she gulped and jumped to repair it.

"Oh! Oh, Susanna, dearest, I never meant that to insult you. Not at all! It was merely a tease to make you laugh! Please, please ignore me. I am too well-known for my tactless sallies! Brodie will attest to that, won't you, Brodie?"

"Indeed," Fowler said with no little sarcasm and threw a what-must-we-do-with-them look at James.

"Nuncheon is served, ma'am," Kait chimed from the doorway, bobbing a curtsey.

James stared. Kait was tricked out in a black dress and white apron and wore a ridiculous white cap about the size of his fist perched atop her mass of wheat colored curls. And she was barefoot, her slightly dirty toes peeking from beneath her hem. She scrunched them out of sight when she noticed him looking.

"Thank you, Miss McLemore," he said gently. "We shall be in directly." She nodded, belatedly recalled her early training and bobbed at the knee. Then she disappeared.

"Shall we?" he asked, offering his arm to Susanna. When she simply stood there looking aghast at his manners, he picked up her hand, placed it firmly on his arm and led her out.

He knew propriety directed that he should have taken Miranda in since she was the female guest and he, the host. She would be fuming at the slight. But he had already deduced that avoiding that woman's touch, even her hand on his arm, was the wisest course of action all around.

And there was, of course, his dedicated resolve to prevent any excuse for that pig-eyed Brodie Fowler to touch Susanna.

Chapter Twelve

"Your behavior was abominable!" Susanna snapped, her whisper harsh in the silence of the upstairs corridor. Their guests had just retired to their respective rooms which lay in the other direction.

James grinned. "Say it aloud, Suz. They know it's true."

She almost twisted the door handle off as she entered her room. "Damn me, you make me so angry!"

He entered right behind her before she could even think to close the door in his face. "Why is that?" he asked, drawling the words, sounding half-foxed.

"Are you drunk?"

"Hardly. Ol' Peafowl kept the bottle busy until it gave out and Miranda soaked up all the wine. Do you suppose they'll leave if the liquor dries up? Remind me not to tell them where the still's located. They'll likely gobble up the fermenting mash."

"Obnoxious boor! Get out of my room!" she exclaimed, pacing to and fro, kicking at her skirts, desperately trying not to slap his face.

He just stood there, arms crossed, observing her. "Are you truly upset with me, Suz? Or with them?"

"You!" she assured him, throwing up her hands. "You insulted them. You refused to entertain them, and—"

"Dance like a trained bear? Suppose they'd asked you to perform a ballet? Would you?"

"Of course not. What I know of ballet you could stuff in a shoe. Besides, I played the pianoforte and sang. I did my part and so did they."

"Hmm." He shook his head. "My ears are still ringing."

She rolled her eyes. "They were only intrigued by what they had heard of a local tradition and wanted to experience it."

"Were they now? A sword dance, they asked for, Suz. You took the only swords in the county to Galioch and hung 'em on the wall. What would you have me dance around, the guns? Believe me, you'd not want me loose in a room with that nodcock and a loaded pistol!" He laughed.

Tears threatened. She knew he was right. Miranda and her cousin had been having their fun at James's expense, thinly veiling their insults in pretended interest. Now she was embarrassed by them, and for James. "You courted their scorn with every word out of your mouth."

"Aye." He sighed theatrically, dropped his arms to his side, then propped his hands on his hips. "I owe you an apology, Suz."

She stopped pacing and glared at him. "I cannot believe it. You are *not* sorry."

He still wore a hint of a smile. "All right." With that, he turned and opened the door to leave.

"You come back here!"

Looking over his shoulder, eyebrows raised, he feigned innocence.

"Why did you follow me in here, Garrow? Did you truly mean to apologize?"

He turned to face her again and then walked toward her until they were standing close. "I've been thinking on it throughout the afternoon, Suz, and what I truly meant to do was this."

When his lips met hers, Susanna fairly wilted. After a token protest, an ineffectual push against the hard planes of his chest—admittedly an excuse to rest her palms there—she gave in.

His mouth engulfed hers, tongue probing until she parted her lips and welcomed it. Hot, wet kisses, one after another, melded lips and tongues and teeth, nipping, soothing, giving, claiming.

Her thoughts gave way to pure feeling. Warm, strong arms and the heathery scent of him surrounded her. The sweet taste of brandy invaded as if she'd imbibed it herself. Her blood sang with it while shivers of pleasure danced along her spine. His hands glided over her back, her sides, her hips, and slid up to surround her breasts.

"Ah, Suz," he whispered against her ear. "'Tis time."

Oh, dear. She grasped his wrists and shoved. "No!"

He caressed her cheek and kissed her chin. "Dinna be afraid."

She stepped back, breaking his spell. "I am *not* afraid!"

He bent his head and blew out a harsh breath. For a long tense moment, he said nothing, then looked at her again. Just looked, as if awaiting an explanation.

She didn't have one. Not really. Perhaps he was right. She might admit to a bit of apprehension, but not really fear. That aside, now was not the time to work on their marriage. Not while there were people in the house. Not people like these, at any rate. "Please, James. Not while *they* are here."

"Well, that gives me incentive to make them welcome, eh? You'll be lucky if I grant them time for breakfast! Hell, I could toss them out right now."

How dare he! "This is *my* house, James. I say when they go. You know as well as I that Miranda will be in danger if we send her back to London! We cannot."

His jaw clenched. "Then pay her damned way to France! Or bloody India, for all I care. We should be rid of these people, Suz. At any cost, we need rid of them."

"Why?"

"Why not?" he almost shouted the words. Then he lowered his voice in what appeared to be an attempt at reason. "Do you not notice the way Fowler looks at you, Suz? He devours you with his eyes. He leers. And she's no better. I felt damned near undressed every time she looked my way!"

Susanna scoffed. "That's because you *were* damned near undressed, with your knees sticking out for all to see and your shirt gaping open to your—your hair!" Her face heated horribly and she brushed at it with her palms.

He ran a hand over his chest and smiled. "Jealous, are we?"

Susanna groaned and spun away, wishing she could scream. She would die before she admitted how jealous she was.

"Good night, Suz. Sleep well," he said in a low, sensuous growl that would melt stone.

She heard the soft click of the door closing, but even then she wouldn't turn around. If she did, she feared she would run after him and surrender everything she was or ever hoped to be for more kisses and...whatever else.

God help her, she hated him. And she loved him.

Madly. He was the most exasperating, frustrating, scintillating man she had ever met in her life. And she knew now, he was also the most uncontrollable.

This entire business of marriage had gotten away from her. He had taken over, a slightly unruly pet turned savage. What in the world was she to do?

She had noticed the way Miranda looked at James, the way she touched his hand or his arm at every opportunity. Susanna wanted to scratch her eyes out. And James was right about the lecherous Brodie Fowler. That one left no room for doubt what he was after. If only the two of them would simply go away.

It surprised Susanna how many of her mother's lessons in proper behavior for a hostess had stuck fast in such a rebellious being as herself. How could she bring herself to go against her father's wish and deny Miranda shelter and protection?

However, many of the lessons on how to be a proper wife had also taken, Susanna realized. James's wishes should be put foremost, shouldn't they? He wanted rid of these people and with sound reason, she had to admit.

What if she refused to banish them from Drevers and Miranda succeeded in seducing James? A man was apt to take what was offered on a silver plate if he grew hungry enough. And James definitely was hungry. His kisses proved that right enough.

There was a simple solution to that, of course. It seemed she would have no choice but to fill that need for James herself. But how could she and still maintain the independence and free will she relished so? Once he had her in his bed, Susanna feared she would never be able to deny him anything. He would hold such power over her, she would agree to anything he demanded of her. A child every year, long nights of energetic lovemaking that would leave her exhausted, and then in addition, she would yet have her other duties as his baroness and her own as mistress of Drevers. Could she manage all of that and still keep some remnant of the woman she had become? There were only so many hours in the day.

She thought of the small statue he had carved in what must have been his lonely hours of leisure after a day's hard work. Susanna wished to heaven she had not left it in Edinburgh at that gallery. She needed it now. If only she were able look upon it again and see the wealth of compassion and empathetic feeling it must have taken for him to create it.

What determination he had wrought upon that figure's face and how fiercely he had depicted her struggle to be free. A man who possessed disdain for what most men considered a woman's weak nature could never have made such a thing of beauty commemorating one. Each time she thought of it, she felt power infuse her whole being. That James Garrow believed women capable of such strength of purpose certainly did enhance her own.

The feel of his kiss lingered as she touched her fingers to her lips. Was it truly fear that Miranda would cause James to stray from his vows that urged Susanna so strongly to offer herself to him? Perhaps it was more on the order of fulfilling her own vows to James. She knew it was the right thing to do, but she had delayed for so long now, he might see it as sudden desperation on her part. And he would surely take it as capitulation. She wanted more between them than that when they finally came together.

This bore thinking about before she took any action.

The following morning, James woke in a foul mood. In addition to the frustration of having Susanna in the next room—knowing he could satisfy the problem by marching right through that dressing room into her chamber and taking what he wanted—he also had to endure Miranda and Fowler. Leaving their entertainment to Susanna was out of the question.

He found that someone—Kait, he guessed—had taken his wrinkled suit and shirt out of the pack he'd carried with him to Beauly and cleaned and pressed them. He washed and dressed hurriedly, hoping for time before the guests awoke to review the accounts and see what needed doing about the place.

Susanna's door opened just as he exited his room. "Good morning," she said in a snippy voice, her lips pursed, her chin high. She wore a fetching yellow gown, simple in cut and highly becoming to her complexion and her figure. He could see that she had taken special care to arrange her hair. Small ivory combs held it in place. His fingers itched to pull them out and watch the fiery mass tumble around her shoulders and over her brow.

He smiled and bowed while keeping pace with her as they walked to the head of the staircase. "What shall we do today?"

"Brodie did express a wish to hunt if we could arrange it."

James lifted an eyebrow and struggled to keep his smile intact. "*Brodie* now, is it?" He rushed on before she could answer. "He'll have to be content to do it afoot and with a pistol, then."

"We have long guns. The other two mounts in the stables are not hunters, of course, but they would probably suffice. Yours certainly looks capable."

"I wonder what you and Miss Durston will be doing while the peacock and I stalk our prey."

Susanna raised her skirts and took the stairs carefully. "You will take her along, of course. I shall remain here to see to the noon meal. What shall you hunt?"

"Pheasant are plentiful. Grouse. We'll not take large game this time of year. It is easier to preserve in cold weather."

They continued to the large dining room where four places had been set with the same modest white dishes and plain, unadorned silver used at supper last evening.

"We shall have to use these until I have the opportunity to order better from London," Susanna told him as he held out her chair and seated her. "Since none of the Eastonbys used Drevers as a primary residence, the fittings are few and not very grand."

"Well, we *must* have grand," James muttered with a grimace, taking his own place in the armchair at the head of the table.

She shot him a questioning look. "You object to grandeur?"

"At the risk of furthering the reputation we Scots have gained for frugality, I do object to the cost of it, aye."

She nodded once. "Then we shall make do with what we have."

Now he felt a miserly grump with no eye for the finer things in life. Fortunately Kait entered just then with their coffee and prevented his having to apologize to his wife for the necessity of denying her the luxury she was accustomed to.

It seemed wrong on the one hand to forbid her buying whatever she wished to buy. She did have money of her own. And on the other, he could not rid himself of the notion that he should support her fully. As man of the house, or houses as it were, he should provide. But women loved their little things about them. His mother probably would have expired without hers.

"Fripperies are fine," he muttered darkly. "If you want them, get them."

"Fripperies?" she questioned, eyebrows raised, looking amused.

He gestured idly at the silver and dishes. "Geegaws. Trappings."

"Ah! What of matched teams of horses?" she asked prettily, and he knew she was pushing to see how far she could go. "A crested carriage, perhaps?"

He set down his cup and sat back in his chair, unwilling to be bated. "Prize rams for the herd and new roofs for your cottars would serve you better."

A loud laugh from the doorway set James's teeth on edge.

"What's this? Talk of rams at breakfast!" Brodie Fowler exclaimed as he joined them. "How positively droll and bucolic! Country life must be dreadfully exciting." He pulled out a chair and sat down, a merry grin on his face.

James wanted to flatten the dandy's beak, but held his temper. This visit could go on for weeks and, while trading punches with Fowler might be the best entertainment he could get out of the experience, James knew it would discomfit Susanna.

He told himself he wasn't going out of his way to please her. It was simply that he wanted to avoid that sharp tongue of hers when he had so many other things on his mind.

Kait brought in a platter filled with sausages, kippers and eggs, which she plopped right in the middle of the long table, out of reach of anyone but Fowler. She promptly left.

Susanna got up from her chair and went to retrieve it and serve. She did so without a word of criticism for Kait's ineptness and completed the task with a smile. Then she set the dish on the sideboard and resumed her seat, all the while nattering on about exhibitions in London or some such.

Kait returned with the bread. This time, Susanna made a smooth, almost unnoticeable motion with her hand and the girl took the bread around and served everyone. Quick-minded, the little maid noted the dish on the sideboard and placed the remainder of the bread there beside it. This time she bobbed a curtsy before she left.

About that time, Miranda made her appearance, dressed smartly in a wine-colored riding habit. "I am famished!" she gushed. "All this fresh air, I suppose. Tell me, does it always smell of…whatever that is?" She wrinkled her nose prettily and directed the question to James.

"Sheep dung. Aye. Mind where you step." He ignored the gasps of the women and Fowler's chuckle and continued eating. He knew she had meant the heathery, piney fragrance that pervaded every breeze and made the Highlands unique. He had missed that dreadfully every minute he'd been obliged to endure in Auld Reekie, the pet name Edinburgh had earned. London was much worse than that, he knew from experience.

"Shall we be hunting today?" Fowler asked pleasantly. "I hear the deer are plentiful."

"We'll be going for birds that nest on the moor," James told him. "'Tis dangerous to hunt the wood unless I give our folk fair warning. There'll be those out gathering mushrooms and herbs."

"What sort of birds?" Fowler asked, folding his napkin neatly beside his empty plate.

James told him, attempting to inject a bit more warmth into his speech since Susanna was shooting him daggers from down the table. Miranda occupied herself with observing that exchange and grinning like a mule with a mouthful of briars.

In short order, they said their good mornings to Susanna who would stay behind, and went out to the stables. James planned to go a distance from any dwellings and well away from the pastureland to shoot. There were usually grouse and pheasant aplenty where he was taking them.

He checked the weapons himself, noting they had been recently cleaned. Colin had hunted, and had maintained the shotguns well. Perhaps they even belonged to him, but James thought not. Though the earl did not frequent Drevers himself, he would see there were firearms kept here in the event he or his friends did decide to visit.

They rode out, Miranda perched sidesaddle upon a sedate mare, Fowler on James's dependable gelding and James himself on the fractious stallion who appeared to be furious with the world for some reason or other.

James felt at one with the beast. They should get on fine.

"How much farther?" became the eternal question. James wondered if these two had ever ridden outside Hyde Park. He supposed they must have done since they claimed to know how to hunt and prated on volubly and at some length about how many customs they were abandoning on today's venture.

James ignored them for the most part, only breaking into their diatribe to point out local points of interest. He was doing his duty. Damn Suz if she drubbed him when they returned for not *doing his part,* as she called it.

These were Eastonby's guests as much as Susanna's,

so he tried hard to quell his instinct that they were up to no good.

Without warning a partridge, frightened by their intrusion too close to the nest, broke from cover and very nearly clipped the top of James's head on her ascent.

Fowler shouted, threw up his weapon and fired twice in rapid succession. Pellets peppered James and his mount. The stallion reared, dumped him off and hared through the bracken like something wild. Miranda screamed, struggling to maintain her precarious one-sided seat while Fowler cried, "I got him! I got him!"

James eyed his own weapon with great longing as blood streamed down his face from a nick in his forehead. Two inches lower and it would have hit his eye. Thank God they were only using birdshot with the damned things or he would be dead as the proverbial doornail. A number of other places stung like hell as he leaped to his feet and snatched the shotgun from Fowler's hands.

"Get down!" he ordered the man.

Fowler paled and dismounted.

"Find the bird."

"But—but I'm afraid I didn't see where it landed."

James glared. "If that's all you're afraid of, you're even dafter than you look. Find the damned bird!"

Fowler trotted off, picking his way through the prickly gorse, muttering obscenities in a barely audible voice.

Miranda dropped her weapon on the ground, slid from her saddle and approached him, her hand out to touch his head. "Oh, James, darling…you're hurt!"

James jerked away and halted her with a cold stare. "That would be *Lord Garrow* to you, madam." He picked up the shotgun, cradling both beneath his left arm. "Remount this instant. And when that poor excuse for a huntsman returns with his prey, he'll ride pillion with you."

She made an apologetic moue with her lips and shrugged toward her mare. "It is a sidesaddle."

"I know." With that, he mounted the gelding Fowler had left standing there and rode off toward Drevers. They could hurry after him or not. As far as he was concerned, they could get lost and rot.

Whether by wise design or happenstance, they maintained a goodly distance behind him all the way home. As he rode, he balanced all three of the shotguns, two of them still loaded, in front of him, taking great comfort in the fact that his charges were now unarmed.

He wondered what Susanna would think of her close brush with widowhood. They really needed to get these people back to London.

James ran a finger above his brow, touching the round little wound that still oozed blood down the side of his face. The bullet's crease above it had only just healed over. This marriage of his was hell on the head, not to mention other parts of his anatomy.

Susanna dropped the silver candlestick and polishing rag the minute James entered the dining room. "Good heavens!" she cried, jumping up and running to him. "What has happened?"

He caught her hand before it could touch his head. "Your English fancy lad shot me."

Speechless, she stared at him, taking in the blood, the ashen color of his skin and his poorly controlled fury.

"Not apurpose," he admitted. "Though I'm none too certain of that, now that I think about it." He laid the shotguns on the table, dirtying the clean white cloth, and proceeded to unload them.

She looked past him and down the hallway. "Where are they? Surely you didn't…"

"Shoot him back?" he asked with a harsh laugh. "Nay, but I was sorely tempted. They'll be along shortly." He carefully stacked the guns in the corner.

"Oh, James, that needs tending immediately. Come with me." She took him by the hand and led him towards the stairs. She put one hand beneath his nearest elbow and slid her other arm around his waist. "Do you feel weak?"

He grunted and leaned on her a bit as they took the stairs, but would not admit to any weakness. Men could be such children.

"I could do with a dose of your favorite medicament," he told her. "For two obvious reasons, staying cupshot for the next week or so holds definite appeal."

"Does it hurt terribly?" she asked. "Of course it does! Do you think Kait would know where to obtain some whisky?"

"I should hope she would. Her uncle is my master brewer."

"I thought she was from Drevers."

"She is. A good many of our people are closely related, Suz. That's why I felt responsible for them when your father did not."

"He did so," she argued. "Only he did not know about Mr. Colin's treachery. He will be appalled when he sees the accounts."

"You've gone over them?" James asked her, looking astonished.

"Of course. What do you think occupied my time while you were in Beauly?"

"Preaching abstinence and painting walls?" he asked, smiling down at her.

Susanna glared at him. "That, too. Sit there," she told him when they reached his chamber and she had led him to his bed.

She went into the dressing room and fetched bathing cloths and brought to the bed the basin Kait had cleaned earlier. She filled it with fresh water from the pitcher and then bathed the blood off his head and face. He endured it silently, looking at her with an approving light in his eyes as she worked.

"Remove that bloody shirt, if you please."

"Bloody? Such language, madam!" he said in a teasing tone.

Susanna quite liked him when his moods lightened. If only he would stay that way. It seemed he would catch himself in a moment of jocularity and, all at once, he'd become the dour Scot again, all frowns and barbs.

Susanna watched him discard his padded weskit and shirt, shrugging out of the one and tugging the other over his head. When she saw his body, she grimaced. There were other circular wounds, several in his right shoulder and another at the side of his neck. That one had been disguised by the blood that covered his neck and collar. "James, this one narrowly missed the vein. You could have bled to death before you reached home."

He cocked an eyebrow. "Or been blinded. The man's dangerous."

"Be quiet. When I've finished here, you should lie down. I'll make your regrets for the noon meal and this evening as well."

"Nay," he objected. "There's naught wrong a bit of salve and a strong drink won't put right."

"Compromise, then. Let me send Kait up with a bite to eat and perhaps a strong toddy. If you feel well enough, you may come down for supper."

He laughed full out. "You're a wee martinet, Suz. They could use you in the Guard."

She daubed witch hazel on the wound at his neck and ignored his hiss of pain. "And you, sir, are a great lump who needs a firm hand to guide you. Be still!"

To her surprise, he obeyed as she continued to treat his hurts. "There now," she announced, tamping the last sticking plaster in place.

He grasped her hand and kissed it. "My thanks, nurse."

She smiled and tugged away to remove the basin and set it aside. "You are quite welcome, but only if you promise me you will try your best not to get shot again."

"My word on it." Though his lips still smiled, his eyes grew serious. "Suz, be careful of Fowler, promise me?"

"That's an absurd and totally unnecessary warning! I know you can't believe Mr. Fowler meant any real harm. He's no more than a pea-brained fool who knew no better than to fire in your direction."

"Ask yourself, as I have been doing, what Fowler might hope to gain if he were rid of me."

Susanna laughed and tossed her head. "Why, nothing whatsoever! Certainly not access to my affections if that is what you imply."

"Access to your person, then. You are your father's heir. A very wealthy heir, I might add. Without my protection you would be completely vulnerable and open to grave compromise or even worse."

"Vulnerable, you think?" she asked, her voice acerbic with the reminder. "Who was it shot Mr. Colin?"

"Mock me, then, but I do not trust either of them, Susanna." His voice was soft, but intense as he said it.

"I know," she replied with a nod of understanding.

"That is the saddest thing about you, James. You trust no one. Not even your own wife."

He looked at her intently, but his expression was unreadable. And he offered no denial of her accusation. None whatsoever.

In the face of his implacability, she relented. "If it eases your mind, I trust them even less than you do."

Chapter Thirteen

James stayed near Susanna as much as possible which meant suffering the almost constant presence of their guests. Fowler did ask about the state of Drevers, though his questions were always phrased as nothing more than idle curiosity. Miranda, too, declared that the place could use a bit of sprucing up, and that Susanna should ask her father for funds to do it if Drevers could not support itself.

Susanna politely brushed off the roundabout queries without giving away what they had discovered about Colin. James answered with a silent glare that lasted until someone changed the topic of conversation.

Then on the fourth day of their visit, Miranda approached him. He was just coming in from the stables where he had gone to speak with Fergus about replacing some of the tack. She rushed to him the instant he entered the door. "Thank goodness! I thought I would never be able to catch you alone!" She pressed a palm to his chest. James looked down at it, then backed away.

He knew that Susanna was in the kitchens with Cook discussing the evening menu. At least that's where he had left her. "Is something wrong?"

She glanced over her shoulder as if fearing they would be overheard, then whispered, "Yes! I must speak with you at length about something of terrible importance. Will you meet me tonight?" There was a deviltry in those dark eyes that sent a different message altogether.

James crossed his arms over his chest and looked her up and down. He had half expected this. Her flirting was not altogether subtle. "Now how proper would that be?"

Again she glanced around. "This has nothing to do with propriety. It is imperative that we talk. Meet me by that copse of oak where the stream enters. You know the place I mean?"

He studied her for a moment, then nodded once. "Aye, I know it."

"At midnight," she declared. "Brodie and Susanna should be asleep at that hour."

"They should."

"Until then," she cast him a gaze of unmistakable invitation, then hurried up the staircase to her room. Or to Fowler.

James slowly shook his head. He probably should tell Susanna about this, but he couldn't see that it would serve any purpose. It would make her angry enough to send the little witch packing, but it might also hurt her to know that Miranda had tried to betray her while accepting her hospitality and protection.

He simply wouldn't go. He'd never said he would. Anything she had to say to him, she could damned well say it in front of Susanna. An hour spent stalking around out there in the fresh air tonight might do Miranda some good. Maybe his not showing up would make her so furious she would leave without being asked. In any event, the results should make for an interesting breakfast.

When morning arrived, however, there was no reaction whatsoever from Miranda. It was as if she had never approached him at all and suggested the assignation. James watched Fowler and tried to determine whether he knew what Miranda had planned.

Two more days passed without incident while James kept a close eye on their guests. Since Miranda had behaved so flagrantly with him, James feared Fowler might have designs on Susanna. He certainly made no secret of the fact that he found her attractive, though he had yet to do anything that could be termed indecent.

James had remained close to Susanna as often as she would allow. When she would not, he had kept an eye on Miranda and Fowler or had David McLean do so. However, nothing untoward had taken place. The guests had been behaving well enough, Susanna was occupied with household matters, so James felt safe in leaving them to their own devices for an hour or so. He had important business with David.

David was a cousin who had recently returned from the fishing fleet out of Moray Firth for a visit. The man certainly had done his part these past few years in supporting his extended family at Galioch. In truth, David had sacrificed the most since he had to leave his wife for half the year while he went out to earn.

James trusted his childhood friend and kinsman implicitly and needed to reward him for his loyalty. He only hoped Davy would view what he was about to do as a reward and not a punishment.

After the noon meal, James sent Kait to find David, who was hanging about the house somewhere, ostensibly serving as the new footman, but actually to keep an eye on Fowler. It was time to offer Davy a position as steward of Galioch since James would have so much to do managing Drevers for Susanna.

When he arrived, James asked him to close the door to the library and have a seat. For some time they simply talked of old times, of how various families at Galioch and Drevers were getting on, and of their respective jobs, taken to help support the clan.

"Are you set on returning to the boats, Davy?" James asked, ready now to approach the reason for the meeting.

David grinned. "When I've only just got the stink of fish off my hands? Nay, if you need me here, Jamie, I'll stay. Catriona will be glad of it."

"Does the stewardship of Galioch appeal to you? Twenty pounds a year to start?"

"Good God, have ye robbed a bank then?"

James laughed with him, glad that David understood the twenty was all he could offer at present. He stood, shook hands across the desk and the deal was done. "Could I sound you out on something that has naught to do with the job directly?"

"Aye. Is it Fowler? Should I bury him in the heather or let the carrion birds at him when I'm done?"

"Neither yet, but 'tis a thought."

"No doubt about it, Jamie, he does fancy Lady Suz," Davy warned.

"Aye, so it seems. We'll be rid of him soon enough. You keep a sharp eye out until he's gone, then you can take up your post at the keep."

James frowned down at the books he'd been examining. "On paper, Drevers looks as bad off as Galioch. Has for years."

David pursed his lips and sighed. "May be, but it's not. There's money here, Jamie. For all that it's been ill spent, it has been made. You helped where you could, but folk still went hungry. The cots are cavin' in. There's those who've been leavin' and not to work and send money home, either.''

There were neatly made comments in the margins of the account ledger that James recognized as Susanna's writing. He glanced up at Davy. "It appears Colin has robbed Drevers of a veritable fortune over the past few years.''

David scoffed. "You don't need account books to tell you that. Look at the size of the herds. Wool alone would turn a nice profit. Probably has done.''

James continued. "Eastonby might not have noticed, but his partner should have. According to the description of duties the earl himself remarked as belonging to the man, the blame falls squarely on Durston, Miranda's father. He handles the business end of Eastonby's estates as well as the shipping enterprise in which he owns stock. Durston is the primary contact for the factors—such as Colin in the instance of Drevers—who are directly in charge of Eastonby's properties.''

"So the earl's in the clear. I'd say go after this Durston and hang him by his—''

James interrupted. "At the very least, Durston's guilty of negligence here. At worst, he's behind it all and Colin's his man.''

"That last would be my guess.''

With a slow nod, James closed the book and rested his elbows on the desk, his hands clasped beneath his chin. "I feared I might be readin' things wrong, Davy, on account of my liking for the earl. He seems decent.''

"Good, since he's family now," David said. "Is that all then?''

"Aye. I'll take the watch for a while. Your Catriona's

still wanting to make up for your months away, I expect.'' He grinned. ''Give her my best.''

''No chance o' that, m'lad. 'Tis my best she'll be gettin'.''

''Be off, then. See you tomorrow.''

James promptly returned to his concern with Drevers's books, assured that Galioch would fare as well in David's capable hands as it would in his own.

Susanna had merely marked in the accounts what she thought might be in error. She would know now, as her father did not, the approximate size of the herds. The numbers recorded were a blatant falsification. So were the entries for repairs and maintenance to the cottages and outbuildings. Even the house itself had received precious little attention, certainly not to the tune of what Colin had recorded in this log.

For a while longer, he studied the figures to see whether he could be overlooking hidden expenses that would explain the huge discrepancies. When he made accusations against Colin and Durston to the earl, he wanted to back them up with specifics.

Satisfied he had come to the right conclusion, James set the account books aside and closed his eyes, trying to piece together what he must report to Eastonby, and whether going after Colin would serve any purpose now. He thought so. Unless Durston had required most of the profits siphoned off Drevers, Colin might have accrued enough to make forced restitution worthwhile.

If Durston had received the money, he would have it invested somewhere unreachable, no doubt. The best the earl might do in that case was to dissolve their partnership somehow and dismiss him with the threat of exposing his theft.

Durston's direct involvement in the scheme might also

mean that Fowler and Miranda had been sent north for a reason other than securing the woman's protection. Both seemed determined to come between James and Susanna. All of this flirting could be merely a distraction. Maybe Durston had sent them to find out whether his embezzlement was likely to be discovered.

Even if Fowler and Miranda were totally innocent and only here for the reason they claimed, they could just as easily find safety elsewhere. Who, with any sense of propriety, intruded on a couple's privacy so soon after their marriage anyway? They had no business being here even if they were likable people, which they certainly were not.

Unfortunately, Susanna wouldn't countenance his ordering them to leave what she considered *her* house. He supposed he would simply have to make them want to go. He recalled having perfected several schemes that proved successful years ago with his mother's guests. With that in mind, he went to see what could be done about the situation.

Unfortunately, Miranda and Fowler were nowhere to be found. And neither was Susanna. He finally went to the kitchens, the only place he had not looked, but there was only Cook and Kait.

"Oh, she was here earlier, but now they've gone off to see the improvements m'lady made at Galioch," Kait informed him. "Left whilst ye was talkin' to Davy."

James dashed for the stables and found the cart and his gelding gone. He quickly saddled the mare and tore off across the fields.

When he rode up, Orvie lumbered up to him before James could dismount. "Th' witch's here!" he whispered, glancing fearfully toward the keep.

James got off the mare and handed the reins to Orvie. "Tether her, would you? I'll see to the witch."

When he entered the hall, it was empty. So were the kitchens. James took the stairs quickly and searched the upper floors, his heart pounding, a feeling of urgency prodding him. They must be on the battlements.

He clambered up the winding stair that opened from the east tower. When he emerged in the open air, he saw the three of them immediately. Both Susanna and Miranda were perched between merlons, though not in the same embrasure. Since the spaces between the crenellations were a good four feet off the floor of the roof, Fowler would have to have lifted them up there. He saw they had also made use of an empty wooden crate someone had left lying about.

Braced with one hand on the stones, Susanna pointed out some view in the distance with the other, probably Drevers itself. Fowler moved toward her, carrying the crate. It looked as if he, too, meant to climb up.

James's breath caught in his throat. He was too far away to prevent Fowler from joining Susanna in her precarious position. The expression on Miranda's face as she looked at Fowler seemed entirely too pleased.

"Ho, there!" James shouted. He meant for them to know they were being observed and if anything happened to Susanna, they would pay dearly for it.

By the time he reached the battlement, Fowler was in place behind Susanna, standing between her and James with a hand on her shoulder. The wall was a good four feet thick, so there was room for two, but Fowler was positioned so that Susanna was too close to the edge for comfort.

"Get down from there!" James ordered in a voice that

afforded no compromise. "And get your hand off my wife if you want to keep it!"

Fowler chuckled, sounding a bit nervous. "We were only seeing the sights. Come join us."

"I'll not be telling you again," James said, pinning Fowler with a glare.

"Oh, this is too frightening! Help me down!" Miranda cried out in mock horror. James ignored her, keeping his gaze locked on Fowler, who slowly removed his hand and eased back from Susanna. James continued to stare at him until the man sat down on the inner edge of the embrasure and stepped onto the box. He made a great to-do about dusting off the seat of his breeches until James shoved him aside.

"Come," James ordered Susanna and lifted his arms. She frowned at him, but allowed him to assist her. With his hands at her waist and hers on his shoulders, he lowered her to the roof, sliding her slowly down the front of his body as he did so.

She trembled and her eyes were wide. Was it because they were touching? Or had she been afraid? He couldn't tell. He could not seem to let her go in either case.

"I was in no danger, James," she told him, her voice steady, but too high pitched to sound as calm as she would have him believe. "Heights have never frightened me."

"Apparently not, but did you consider the age of these stones and how easily they might crumble beneath your feet?" He could hardly bear to think about it. His heart was still racing.

Miranda complained until Fowler dragged the box over and helped her descend as well.

Susanna removed her hands from James's shoulders

and placed them on his chest, gently pushing away. "I am fine, I tell you."

He reluctantly released his grip on her waist. "Well, I am *not* fine," he admitted in a low voice only she could hear. "I need to speak with you privately as soon as may be."

As they started down the steep, uneven stone stairway that led from the roof to the lower floors, James insisted that Fowler and Miranda go first.

When they returned to Drevers, it was late afternoon. Fowler and Miranda excused themselves and went to their respective rooms to rest before dressing for dinner. James escorted Susanna to the library and closed the door.

She took a seat behind the desk and he paced, trying to decide how much to tell her and whether he should couch it as fact discovered or the mere supposition that it was.

"Not only do you dislike and mistrust them. You suspect them of something," she declared, cutting right to the heart of the conundrum.

"Aye, I suspect they've been sent for some purpose other than what they pretend. I doubt Miranda was under any threat at all in London. Durston could have used that plot against your and your father's lives as a good excuse to send her here."

"But why?"

"To see whether I suspect what he and Colin had going perhaps." James proceeded to explain what he had deduced from the account books and how the steward, Colin, would have reported directly to Miranda's father, not Susanna's. "I could be wrong, I admit, but your father needs to be made aware of the possibility that his own partner has been cheating him out of his due for years. In the meantime, we should get rid of the spies Durston sent here. Do you agree?''

She sat sideways in the chair, one elbow resting on the desk, tapping her chin with one finger as she considered what he'd said. Then she straightened and faced him. ''I can't think Mr. Durston's involved with embezzlement, James. Why would he be? He is certainly no pauper. When Father met him, he had just made an enormous amount of money in the Exchange. He is a very wealthy man.''

''So was my father at one time. Circumstances can alter, Suz. Investments turn sour. There are any number of ways for fortunes to be lost in the blink of an eye.'' And ways for them to be gained as well, he thought darkly. ''How long has your father been in business with Durston?''

''Since I was twelve, I think. Yes, that's correct. Miranda joined me at Throckmorton School when we were exactly that. Father vouched for her so that she would be admitted. It is an exclusive school and unusual for a girl of her station to be allowed in.''

''The recommendation of an earl plus a hefty amount of blunt made it all possible,'' James guessed.

''A fact of life, I'm afraid,'' Susanna said with a wry smile.

James smiled back. ''Another fact of life is that we need to oust your friends before I do bodily harm to Fowler.''

''Jealous, are we?'' she taunted, as he had done to her regarding Miranda.

''Aye. I am that, Suz. So much so that I might be seeing treachery where it does not exist. Humor me and let me send them away.''

She left her chair, came around her desk and headed

for the door. ''I doubt I can stop you if that's your intent, but I hate having to explain it to Father when we have no excuse other than unfounded suspicion. After all, he requested that we give her protection here. Suppose you're wrong?''

He caught her arm as she passed by him. ''Suz, I do see your point, but it could be dangerous to let them stay. Dangerous to our marriage, if nothing else.''

She shrugged. ''I have to grant you, Fowler is either a crafty devil or incredibly stupid. And Miranda… Well, let us say she learned very little at Throckmorton in the way of behaving as a houseguest.''

''I know you are not good friends now,'' James stated. ''Were you ever?''

She laughed. ''Hardly. And it had nothing to do with station or lack of it. We tolerate one another at best. Until this visit, I thought she only possessed a strange sense of humor that rubbed me the wrong way and I tried to ignore it.''

''And now?'' James asked, sliding one hand up her arm to rest on her shoulder, as if he could erase Fowler's earlier touch.

She met his eyes, hers sparking with an inner fire. ''Now I believe she would like to insinuate herself into your affections, to come between us somehow. She wants me angry with you.''

''Are you?''

Her sigh sounded incredibly weary. ''No. I cannot believe her when she relates, laughingly, how you look at her when I am not observing. Or that you requested that she meet you alone and she, out of friendship to me, refused you.''

James could have strangled Miranda at that moment. ''Suz, I swear on my life those are lies. I want her *gone*.''

"Knowing her as I do, and unless you give me good reason not to do so, I believe you."

He moved his hand from her shoulder and cradled her chin. "You trust me."

She grinned. "It is more like I credit you with better taste."

James laughed and offered her his arm. "Then we are in complete accord, lass. May I escort you to your room?"

"I could use a lie down until supper," she admitted. "What will you do about them, James?"

"Leave them to me and don't worry your bonny wee head about them any longer."

"My bonny wee head?" She shot him a frown, her voice rising with every word. "My bonny wee witless *woman's* head? Is that what you mean?"

James winced. "Suz, please! I never said—"

She snatched her hand from his arm. "I should have pushed *you* off that parapet, you brainless...*gorm!*"

"Suz! Wait!" he called as she ran up the stairs, skirts lifted and petticoats rustling. But she did not wait. She never even looked back.

"Gorm?" he muttered to himself. Well, at least she was learning Scots.

Susanna took her time dressing. Though she had been engrossed in writing to her father, the time still dragged by. The clock had just struck seven. She had an entire hour left before that which she had designated for the evening meal. Eight was early for supper, but City hours made no sense given that rising at dawn here in the country was a necessity rather than a choice. There was so devilish much to do.

She donned the soft rose silk since it was easily fastened and required few underpinnings. Kait would be too busy below with Cook to assist her in dressing. That done, she stepped into her matching soft-soled slippers that required no buttons or ties. Impressing Miranda and Fowler, or even James, took second place to comfort this evening.

Getting rid of their houseguests would not be a pleasant undertaking. Susanna almost hoped James would delay doing so until morning so that they could pack and be away immediately. There were bound to be hard feelings. Not that she cared, but she did not relish facing them over breakfast.

Though she did not mind seeing the last of either Fowler or Miranda, she still worried what might happen to Miranda if James was proved wrong. Perhaps Mr. Durston had no knowledge of Colin's thievery and was totally innocent of any wrongdoing. Unlikable as Miranda was, Susanna hated to expose her to any hurt or worse by denying her sanctuary here.

The sound of subdued voices emanated from the library as she approached it. She stopped outside and listened. Glass clinked against glass and liquid burbled as if someone were pouring a drink.

"One more day like today and I shall go mad!" Miranda was speaking in a low voice. She sounded angry. "At this rate, we'll be stuck here in the damned Highlands forever."

"This is not as easy as you said it would be," Fowler complained.

"You've muffed it, Brodie," Miranda accused. "You certainly had your chance. More than one."

"Look, money is the primary objective, isn't it? Suppose we could obtain the property, perhaps both properties while we're about it? Those could be sold or mortgaged. That would take care of the immediate problem,'' Fowler told her.

"Shh," Miranda warned. "Keep your voice down." She paused. "Very well, we shall go for what we can get and be done with it. Maybe that will suffice until we can think of something else."

"I think I have a plan. How clever at cards do you think Garrow is?"

Susanna heard Miranda scoff. "Living here in the back end of nowhere? How clever *could* he be?" She laughed. "I see you're up to no good."

"To *our* good," Fowler declared. "This way, if the other plan goes awry, we are not culpable in any way. Here, finish this if you want. I'm going up to study my tricks of the trade. Prepare to be highly entertained this evening."

"Of course, darling, I expect no less of you," Miranda cooed.

There was a short silence and heavy breathing. "And I expect a greater reward than that later tonight," Fowler said suggestively.

Susanna dashed away and hid in the alcove beneath the stairs.

Good heavens, James was right! They were up to no good. And they were planning to gull James out of Galioch and her out of Drevers!

Susanna crouched out of sight and worried her forehead with her fingers, trying to think what else Fowler and Miranda might have had planned that had not worked for them. Had Fowler some addlepated notion she would leave James for him? That James's supposed attentions to Miranda would cause her to leave Drevers and go back to London?

That almost made sense from Mr. Durston's perspective, if he were guilty of stealing from the estate via Mr. Colin. If she were not here and relieved James of the responsibility of her property, the theft could resume. Yes!

She must warn her father as soon as possible and have the man arrested. The account books might be enough proof. But they would only incriminate Colin.

Now, however, she must quickly decide what to do about Miranda and Fowler. He had mentioned cards and winning property. She had to prevent his relieving her of Drevers, and James of Galioch. She must warn James not to engage in any game of chance. Fowler sounded altogether too confident of his ability to win.

She and James could confront them. He would know what to do about this. She had to speak with him immediately.

Susanna crept from concealment and rushed up the stairs, praying Fowler would not come out of his room and see her before she made it to the master chamber. When she reached it, she didn't pause to knock. She simply whirled inside and closed the door behind her, turning to lean against it. "James! There's trouble afoot and— Oh!" She jumped, startled.

He had just emerged from the dressing room and wasn't wearing a stitch. In one hand he clutched his kilt and in the other, a shirt. It was a wonder she even noticed his hands at all.

"Suz?" His shock was nearly as profound as hers. She forced herself to shut her eyes and turn away.

"Forgive me, I can't—can't leave the room…right now," she gasped, pointing in the direction of the dressing room that separated their bedchambers. "Could you dress in there, please?"

He laughed. "Nay, I can scarcely turn around in that wee cupboard. What's amiss?"

Susanna cleared her throat and remained as she was, facing the door. She heard the rustle of fabric and prayed he was putting on his clothes. How was she ever to think if he was standing there naked? "We must t-talk," she told him, frustrated by the waver in her voice.

"Well, turn around, Lass. It won't bite."

It? She shook her head, highly impatient with his joke. But she did turn to look in spite of herself.

He was now wearing a shirt of pristine white, a simple lace jabot at his throat and a carefully pleated plaid that reached midknee. Instead of the faded greens and blues of the old kilt, this red-and-black garment looked smart as any she had ever seen on a Scottish soldier.

As she watched, he buckled on a smooth, black leather belt with a huge silver buckle. His lower legs and feet were still bare.

"Take a deep breath," he advised, "and do sit down somewhere before you topple over. What's got you so fashed?"

Fashed. That's precisely how she felt. Since he was now standing in front of the only chair in the room, she walked hesitantly to the bed, stepped up and seated herself primly on the edge facing him. "We have problems, James."

"Aye, I'd say we do if the sight of me still upsets you so."

Only now that she was seated did he sit, promptly taking up the knee-length stockings of clockwatch and preparing to put them on. She averted her gaze again, unwilling to observe such an intimate act. They might be wed, but she still found this sort of thing highly unsettling.

"I overheard them plotting," she told him, her voice little more than a whisper.

"Not surprising. You're a deft hand at eavesdropping as I recall. What did you find out?" He also kept his words low enough that they would not be overheard through the door in the event anyone was listening.

She told him word for word as correctly as she could recall. "And I believe they plan to acquire our properties, either for their own or for Mr. Durston's gain, so you must not agree to anything Fowler proposes in the way of gaming."

"Oh, I'll be giving him no time for that. They'll be on the road within the hour." Her gaze flew to him just as he pulled on his second stocking and fastened it at the knee.

Susanna forced her mind from his bare knees back to more important matters.

"Ordering them away tonight worries me," she admitted, twisting her ring on her finger and nervously swinging one foot. "Could we wait until morning to ask them to leave and concoct some excuse other than the real reason?"

"Why?" he asked. She liked that he was willing to listen to her, rather than laying down the law.

"Because they are most probably in league with her father, just as you suspected! But we have no actual proof and cannot hold them accountable in the courts for it. If they do not know that we know, we would have time to apprise Father of what Durston has been doing. Perhaps then he would have time to find proof against the man there in his own office and have him apprehended. What do you think?"

For a moment, he said nothing, then replied. "You could have the right of it. The minute they're off, I shall

have one of the men ride hell-bent to the nearest telegraph with a message for your father. He needs to be told
about Durston as soon as may be.''

"But suppose Durston receives the message instead?
He will know we're on to them and might become desperate enough to do something rash to escape being revealed for what he is!''

James shook his head. "Brilliant, Suz. I hadn't thought
of that. Then I will telegraph a friend in London and have
him inform the earl personally. For now, I'll get the vi-
pers out of our nest. That's the first order of business.
Are we agreed?''

"Agreed," Susanna declared, her gaze fixed upon him
as he leaned over to straighten his shoe buckle.

"There," he said, standing. "My humble modesty's
preserved. I'm decent," he told her.

Indeed, she thought as she looked at him and very
nearly sighed at the sight. James, Lord Garrow, stood tall
and was every inch the romantic Scots laird of novels
and poetry, exuding authority and demanding attention.
And making one wonder what deviltry went on behind
that dark-eyed look of intensity and the barely concealed
smile. Damn him, he knew exactly how he looked and
how it affected her.

He wore a short, dark jack trimmed with ebony buttons
that contrasted dramatically with the snowy white lace at
his throat. Knife sharp pleats clung to his narrow hips, a
swath of matching plaid secured to his left shoulder with
a large brooch set with stones. His sporran, embossed
with silver gilt, hung suspended from chased link chain
attached to his waist. Silver-buckled shoes encased his
feet, and his legs were covered with the patterned hose
held up with flashed garters below the knee. He had
tucked a small, black-handled knife in the left one.

She caressed him with a gaze of longing she could not deny feeling or showing at the moment. He set her pulse racing and stole her breath, he was so handsome.

On some level of consciousness, Susanna realized he was perusing her as voraciously as she was him.

"How lovely you look, lass," he told her, his voice more sensual than she had ever heard it. "You're wearin' a beautiful dress tonight."

She smiled at him and inclined her head in response to his compliments. "Thank you, my lord. So are you."

His laughter rang out and she joined in as she took the arm he offered and let him lead her to the door.

"Damn me, but you're bound to have the last word, eh?"

"A failing I admit," she replied, then grew serious as they reached the stairs. "James? Promise me you'll not take up any challenge, even if Fowler pricks your pride? He mentioned the cards, so you should especially avoid them."

He looked down, his smiling expression unchanged. "Perhaps a game or two would teach him a lesson about prejudging his opposition."

She stopped in her tracks and halted him as well. "You *never* play cards! He'll trounce you, James! No, I won't allow it."

He touched a finger to her lips to hush her. "Trust me, Suz." Before she could utter a word of protest, he replaced his finger with his mouth and kissed her.

Her wits evaporated like spilled perfume. All she could think was how desperately she wanted him to continue, never to stop, to deepen his foray and crush her closer until she became one with him for all time, inevitably joined and inseparable. The heat rushing through her demanded he increase it, feed it and burn with her. It was unfair, so unfair, and so deliciously wonderful she could scarcely breathe.

When he released her, she uttered an oath her father would have surely rebuked her for.

He laughed. ''There's no havin' the last word with you, is there, lass?''

As last words went, Susanna admitted it was not one of her better offerings.

Chapter Fourteen

The dreaded moment when supper was over arrived all too soon. Susanna wished she and James could go up the stairs now, lock their doors against Miranda Durston and Brodie Fowler and never see the pair again. But James would have none of that and she knew it.

The thing was, their guests appeared so guileless this evening. At least at first meeting and during the meal. Susanna felt incredibly relieved to know that the two of them would soon be gone. The very idea of what they had planned made her want to fetch James's pistol and send them both the way of that wretch, Mr. Colin.

Fowler apologized again, quite profusely, for the so-called accident with the shotgun. Quite a mistake on his part, bringing that into the conversation, Susanna thought to herself. James was smiling. A wolf's smile, she decided.

Fowler's dress and manners looked impeccable, as usual, though he paled in comparison to James in his Scots finery. Obviously, Miranda agreed. Susanna kept watching for her to drool.

While James said very little, Fowler spent the duration

of the meal deferring to Miranda and herself, dishing up flattery more sugary than Cook's jam tartlet dessert.

Miranda basked in his praise and tried to elicit—with some little success, too—a tribute on her appearance from James.

"Aye, I think that green you're wearin' becomes you, Miss Durston. You've the look of a true London lady and that's a fact," he said pleasantly.

It took Miranda a moment to realize his was a back-handed compliment, that she *looked* the lady, but that all present knew very well she was not. Her preening smile grew quite calculating then, as if she knew revenge was in the offing and relished it to the extreme.

Fowler's air of superiority increased. "Ah, yes, Miranda is quite popular in Town. Runs in the most exalted circles and is loved by all who know her. Why, even the Duchess of Runesbury invites her to each and every salon she holds. Miranda is a favorite of hers, y'know."

He heaped even more praise on Miranda, like mounds of sweet clotted cream atop rotten raspberries. Susanna thought she might gag.

Instead she found she was fighting a smile. Everyone who was anyone knew the duchess he spoke of was nothing more than an incredibly wealthy cit's daughter who had snagged herself an aged and impoverished duke who had fallen out of favor long before his wife had been born. The woman's salons were reportedly a disguise for attending her gilded den of iniquity.

To Susanna's disgust, she discovered she possessed the most frightful urge to impart that bit of gossip to her husband and laugh with him about it. Not the most lofty of thoughts, she admitted, but there it was nonetheless.

Yes, just as she performed her own little niceties with reluctant deftness, James did perfect duty as host, though he seemed to go out of his way to mislead Fowler into thinking him more provincial than he actually was. She did not have to be terribly canny to understand what all of this was leading to. James actually *wanted* the man to meet him over cards.

Susanna feared the worst, that her husband was over-estimating his own talents. How could he possibly be certain that he would win, even if he truly was as proficient as he must think? So much depended upon sheer luck. And who knew how much of that Fowler would have tonight?

Too many times, she herself had been so caught up in a game with her father that she completely forgot the consequences of losing a bet. Had she not wagered her freedom against her father's right to choose a husband for her? Of course, she had never really believed at the time that he would hold her to such a wager if she lost. Never mind that she would have expected him to honor it, had she won. With that hand she'd held, she had been so certain of victory. But that had only been a game between parent and child, meant to entertain. Or perhaps teach a lesson.

She had known full well her father would never force her to marry. For one thing, it was against the law. For another, he was, at heart, too kind. His insistence that she marry James had surprised her, but even then, she had realized that if she had objected strongly, he would have relented. That aside, she had indeed toyed with fate. It had not been wise to wager.

People who gambled more than they could afford to lose could be beggared in one evening. In one game, if they were so foolish as to stake everything at once. Though he did not show it at the moment, she knew

James seethed with anger. That very thing could be his undoing. And hers.

"Shall we have an evening of music?" she suggested, hoping against hope everyone would agree.

"Well, we have done that to death, haven't we? Why not a friendly game of chance?" Miranda countered.

Oh, there it was, Susanna thought, her heart sinking.

Miranda continued. "We've not done that yet. We could play for—oh, let me think—dried beans, I suppose."

"Now there is a brilliant idea!" Fowler chimed in with exuberance.

"We haven't any cards," Susanna announced.

"I have a deck," Fowler said, not surprising anyone.

"Very well, then. I shall get the beans," Susanna offered, vastly relieved they would at least begin with that. Perhaps she would have some notion of James's expertise before he risked anything of value.

"Nay, dinna bother," James told her, shaking his head as he rose from the table. "'Tis not as if I've naught to wager with. We play for worthy stakes or not at all." He smiled at Susanna, an obvious dare for her to protest further. "Shall we retire to the parlor?"

Fowler clapped his hands once and rubbed them together. "Excellent! My deck of cards is in my case upstairs. I'll be back in a trice." He rose and promptly left.

"And I," Miranda said with a cheerful lilt, "shall pour us each a tot of sherry!"

"There is none," Susanna absently reminded her. "You finished it off."

"Oh, but we *do* have more! I went exploring yesterday afternoon and guess what I found! Through the kitchens, at the back of the buttery, lies the door to a perfectly lovely old wine cellar. Not fully stocked, by any means, but neither was it empty. And to think, all this time you had no notion...." She shook her head as if disbelieving Susanna's ineptness as a hostess. Waving one hand, she swept by them to take the lead in leaving the dining room.

"All this time," Susanna parroted with a roll of her eyes. "Trust *her* to sniff it out." And after going to such pains to keep it secret. She looked at James. "Did you know of it?"

"Aye." Then he slid his palm along the back of her waist and leaned close to her ear. She thought he would kiss it—almost hoped he would—but instead he merely whispered, "When I wink, you are immediately to do whatever necessary to distract her. Both of them if you are able, aye?"

Susanna shot him a questioning look, but said nothing. When she saw the sly gleam in his eye, she gave an assenting nod. Whatever he was planning?

In the center of the parlor, James set up the playing table, a lovely old three-footed pedestal affair with a round top that tilted up so that it could be stood in a corner when not in use. They drew chairs up to it, but did not sit yet. Instead, they waited for Fowler. Susanna assisted Miranda in pouring the drinks while James lit a small blaze in the fireplace to take the chill off the room.

Fowler returned shortly, flourishing the deck of playing cards. He strolled over and placed them on the table. From his pocket, he withdrew a small pad of paper and a pencil for keeping score, and put them down beside the fancy cards. It looked to be a rather expensive deck, edged with gold, the backs decorated with an ornate and colorful paisley design.

"D'you mind if I count 'em?" James asked politely,

raising an eyebrow at Fowler. "'Twould be a shame to void a game on account of a missing card or two."

Fowler quickly picked up the deck again and riffled through it several times before handing it over to James. "There you are. But I'm certain the deck is intact."

Susanna would bet it was. *Now,* at any rate. Had he been palming one or two of those cards?

James looked him up and down with an expression that revealed nothing of what he was thinking. "Have a drink whilst I make certain," he said to Fowler. "I'm no novice at this, y'know?"

Susanna marveled at how his words conveyed exactly the opposite impression. He seemed the epitome of the proverbial mark to her, a man who knew as much about cards as a monkey in a zoo. Standing beside the table, he proceeded to examine every card, laboriously laying them out according to their values in small stacks before him. Fowler paced and sipped his sherry, obviously eager to get on with it. Small wonder.

"Allow me to freshen that for you," Susanna said to him, approaching with the bottle. She wished for the green whisky instead of sherry, something powerful to deaden the man's devious mind in a hurry, but there was none to be had at the moment.

Fowler held out his glass and she poured. "Do you play often?" she asked, hoping to determine what they would be facing. The games with her father provided her some experience, but judging by the awkward way James handled those cards, he appeared all too new at this. The thought of having the task of saving Drevers and Galioch resting with her own abilities made her incredibly nervous. She was not that good.

"I play now and again, as leisure permits," Fowler admitted. "And you?"

"She's sworn off," James announced, still clumsily sorting the cards.

Everyone turned in unison to stare at him. "What?" Susanna demanded, her outrage nearly gaining the upper hand.

"Aye, you did make a solemn vow to me when we agreed to marry. I strongly disapprove of women wagering."

"But...then how are we to play partners?" she asked, delaying for the moment her reaction to his imperious and implacable tone.

"Fowler and I will play. You and Miss Durston may observe if you like." He winked. "But not advise us."

Damn the man! Was that the signal he was giving for her to distract Miranda from what he was doing? Or was he simply being condescending? Reluctantly, she gave him the benefit of the doubt.

She took Miranda by the arm and attempted to guide her toward the chairs beside the fireplace. "Come, if they are to be that hypocritical, you and I shall find something else to entertain us."

"No, I wish to watch and cheer them on!" Miranda pulled away and proceeded to seat herself in one of the empty chairs.

James glanced at her, then at Susanna as he gathered the cards back into a stack. He nodded towards the empty chair to his other side. Susanna swept around him and waited for Fowler to seat her.

"Piquet?" Fowler asked politely, taking his own chair.

"Nay, *vingt-et-un,*" James declared. "I know the rules to that."

"Every *child* knows the rules to that," Miranda commented wryly. "All you need know is how to count to twenty-one. How boring is that?"

"'Tis quick," James retorted. "I've no patience for tallyin' up points, tricks and such. 'Tis no game for men."

"I beg to differ, but...as you wish," Fowler said with a smile.

He reached across and took up the cards. His long, pale fingers performed several expert shuffles and a final fanning that was all for show. Damn the man. He was a card shark if Susanna had ever seen one. Even her father could not do that.

"Cut for the deal?" Fowler asked, not even looking at the deck as he cut it, holding up a ten of spades.

James reached for the deck and came up with a four of hearts. "To you," he said and sat back with a disappointed sigh. "What stakes, then?"

"Two pounds," Fowler suggested.

"Suz, keep th' score," James ordered.

Fowler dealt two cards each. James peeked at his and asked for another, while Fowler announced that he would stand with his two.

"Twenty-four!" James exclaimed, tossing his cards down with a grimace as he saw Fowler's two face cards.

Susanna had a sick feeling in the pit of her stomach as she wrote Fowler's winnings below his name on the tablet.

Thrice more, James lost. Five pounds, then ten. The stakes were escalating and he grew more dour with each defeat.

He gathered up the cards then and shuffled them since it was his turn to deal. "This grows old, Fowler. Let's be done with it. What are you worth?"

The man's eyes went wide. "What do you mean?"

"How much d'you own? What are your assets?"

"What a rude question!" Fowler exclaimed. "I'm aghast that you would even put forth such a query!"

James smiled. "Right now, all I'm certain of is that you're good for thirty-four pounds, every jot of that on paper. Now what are you worth?"

Fowler glanced at Miranda, seemingly at a loss for words.

"I shall stand good for whatever he might lose," Miranda said with a cat's smile. "What are *you* worth, Garrow?"

Oh, God, Susanna thought. She had to stop this.

"One thousand, seven hundred, sterling," James said without hesitation. "And Galioch, according to the tax assessor, amounts to eighteen thousand. Can you match it all?"

"I can," Miranda stated haughtily. But Susanna noted the small hesitation in her voice, the flicker of doubt in her eyes as she looked away.

James took the pad of paper, ripped off the upper sheet and shoved it in front of her, an outright dare. "A marker, if you please."

Miranda looked to Fowler for assurance and he smiled at her with overwhelming confidence. He even offered her an almost imperceptible nod.

Slowly, she took the paper and James handed her the pencil. In a swirling hand, she wrote out the amount and signed it. With deliberation, she took the page and pushed it to the center of the table.

James appropriated the writing implements, listed his assets and placed the paper, along with the tally Susanna had made on top of Miranda's. "There."

Susanna thought this had gone quite far enough. Next he would be wagering Drevers and she could not have that. "James, I protest. This is worse than foolish. It is mad! Neither of you can afford—"

"My deal, I believe," he said, ignoring her. He picked up the cards and shuffled them as expertly as Fowler had ever done. To go him one further, he performed a maneuver Susanna had never seen before. She watched in amazement as the entire row of cards seemed suspended in midair, then came together again as if by magic. He fanned them, then did it again.

Miranda gasped. Fowler's face fell. James dealt so quickly no one had time to speak. He raised the corner of the card lying facedown beneath his ace, smiled and looked at Fowler. "Card?"

Slowly Fowler looked up from his own cards and nodded.

James flicked one off the top of the deck—at least she assumed it was from the top. "One to me," he said and slipped another toward himself. He waited a beat until Fowler had looked at his, than asked, "Another?"

Sweat had broken on Fowler's forehead. He brushed two fingers over his mustache, grimaced, glanced at Miranda and then gave one succinct nod.

James slid one more card in his direction, then turned all of his face up. Two kings and an ace. Fowler threw his cards down and leaped up. "You could not possibly have won! You cheated!"

"Duelin' words, friend," James remarked, picking up the two sheets of paper, folding them neatly and tucking them into his sporran. "And, believe me, I'm a damn sight better with weapons than I am wi' cards."

Reckless now to the point of stupidity, Fowler raised a fist and slammed it down on the table. "You *had* to cheat!"

"Now how could I help myself when you marked the

cards so clearly?'' James asked with a smile, all trace of his brogue subdued. He turned to Miranda. "Shall I call upon your father or will you settle this debt yourself?"

Miranda screeched. "I'll not pay you one damned farthing, you deceptive oaf, and neither will my father!"

"Ah, ah, ah!" James cautioned her with an evil grin and a wagging finger. "That charm of yours is slippin'."

"I'll not remain under this roof one instant longer!" she declared, marching angrily toward the doorway, her chin held high.

Fowler snatched up the cards and rushed out behind her without a further word.

James winked at Susanna and dusted his palms together. "A job well done if I do say so."

Susanna slowly sank back down in her chair, covered her face with her hands and put her head on the table. "Never, *never* put me through such a thing again," she pleaded.

He rested his broad palm on her back, then slid it up to caress her bare neck with those magic fingers of his. "Ah, lass, will ye ne'er coom ta trust me then?"

"I might coom ta kill ye, Jamie Garrow, do ye gi' me another such fright!"

His laughter boomed out, filling the room, calming her fears and stealing her heart as quickly and as surely as he had just stolen £19,717.

Chapter Fifteen

James poured them another sherry and he and Susanna toasted his success in besting Fowler at cards.

"Will you actually try to collect your winnings?" she asked with a grin as glasses touched and crystal pinged.

"Why not? Though I hold precious little hope of success." He finished his drink, set down his glass and took hers from her hand.

Letting her clearly see his intent, he lowered his head and pressed a kiss on her waiting lips. Waiting, open and inviting lips. God help him, he could not bear many more such teasing interludes. He would either have to take her or leave her completely alone.

She drugged his senses like opium and sent very nearly the same forbidden euphoria rushing through his brain and body. He had not taken to the deadly poppy of his own volition, but by another's hand. He now staunchly avoided all contact with it, knowing full well how it could skew a man's—or a woman's—life and destroy it and those around it. But even if she proved an equal threat to his survival, James knew he would never be able to deny the sensual beckoning that was Susanna. She was in his blood, filling his heart and his thoughts, every day, every night now. He was lost to her and there was no going back even if he wanted to. Where could he find protection from such an obsession? Was there any to be found?

When he drew back, she looked as dazed as he felt.

"How—how will they leave?" she gasped.

"Who?" James shook his head sharply, trying to clear his mind enough to think. "Oh."

"The pony cart," she suggested, obviously not quite as lost in the fog of passion as he was.

That piqued his anger more than a bit. "Aye. I'll see to it now," he snapped, releasing her.

"James!" She grasped his hand when he would have stormed out.

"Aye?" he felt her fingers curl inside his.

"Hurry them off, would you? Then we can...talk again."

"Talk?" he asked, a smile of anticipation threatening to break free.

She ducked her head and blushed.

"What are you saying, Suz?" he asked, drawing her close again, fiddling with the wispy red curls that tickled her ear.

Reluctantly, she raised her eyes to meet his, a heady promise in their emerald depths. "You said it yourself...'tis time."

He kissed her on the nose. "I'll beat them down the road with a buggy whip. Wait right here."

Her merry laughter followed him as he left.

The departure of the guests went virtually unremarked. James hardly stayed to see them seated in the cart. Old Parlan MacNee was at the reins, the sturdy gelding eager in his traces and the bags piled high in back like stacks of peat. There were no farewells, only glares in the lantern light.

The moon overhead was bright enough to cast shadows and stars winked as if they were happy.

"Safe trip and a fair night, Parlan," James said, placing several coins in the fellow's hand for a good rest in an inn before his return. "Slow does it where the ruts are deep, aye?"

"Aye, Jamie. I ken."

Without further ado, James hurried back inside, the departing guests and everything other than Susanna promptly forgotten. He had promised himself he would never allow her to hold such sway over him, but he supposed the heat of pure lust could overcome most anything, to include good sense and self-preservation.

Lust was transient. But loving her was permanent and he was too well caught up in that not to worry about it. If she knew, she would try to use his feelings to her advantage, of course, and he couldn't blame her for that. It was human nature.

His mother's voice rang out of memory. "Garrow, darling, if you loved me as well as Bonwell does, you would come with me to Venice. Everyone is going and it is so dreadfully boring here."

And his father would hurry to make travel arrangements, knowing that if he remained behind, Lord Bonwell would supplant him, at least for the duration of the holiday.

"Trent bought me these emeralds," she would say. "Are they not wonderful? He says he loves me, but of course I told him you love me more. You do, don't you, Garry-love?"

His father would buy diamonds to prove it. All the

while knowing she would flit elsewhere before they grew warm against her skin.

She had been such a feckless, self-centered child, even into her thirties. His father had been little more than that. Neither had ever known a hardship unless one counted the unruly lad they had created together in the first blush of passion. Him, they had relegated to the status of house pet. Patted on the head and shown off one minute, banished the next into the care of some retainer.

James sighed as he reentered the library, only to find Susanna gone. She must be waiting above for him, ready and willing to make good on their vows. He headed for the stairs, now in no rush to meet his fate. God knew he wanted her. Far too much. But he was different from his father, James decided. Stronger. Made wiser by his experiences. Able to manage a woman.

Susanna was also different from his mother. He knew that. However, she shared several traits. Beauty, for one, and a spiritedness that entranced a man. All men, probably. Certainly her own father had been unable to deny her much.

She was spoiled, determined to have her way. However, James had noticed a quality in Suz that his mother had never even thought about, much less possessed. Susanna cared about people. She showed concern, compassion and a willingness to help.

Also, she had not grasped at the perfect chance provided for her to escape him and this marriage. How easy it would have been for her to blow Miranda's flirtation with him out of proportion and use it as her excuse to effect a separation. She had the means to live independently, wherever she wished to go. What held her here? He wondered.

No point belaboring her motive. She seemed to want

him. Was this that first blush of passion his parents had once known at the beginning of their marriage? Would he and Susanna eventually make a child who would spend its youth clamoring for scraps of love and attention?

He entered his bedroom, heart-heavy and more than a bit wary of testing his resolve now that the long awaited opportunity had arrived.

"Have they gone?" she asked.

"Aye," he assured her, taking in the alluring picture she made, sitting in the midst of the oversize bed, already in her fine lawn nightrail with its tucks and tiny ruffles, waiting to offer her virginity on the altar of wifely power.

She looked uncertain. Her dark-fringed eyes were wide and her full lips trembled a bit. Dainty hands with their carefully buffed nails gripped the heavy counterpane to her chest.

"We could wait if you've changed your mind," he told her gently, knowing he was granting her more than was reasonable in the effort to ease her mind. Why did he insist on doing that? James could have kicked himself for it, knowing it was the very sort of capitulation he had determined he would avoid.

She shook her head, a jerky motion that seemed wrung out of her against her will. How could he take her when she was so obviously frightened?

He walked over and sat down on the edge of the bed, turning his head so that she could not see the desperation that must be written all over his face. "Susanna, maybe we should talk—"

"But you—you seemed to want to," she said in a small voice. "And I…well, I think perhaps we should. Now."

"Not this way," he insisted, still not looking at her. She stirred restlessly.

Suddenly a pillow slammed against his head almost knocking him to the floor.

"Damn you!" she cried, throwing herself at him, beating against his shoulder with her fists, sobbing with fury.

He caught her fast and held her, burying his face in the wild curls loosed from her pins. She writhed within his arms, her body exciting him to fever pitch with her struggles. If he let her go, she would flail at him again, perhaps hurt herself, but if he did not, there was a danger he would forget her anger or, worse yet, use it. "Suz, please!"

She stilled. He backed away a bit and looked down at her upturned face. There lay a mixture of frustration and longing so great, he could not resist it. Slowly, he lowered his mouth to hers and tasted her. None too carefully at that, after the first instant. She wouldn't allow it. Any gentleness he had planned flew right out the window like a caged bird let loose. The wait had been too long, his dreams of her too vivid, his fantasies too wild.

Her arms encircled his neck. Eager fingers threaded through his hair, tugging, pressing, demanding. He eased the kiss, reangled it, nipping her lips, tracing them with his tongue and encompassing them again for a deeper foray. She responded, invading, giving as good as she got. Better, he figured, delving deeply into her mouth again, crushing her breasts to his chest and mapping her every luscious curve with his hands.

The pleaful sounds she made reverberated through him, inciting an urge so primal and undeniable, he feared he would hurt her. "Wait," he said, breaking off the kiss to suck in a deep breath, to get himself under control before he did the unthinkable.

"No," she rasped and found his mouth again. Her hands tore at his shirt, pushed frantically at his jacket. One found its way beneath his plaid and sealed her fate.

He groaned, pushing her flat against the bed as he raked up her nightrail, feeling for the first time the incredible hot softness of her body against his palm and fingers. His face buried in the curve of her neck, he breathed a broken spate of the old language, searing words he knew she would not ken, nor did he want her to. But the feelings inside him would not stay silent. She answered with incoherent murmurs until their mouths met again and words turned to sounds of need.

With an effort so taxing it pained him, James broke away long enough to yank off his belt, tossing it and the sporran aside. While she pulled up his shirt, he unfastened his kilt. Then slowly he peeled her nightrail away and looked down at perfection. The sight of her stole the last of his sanity and any words he might have formed to praise her.

With one hand, none too steady when faced with touching such treasure, he cradled her face, then slid his palm sinuously down the curve of her neck and over her breasts, first one, then the other, watching as they beckoned his mouth to take them. He leaned forward and tasted, first gently, then with greater eagerness when she arched herself more firmly against him. That sufficed for a while, pleasuring her, exciting himself to greater heights than he'd ever deemed possible. She demanded more and he gave, denying himself the completion his body craved as he explored that part of her he would soon claim.

So soft she was, so open and already weeping for him. He slid down her body, brushing his lips along the curve of her hip, his tongue tracing the crease of her thigh.

He drew in the scent of her as he brushed his face against her nethercurls and then exhaled with delight, knowing the warmth of his breath would caress what he had not yet touched.

She cried out, an almost painful sound, and writhed sinuously as he kissed her, delving deeply, relishing the sudden tremors that shook her. Unable to wait a second longer, he slid upward along her trembling body and entered her carefully, exerting every ounce of his control until she grasped his hips and lunged upward. Her nails bit sharply into his skin, a counterpoint to her own small hurt. Again she shuddered and cried out, in full completion this time, he thought with supreme satisfaction. He withdrew slowly and stroked deeper, repeating again and again, the excruciating effort to hold back his own release a pleasure-pain so intense he could hardly endure it. At last, at last, the rhythm of her response increased.

He found her mouth with his and devoured her with a kiss so deep he got lost in it. Suddenly her inner body gripped his with such sweet force, he let go his control and soared like a hawk straight through the clouds and into the sun. Dimly, he heard her cry out, a joyous sound that voiced his own sensation so clearly, he felt they were one, even in the euphoric, floating descent.

He lay spent against her softness, his heart thundering so hard, he thought death was imminent. And couldn't care. Struggling for breath seemed a futile waste of energy. But she might not think so. He slipped out of her and shifted to her side, his arm draped over her. One breast lay hot against his forearm, the swift rise and fall of her ribs beneath it. He moved his palm over her heart and felt it echo the rapid beat of his own.

''That...was,'' she said, her voice languid, interrupted by a heavy sigh, ''unexpected.''

James smiled against her shoulder. "Aye." He brushed a finger over her left breast. She had no idea *how* unexpected it was to him, and he was not about to tell her.

"Is it always so...?"

"Aye," James repeated. Though it was a blatant lie. She would find out soon enough how unusual it was, he supposed. A man would be hard put to live up to such a standard on a regular basis. He had never reached such heights before with any woman, even in his randy youth.

This raised his confidence as a lover way over the moon, but he was not quite so self-important as to be sure he could sustain it forever. Tonight had combined too many factors for there to be an exact replication of it. It was her first time. It was his first in a long while, six months or more. And she had been innocent, so he had been careful with her.

He smiled again, unable to hold on to any worry at the moment, even that of eventually disillusioning Susanna. Who knew? Maybe, if he put his mind to it, he could go one better than a mere repetition. There were things he could teach her. Each time would be different, each new to him because it would be new to her. Already, he wanted her again and those fantasies of his were drifting across his mind like tickling feathers.

She propped on one elbow, dislodging his comfortable position against her shoulder as she looked down at him.

He raised an eyebrow in question.

"How...often do you mean for this to happen?"

His smile grew wider, his pride swelling in tandem with his desire, perfectly ready and willing to accept any challenge. "How often would you like it, Suz?"

Her brows drew together and her lips pursed provocatively as she considered that. Then her face relaxed into a small moue of uncertainty. "Every three years. Shouldn't that be sufficient?"

James stared at her in disbelief. His mouth hung open, but no words would come out. *Every three years?* His mind shouted. Both his pride and other wounded attributes deflated like hot air balloons.

She waited, biting her bottom lip, eyebrows raised, gaze trained on his face.

James rolled off the bed and snatched up his kilt, draping it around him like armor. "Three years will be just fine!" With that, he stalked out of the room to find that damned wine cellar.

Susanna snuggled into the pillows, inhaling deeply of James's scent. Wild and sweet and intoxicating, she thought, just like the man himself. That she could feel so incredible after such an experience astounded her. Why had no one ever explained what it was really like? No words would suffice, she supposed. How on earth could anyone truly describe it?

Though fully aware that she had angered him with her last suggestion, and none too happy with the necessity of making it, Susanna meant to hold him to his reluctant agreement. He would honor it, she knew. The question was, could she?

The thought of bearing a child every year should keep her senses about her. But, oh, it would almost be worth it to enjoy this feeling as often as she liked, as often as he was able. Instinctively, she realized that the ability to make her feel this way was unique to him alone.

She admitted some pride in the fact that she had not been the only one to relish this night's event. James had been pleased with her, no doubt about that. He was not one to conceal his pleasure. She smiled just remembering the ecstasy on his handsome face. The piercing need to see it again almost overwhelmed her with its intensity. How could she not wish to? She loved him and wanted more than anything to make him happy. But at what cost?

This once was enough to make a child, she thought as she pressed one palm to her abdomen. That fact was preached far and wide to every young girl. It only took once and you were caught.

Caught. The idea did not trouble her as it ought. One child would be fine. They needed to have an heir. In a few years, another should not sap her strength too dangerously. Three children were enough for anyone. Perhaps she could stretch that to four, unless she grew weak as her mother had. Then James would have to forgo coming to her at all.

She sighed, feeling dejected. James was not the only one who would miss this.

As for now, would a second time make twins? She thought not, but was uncertain. She needed to study this if she could find a book that would tell her. Would anyone even be bold enough to put such things in a book? Perhaps she could ask someone. But whom could she ask such a forbidden question?

She sat up, drawing the covers to her chest and locking her arms around her upraised knees. A second time could not make twins unless it came soon after the first. Could it? Once she knew she was increasing, could they do this again and again without any consequences? Slowly she shook her head. Surely that would not be safe for the child. He probably would not wish to if she grew fat as women did when they were with child.

Not for the first time, Susanna cursed her own ignorance and the inability to gain the proper knowledge of her body and its workings. When she had attempted to research the matter for her talks to the women in London, she had asked Dr. Robbins, the physician who had always served their family, to explain the effects of frequent childbearing. He had been horrified and chastised her soundly for broaching subjects unfit for a young lady to dwell upon, especially one who remained unwed.

She had gone to a midwife and frankly stated her need to know. The old woman had merely shrugged and told her she would find out soon enough. Susanna had gotten virtually the same answer from her only aunt who had borne two children and stopped with that. It seemed there was a code of silence among all those who had the answers. She had been forced to draw all of her conclusions from her observations.

Those had become all too clear with respect to a woman's health dwindling in direct consequence to the number of pregnancies. Whether wealthy or poor, the more one had, the worse off one became. She had seen exceptions, of course. There were always exceptions to every rule. More among these Highland women, she thought. They were a sturdy lot.

Susanna sighed again and slipped out of James's bed. It would not do to be here when he returned. She might weaken and justify another bout of lovemaking by convincing herself that she was a Highland woman now and every bit as strong as these women who had six or more bairns. She must remember always that she was her mother's daughter, smallish and slender, delicate looking and likely no hardier. What good would it do to produce a houseful of children and not be alive to rear them properly? Or worse yet, to endure the heartbreak of having to bury the poor little stillborns as her mother had done?

Reluctantly, Susanna picked up the nightrail James had so eagerly whisked from her body and went to her own chamber.

Chapter Sixteen

An hour later in the wine cellar, James sat on the dusty bench, leaned on the small trestle table and nursed a bottle of truly bad wine. Damn stuff was weak as bloody tea and about as effective. He upended it, drank deeply and grimaced.

He fully understood Susanna's three-year suggestion, of course. Once he'd gotten over the knock to his pride, he recalled her advice to the women that day he had overheard her speaking to them. But it was not having a child that worried her so much. It was having them frequently. Ruining her health, which he admitted it could do.

They could get around that problem easily enough if he could convince her he knew what he was doing. Nothing short of abstinence was foolproof, of course, but he hadn't produced any bastards that he knew about. Considering that, he felt fairly confident he could manage.

He smoothed down his kilt and tried to put desire out of his mind. Denial was good practice, he assured himself, for when Susanna eventually began to use his need for her in order to bring him to heel. It was bound to happen, so he might as well be prepared for it. Come to think of it, wasn't she doing it already, trying to mold him into the sort of husband she wanted instead of accepting him the way he was?

She was a determined, opinionated woman, just like his mother, at least in some respects. And he was—much as he misliked admitting it—his father's son, a man inclined to love blindly and offer whatever it took to have it reciprocated. He kept vowing to himself he would not go out of his way to please her and yet everything he did seemed aimed toward that end.

He could deny that he loved Susanna. He could say it and sound convincing if he had to, though he didn't think that would be necessary. Not yet. She wouldn't require it because she didn't love him. Hell, she barely even liked him, though obviously she was making an effort.

He certainly didn't love her *blindly* since he could clearly see all her faults. Trouble was, he loved her in spite of them, maybe even because of them. But he should never be so stupid as to admit that out loud to her, no matter how delectable she was. So what if he did it in Gaelic in the heat of passion? She hadn't understood a word.

Eventually, James went for a second bottle of something. Anything would do at this point. He needed oblivion for a while. As he bent over the dust-coated bottles, he spied a tiny glint of gold hidden half beneath the edge of the bottom rack. He knelt and discovered a gilt-framed cameo attached to a thin broken chain.

Pulling it free, he wondered if Susanna had dropped it. He took it over to the table and held it close to the lamp. He had not seen her wear this before. It was a rather nice piece—Italian, he thought—not very large, but obviously well made. The woman's profile on the face of it was carved in either ivory or bone. Delicate workmanship. He admired it for a moment.

Then his finger brushed over the tiny catch on one side. A locket, he realized, releasing the mechanism so that it popped open like a small book. Inside were two incredibly well done miniatures, one of a beautiful dark-haired woman. Miranda?

The other was of a man.

He froze. The familiar face of the man pulled the entire puzzle together like an evil mocking hand. Durston. The locket was Miranda's. And her father was the man he had seen in the public house in Edinburgh. The one who planned the earl's murder.

James rushed out of the wine cellar, through the buttery and kitchen and took the stairs two at a time.

"Susanna!" he shouted. "Suz!"

He quickly discovered that she had left his bed, so he burst through the dressing room into her chamber. She was already up, donning a dressing gown, her face a study in consternation. "What is it? What has happened?"

"This," he said, thrusting the open locket at her. "It's Miranda's. I found it in the wine cellar. Durston's the man I overheard planning the attack in Edinburgh. Your father must be warned."

"God in heaven!" She covered her mouth with a trembling hand, her eyes beseeching. "What if he is already—?"

"We would have been notified if Durston had already struck," James told her, drawing her into his arms. "It would do him little good to get rid of the earl first. If he did, you would inherit. Then—through you—controlling interest in your father's business would rest with me. Remember that Durston also meant to be rid of *you* that night your father was attacked.''

''Yes, but—''

James pulled back a bit so that he could see her face. He brushed a thumb over her cheek. ''I believe he sent Fowler and Miranda here to dispose of both of us. Then the earl would have no heirs, am I right? Durston could safely murder your father then and, as partner in the shipping company, everything would revert to him.'' James hated to spell it out so bluntly, but she needed to know. At least it might relieve her immediate worry.

''But they've given up on that,'' she said. ''Fowler apparently hadn't the fortitude for murder and Miranda lacked the skill or strength. She also said she thought the risk too great for what they had been offered to do it. Now I see what they meant! And all the while I thought they spoke only of seduction and thievery by cards.''

''You are not a reader of thoughts, Suz. How could you have guessed such a thing?''

Her eyes were bright with tears. ''James, what if Mr. Durston becomes desperate with their failure, sees an opportunity to kill Father and does it anyway? He could always send someone else to kill us. I say we must face this head-on, go to Father with what we know and join forces to eliminate the threat altogether. We must go immediately.''

''He has charged me with keeping you safe, Susanna,'' James reminded her. ''You're less at risk here than anywhere else. I'll telegraph my friend in London who will go and speak with him personally.''

''Then you renege on your promise to allow me to go where I will and do as I wish?''

God, she sounded so disappointed in him, as if he had betrayed her somehow. James sighed and shook his head.

"I only mean to protect your life, Susanna, not impinge upon your precious rights."

She looked up at him. "It seems I have none of those, save for the ones you see fit to grant me. That aside, how will you communicate everything we've learned to Father in the few words the telegraph allows? And what if Durston is the one to receive the message? He is most at the offices and handles much of the correspondence. Besides, suppose Father is not even in London. What then? He did have unfinished business in Edinburgh and might have returned there by this time."

"Entirely possible. Even probable. And I had not thought of it."

"Well, I am going to find him whether you come or not!" she exclaimed.

Despite her vehemence, she looked damned near ready to faint. James doubted she would make it from here to the road in her present state.

However, he granted she might be right about finding Eastonby and settling this once and for all with Durston. If they stayed here, the man could send someone else. That someone could hire any cutthroat hereabout who needed the money badly enough. The level of poverty being what it was in the Highlands, who was to say how tempting that might prove? It could even be someone he knew and would not suspect until too late. Susanna would never be completely safe unless they knew precisely with whom they were dealing. Better to go after the brains behind the plot, he decided.

"Are you able to ride?" he asked.

She tugged away and straightened her shoulders, wiping angrily at the tears she'd just shed. "What sort of faintheart do you think me, Garrow? Of course I can ride!"

The Scot

"I only meant to ask whether you are well enough after…"

"I'm perfectly fine," she declared, already rushing to the armoire and searching through her wardrobe.

"Old Parlan is driving Miranda and Fowler the twenty miles into Beauly. That will take a while. Then they will either take ship for London, which likely will mean a wait of a few days—or cross the firth and go down the coast by rail. I doubt they'll be in any hurry to admit their defeat to Durston, but we'd best not count on that. We need to warn your Father before the three of them concoct another plan. God knows what that would be."

"If only we knew for certain where Father is at the moment."

"We'll find him." With a hand on her arm, he stopped her when she kept pulling dresses out of the wardrobe and tossing them on the bed. "Pack only one change of clothing, Suz."

"One?" she asked, distracted from her task.

"One," he declared. "We'll need to ride hard. Speed counts and the extra weight of baggage will slow us."

"I understand," she agreed. "One case it shall be."

"A pouch," he said with an admonishing look. "A small one."

She rummaged until she found her tapestry bag, dumped out the knitting things and began rolling up a plain gabardine gown to replace them. "Shall I pack for you?" she asked as she hurriedly stuffed the gown into the bag.

"I'll do that while you change. Choose something substantial to ward off the chill."

She brought a hand to his face and rested it there. "James, we will succeed?"

"Aye, never doubt it." He took her hand in his and

quickly kissed her palm. Then he hurried from her room before he did anything else to show her how dear he really held her.

A half hour later, they were on the road. He rode the stallion and Susanna rode the mare. His gelding was hopefully plodding slowly toward Moray Firth with their former houseguests in tow. With any luck, he and Susanna would arrive first.

James had left written instructions for David, who would see to Galioch and Drevers while they were away. He had ordered him to sell off part of Galioch's herd, purchase more food for the winter and make necessary repairs to the cots before it snowed.

What James had left of this season's earnings were in his pocket for this journey. He would not have to use any of Susanna's funds yet, though he knew it might come to that in the near future. Would she see that as his spending what, by her lights, belonged to her alone?

A woman, even a wife, should have the opportunity to refuse or grant what was hers as she saw fit. If she had that choice, he would not mind asking her for a loan. Well, he would not mind half so much. Why the devil had he ever believed he could be content marrying for money?

Drevers would prosper anyway. And Galioch might survive a while without his begging, but there were additional mouths to feed now and less money arriving from the usual sources. Many of the people working elsewhere and contributing to their families' upkeep had already come home. He would have to conquer his pride soon and appeal to Susanna for help. That was, after all, why he had married her. It stuck in his craw like grit. It smacked of using her for his own gain and he hated the very thought of it.

She deserved more from a marriage, especially since she had been reluctant to wed in the first place. He pushed the thought aside and concentrated on the immediate problem.

True to her word, Susanna had brought only the one pouch of clothing, though she had added another of about the same size bearing food to sustain them on the trip. Draped over the back of his saddle was a pack with his suit and a flagon of something or other he had grabbed from the wine cellar as an afterthought.

He worried their pace was too rapid for her, seated precariously as she was on the side saddle. But Susanna rode as she did most things, with grace and proficiency. Pride in her filled him. How could he not love her? He was very nearly sick with it.

Thankfully, there was little opportunity to talk as they rode, so he made no stupid admissions of how he felt. He limited his own words to questioning now and again if she fared well or would like to rest. She made do with a decisive shake of her head. James had the feeling she would fall off from exhaustion before admitting she needed to stop. He could hardly blame her when her father's life was at stake.

Only when they stopped halfway to rest the horses did she agree to dismount for a respite.

''Try not to worry.'' Concerned, he reached out and took her hand, winding his fingers through hers and holding it to his chest. He wanted so much to hold her and reassure her, but knew he had best not if they were to make Moray Firth by daybreak.

He had no intentions of waiting three years to hold her

again, but now was definitely not the time to settle the problem.

"What happens when we reach the firth?" she asked.

"We cross as soon as we can hire a boat, then take a private coach to the railhead. That will put us in Edinburgh faster than sailing around the Head of Kincaid. If your father has come back to Scotland, it's a sure bet he did not advertise his intention." However, as his partner, Durston almost certainly would know. Though James could see the same thought reflected in Susanna's worried expression, neither of them voiced it.

"When we reach Edinburgh, we'll go straight to the Royal Arms. Even if your father's not there, at least we can rest for a few hours before heading on to London."

She nodded and started to remount, obviously eager to resume the journey. James lifted her to the saddle, mounted his stallion and they rode on.

Soon after, he spied the pony cart ahead, trundling the winding road which tracked around the hills and berms. He motioned for Susanna to follow him as they cut across the heathery landscape, through the trees and came out ahead on the road. Then they rode at a gallop, determined to reach the firth by sunrise.

Exhaustion had claimed her completely by the time they made the dock. James found a tea shop that looked fairly respectable and urged Susanna to sit with their belongings while he arranged stabling for the horses and passage across the firth.

When he returned a quarter hour later, she had fallen asleep on the settle where he had left her. Their bags were stacked in the corner of the bench against the armrest and she leaned against them, her head propped against the wall. Her untouched tea had grown cold.

James drank it while they waited for the time to board and let her sleep.

She looked childlike and innocent, too much so to be caught up in this intrigue. But there was not a cowardly bone in that small body of hers, he thought with pride. Not his Suz.

He had been thinking all the way about how he might be misjudging her. Certainly, she was a beauty like his mother had been. She liked the things money could buy. She spoke her mind and believed she was always right. But there were also differences he could not ignore.

Susanna cared for him. In the short time he had known her, she cared much more than his mother ever had. She was fair, just as she had promised she would be. She kept promises. James had the feeling he might be selling her short.

But if he confessed how he loved her and wanted her to love him, would she use that to try to change him? God knows, his mother had. And because he had loved his mother and wanted her to love him back, he had changed. Drastically.

His mother had disparaged his father so, James had struggled to be as unlike him as possible. He had denied his urge to paint and sculpt. He had turned whatever talent he had toward more manly endeavors that required as much or more brute strength than mental creativity. And she had not even noticed.

At least that had prevented his living holed up in some studio and looking inward at himself.

Only now, at this particular juncture, did James begin to realize that there had been another very good reason—one probably more important to him than his mother's love—that had made him so eager to set himself on a different course. He had not *wanted* to become a replica of his father. How had he not understood that before? Why was it so clear to him now?

At any rate, James vowed he would never reverse those changes he had made then, no matter how refined or gentlemanly a husband Susanna might desire for herself. Damned if he would allow anything—or any woman, strong-willed or not—to reduce him to what his father had been, a smitten man who relinquished his will, his entire fortune and even the respect of his only son, just to allow his wife everything she thought she wanted. It had killed them both in the end and left James with nothing but bitterness and a mountain of debts.

As far as he was concerned, the stronger the woman, the more she needed a firm hand to guide her. Though it went contrary to everything Susanna believed, he knew it to be true. But he also knew he couldn't say that out loud, either, or he wouldn't have a woman to worry about.

Handling Susanna would require finesse, if he could conjure up any of that when he was around her. She could be so damned unpredictable and was forever catching him off guard.

They had consummated their marriage now. He could see no problem with making love to Susanna, so long as he kept his wits about him.

She would have his children, of course. And he would see to it that she showed them all the love and attention they were due. It might be asking too much that she love him as well, given her attitude toward men in general. James supposed he would have to resign himself to infrequent sex and what little affection she could muster. He had promised himself he would never solicit love from anyone, ever again. He had learned to do without it very well.

For now, he should put all thoughts and decisions about his marriage and his feelings on hold until he had ensured the safety of Susanna and the earl. That was the first order of business. Unlike his father, James intended to mind his responsibilities and fulfill every single obligation to the utmost of his abilities before he took his own needs into account. It was a matter of honor.

And, he admitted privately, it was also a matter of how much he loved Susanna, even if he couldn't tell her.

Chapter Seventeen

Susanna awoke with a start as James shook her gently. For a moment, she could not recall where they were. The odor of scorched pie crust mingled with that of cheap lamp oil and dead fish. Ah, they were in a mean little tea shop near the docks. She had fallen asleep.

"Is it time to go?" She brushed her hair back with both hands and resettled her hat which had shifted askew while she slept.

James reached out, straightened it and smoothed out the brim. "Aye, we're off." He rose, assisted her up and then lifted their bags of clothing, handing her the lightest one containing hers.

"Have you eaten?" she asked. He looked rather pale.

"Nay, and I'll not until we reach the far shore. I've bought meat pies, but I would advise against eating anything until after we land. The firth's likely to be choppy during the crossing. It must be coming up a storm."

She nodded and preceded him out of the shop and down to the quay. There, they boarded what was obviously a fishing vessel with a crew of four.

"I'm yer captain. Jock Menzies is m'name. That'll be two pound, four pence," he said holding out his hand palm up. James fished in his pockets for coins and paid the man.

"Take yer lass below and keep 'er there," Menzies ordered. He was a short burly fellow with arms twice the size they should be and a ripe odor that would have felled people in a closed room.

James ushered her into the small cabin built into the deck amidship. She noted a trapdoor near the entrance to it that she supposed was the hold where the expedition's catch would be contained. The overpowering odor of fish almost rivaled that of the captain. She coughed and took a scented handkerchief out of her reticule to cover her nose.

"Breathe shallow," James advised. He brushed off the bench nailed to one wall and indicated she should sit there. "Be as still as you can and try not to close your eyes."

His voice was curt, his movements tense as he joined her and braced his hands on either side of him. Susanna followed suit. The boat already rocked dangerously and they had not yet left the dock. "Is this wise?" she asked. "Are you certain this craft is seaworthy?"

"As a bloody cork," he assured her on a weary sigh.

In a few moments, she felt the wind take the sails and they were off. The captain's orders rang out above them, mixing with other voices, the inevitable creaking of timber and squeak of ropes.

Scarcely a quarter hour had passed when he left her for the deck. Susanna had no need to ask why. He looked perfectly green. No matter how capable James might be in other circumstances, it seemed he was no sailor.

Susanna fought a smile. There was nothing at all humorous about seasickness, she knew. It could be quite debilitating, a fact she had witnessed in others the few times she had sailed with her father across the Channel and up the eastern coast to the islands. However, this trip would be of short duration and its effect on her husband at least provided her with one small reason to experience superiority of constitution.

He returned a while later and carefully resumed his seat beside her.

"Feeling better?" she asked brightly.

"Aye," he growled. "Damn me, I hate boats."

"Why is that? Have you not sailed before?"

"Merchantman out of Dornoch." His words were clipped.

Susanna turned to look at him in disbelief. "You were a seaman?"

"Cabin lad," he corrected. "I was eleven."

"Ran away from home, I'll wager."

"Walked," he informed her. "No one bothered to give chase."

"How long did you last?" Not long, she suspected.

"A year," he answered.

"Oh, my! Were you always…?" She broke off the question and looked toward the deck.

"Nay." He clenched his eyes shut. "Leave off now."

She did. For some reason she could not explain, Susanna found herself as reluctant to hear about this trial as he was to repeat it.

She kept envisioning him as a young boy jumping with excitement, filled with romantic tales of a life at sea, only to endure the next twelve long months fully expecting to die. Poor little fellow.

She looked at him sidewise. Poor *big* fellow, she thought. He was suffering like the damned. Gently, she placed a hand over his where it clutched the bench upon which they sat and gave his fingers a comforting squeeze. "Not much longer now, I expect," she said. "Be brave."

His tight lips quirked up at the corners and his squinting gaze met hers. Though he said nothing at all, Susanna felt his chagrin. She also felt something else, a warming that defied description seemed to blossom between them, an intimacy almost greater than when she had shared his bed.

"You mustn't mind this or that I've learned of it," she told him. "We all of us have things we simply cannot abide."

"Do you?" he asked.

"Certainly!" she assured him. "For me, it is places that are too closed in." She glanced around her. "Now this cabin is not so terrible, for there are portholes to see out and a clear way up to the open air. But, on the other hand, if I were confined to the hold or somewhere similar..." The look on his face stopped her midsentence. She gasped, her eyes never leaving his. "Oh, James, never say they did that to *you!*"

He drew his hand from beneath hers, rose swiftly and headed back up the gangway.

Susanna leaned her head back against the wall of the cabin and released a sorrowful sigh. Why, oh, why had he elected to cross the firth instead of riding around it to the bridge at Inverness? Because speed was of the essence, of course. Her father's life might well depend upon their reaching him before Miranda and Fowler met with Durston, that was why.

Every blessed time she decided that James was like all the others of his gender—hell-bent on having his own way and casting all else to perdition—he had to go and do something noble like this.

When they disembarked near Kinloss, James swore, as

he always did, that he would never embark on another voyage as long as he lived. He knew full well he would have to eventually. There were bodies of water to get across and unfortunately, a boat was the only way when there was no bridge. A sorry fact of life and one he devoutly ignored until necessity forced him to recognize it.

"We'll hire a coach, then take to the rails from Elgin," he told Susanna, rushing her along in the direction of the nearest inn. The captain had said there was a hostler there.

"We could ride. It would be faster," she told him.

"Too hard on you," he argued.

She stopped to get a better grip on her tapestry pouch. "Balderdash. We can rest on the train. Unless you are not up to riding." A challenge if he had ever heard one.

He gave way without another word and rented two horses, knowing full well she had goaded him into it. It was not a long ride, anyway, and he would just as soon have done with it as to fool with a coach. They ate the pies he had purchased and shared a flagon of decent ale while they waited for the mounts to be saddled.

Susanna seemed refreshed rather than done in by their hastily cobbled journey, he thought. She took to the saddle with only the slightest wince and tried to hide that from him. He knew she must be in pain, unused as she was to riding since she had been in the Highlands. Even so, she hid it well and sat a horse as if born to it. And did it without complaint.

Her cheeks fairly glowed despite the lack of sunshine to reflect off them. The heavy dampness was fast becoming rain. James wished for oiled capes to protect them from it as they rode, but none were to be had. That silly hat of hers, a lady's version of a gentleman's top hat, would only serve to collect a pool and direct it down the

front of her frock. He expected they would be wet clear
through by the time they reached the railhead and
boarded for Edinburgh.

The train was not to be what Susanna was used to,
either. They would be lucky if they were able to ride
inside instead of in the open cars that doubled as cargo
transport. Damn his eyes, why had he ever agreed to
bring her along? Next time he objected to one of her
demands that she be in the thick of things, perhaps she
would listen to him.

Once they reached the railway station, she went inside
while he took their rented mounts to the nearby stables
where he had been instructed to leave them. By the time
he joined her, she had plunked her reticule down on the
small ledge beneath the master's caged window and retrieved several bills. "Two tickets for Edinburgh,
please."

James stood to one side, arms folded over his chest
and said nothing, rather than cause a scene. His mood
darkened even further. He recalled something Susanna
once said to him about a woman's lot, having to rely on
a father or husband for every expenditure, no matter how
insignificant. Was this how they felt when obliged to depend on the generosity of some man? How did they abide
it?

She turned and smiled at him. "There were few seats
left on the next train, so it is fortunate we rode instead
of coming by coach, you see?"

"I see," he said, looking away.

"There will be a half hour's wait. Would you excuse
me while I freshen myself and try to wring out a bit of
this water?" She pulled a wry face as she brushed at the
soaked bodice of her traveling costume. It was of medium
weight wool and probably weighed heavy as lead when

wet, especially with all those sodden petticoats beneath it.

If only they had time to take a room at the inn where she could undress completely and crawl beneath warm blankets. And into his arms. Not bloody likely, he thought, frowning at her determined cheerfulness.

She had been offering nothing but bright smiles and challenges since he had disgraced himself on the damned boat by having to go topside not once but twice. Better her pretense of high spirits than frowns of pity, he supposed, but it did nothing to lighten his own dark mood.

James watched her disappear into a room apparently set aside for the comfort of female passengers, then took himself out back to tend to his own business before boarding.

Susanna endured. That was all the success she could claim when it came to travel by train. The ever present rumble and clacking of the wheel pistons lulled her once she was used to it, but the vibration of the hard wooden seats beneath her saddle weary bottom kept her wide-awake.

Poor James, she thought. At least she had the cushioning of several petticoats. At the last, she even resorted to sitting upon the tapestry bag that contained her only other gown. If Father was there, he would be appalled at her appearance. If they must continue on to London to find him, she would need appropriate clothing for Town.

James seemed to have cast off the worst of his melancholy, but it was hard to tell with him. He wore a sort of non-expression, polite and distant, uncommunicative. When she tried to converse with him to pass the time, he only answered in monosyllables.

She might not know much of men, but she did know

how to placate him. The only problem was, she respected him too much to play with his self-esteem and puff it up. He had always been painfully honest with her, as far as she could tell, and she owed him no less.

She leaned close to speak to him since the car was crowded with other passengers who might overhear. "We shall arrive in Edinburgh within the hour," she said, pointing out the obvious. "We should establish how we are to go on once we get there."

He turned to look at her, his brow creased in question.

She stretched out the drawstring of her reticule and drew out all the bills within it. "You must take charge of our funds. I fear to carry so much about." She took one of his hands, put the money in it and closed his fingers around it. "I can see it troubles you not having any, but it is your own fault."

A muscle flexed dangerously in his strong square jaw. She hoped his teeth didn't crack.

When he offered no answer, she continued. "By that I mean you should have drawn on our account when you were last in Beauly. It is up to you to secure your pay for the stewardship since I have no power to access what belongs to us."

"What belongs to *you*," he snapped through gritted teeth.

She leveled him with a glare. "No, James. By law, it is yours alone. Only by your generosity will I possess even a tuppence to call mine." She put it to him baldly as she could. "I know well what this costs you in terms of pride."

"Do you?"

"Of course I do. But if Galioch and Drevers are to prosper, you must do what you first intended when we married. We shall both benefit eventually so it will not be as though you are taking anything away from me. As for this money," she said, tapping his hand that held it, "my father gave it to me before we left Edinburgh. How better should we spend it than finding and warning him? So take it and be damned to this 'yours and mine' folderol."

"I never brangled about that, Suz," he argued. "Have I said a word?"

"Not aloud. But you certainly do go all frost and icicles when I take out a pound to pay! Did you think me oblivious to your glares at the ticket window? Or when we paused to dine at Warkworth?"

He huffed and tore his gaze from hers. "I *had* th' money."

"You see?" She laid her hand on his arm. "James, we have much more important matters facing us. This is no time to be at loggerheads over a bit of blunt."

His free hand closed over hers. "Aye, you've the right of it. If I'm a kept man, so be it."

"Better kept than discarded, wouldn't you say?"

His eyes met hers again. "Did you consider it? When Fowler made his pretty speeches and threw the idea in your path, were you tempted to chuck it all?"

"Not for an instant."

He grunted. "Better a Scotch pauper than a ne'er-do-well English dandy, eh?"

Susanna nodded emphatically, then added for good measure, "Especially when I'm well aware of how you came to be without the riches to which you were born. I have heard about your parents and how hard you have labored to restore what they squandered, James. I admire your fortitude and your sense of duty."

"Late in coming, I can tell you." He did not remark on the fact that she had questioned the people at Galioch and nosed into his past like a pig digging truffles. She applauded his tolerance for she would have been incensed if their roles had been reversed. He was a tolerant man and fair. With everyone but himself.

She could not help but say, "It is time you forgave them and yourself. Even if you resent marrying for wealth, you will nonetheless make use of it to better the lives of others for whom you feel responsible. A lesser man might not, James, but we both know you have no choice."

He knew she was right. She could see it in his eyes. But she could also see the distress. "It is I," he said with emphasis on the last word, "who should be supporting you. That's the way it should be."

"And who decreed that?"

"It just *is,* that's all."

She punched him with an elbow, furious because he would not admit to reason. "That's a devilish poor argument, James! Only suppose your parents had acted more wisely and you were the one with the fortune instead of me. It still would not be *you* who financed what we need. It would be your father's bequest."

"Better mine than yours."

"But it is not even my father's, not entirely. Can't you see? Most of it is my grandfather's and his father's before him and so on, ad infinitum. What does it matter who accrued it? We need it, we use it."

"It matters to me," he assured her.

"Well, it should not," she announced, struggling to control her frustration and keep her voice low. "You are duty bound to follow through with this, James, and do your part. This pouting about it will not change a thing."

He smiled, though it appeared tight and somewhat wry.

"Ever the practical wife. And very plainspoken, I might add."

"Guilty," she admitted with a shrug. "You know, I could have wept today and played the brainless twit, puffing up your pride, falling on your mercy as my big, strong protector."

"But you spared me."

She simpered on purpose and affected a breathless whine. "Oh, please, please, I cannot for the life of me figure how to count out these bills! How shall I know if the change is correct? Someone might cheat me if you will not take charge of it." With a hand to her forehead, she lolled her head to one side and looked pitiful.

He tried to contain a laugh and his great shoulders shook with it. "Ach, Suz. You are death to a man's conceit."

She assumed a prim pose and shook off her acting. "Well, I should hope so! Heaven knows you are overly endowed with it, sir. Amour propre could be your by-name."

Again he laughed as he pocketed the money she had given him. "Deliver me from a righteous woman," he said dryly.

"No chance of that. Is my hat on straight?"

He leaned back and assessed her. "Nay, it sits at a rakish angle that quite becomes you and your hair is curling like a bonny bairn's. You look so delicious, I wonder some lecherous bloke has not snatched you up and devoured you."

She grinned and preened. "One has, if memory serves."

He raised an eyebrow. "Be warned. He's voracious and you've merely whetted his hunger."

That reminded her of another problem she needed to

solve. "James, when this business with Father and Durston is settled, I should like to broach some questions. Things you might find...well, inappropriate. Perhaps even embarrassing. However, I shall expect complete candor since I have afforded you that regarding our financial affairs."

"Questions? About what?" he asked with full alertness.

She paused and glanced around at their fellow passengers to see whether anyone was listening. Assured they were not, she answered him in a lowered voice, "The topic dearest to my heart these past few years."

He appeared surprised. "The rights of women?"

"The lack of them to be precise."

"Any one in particular?"

"Yes, one in particular."

"May I know what it is so that I can be forming clear answers?"

"Not here," she replied, shooting him a meaningful look before she leaned very close and whispered in his ear. "But it has to do with that hunger you mentioned."

She had rendered him speechless, Susanna realized as she sat back and observed his astonished expression. At least now he would have something else to think about.

Trouble was, so did she. The rhythmic motion of the train and his warm hand squeezing hers did not help soothe her mind at all.

Chapter Eighteen

"His lordship is not here at present," said the manager of the Royal Arms. "However, he did post us that he will be arriving on Thursday or thereabout."

"From London?" James asked.

"No, m'lord. From the Orkneys, I believe."

"Thank you," James replied. "We'll be requiring rooms to await him."

"The earl's suite is at your disposal, Lord Garrow," the man declared with disdain, as if James should be well aware of that already.

Susanna stepped forward, her manner putting the manager's haughtiness to shame. "Lord Garrow and I prefer our own suite, if you please. We have no way of knowing whether the earl will be traveling alone or in company."

The man cowed at once and bent at the waist, suddenly all subservience and humility, "Of course, my lady. Whatever you wish." He hurriedly tugged on one of the bellpulls behind the desk.

James quelled a smile as Susanna cast a glance around the lobby, all grace and poise, her nose in the air. She looked queenly as Victoria and yet bedraggled as a beggar, wearing the horribly creased traveling ensemble in which she'd spent the entire journey. He was even worse in his second-best suit, his linen grayed and his shoes covered with dried mud and dust. They both smelled of horse sweat, wood smoke and probably worse.

Thomas appeared almost immediately. "Lord Garrow! My lady," he said, greeting them with a smile and a perfunctory bow. He took their pouches from James without asking and accepted the key the manager held out to him. "I shall show you to your rooms. How good to see you again."

James nodded. "Thomas."

Only when they reached their chambers did he take Thomas aside. "I need a great favor of you. Do you know the Shipman's Inn?"

"Not well, but I know the location. Why?"

James fished the locket out of his waistcoat pocket and opened the catch, showing the miniatures. "I need to find out whether this man is lodged there. If not, I want someone sent to inform me the moment he appears. It's crucial, Thomas. Bribe someone there. The earl's life could depend on it." He took out a few of the bills Susanna had given him and thrust them, along with the locket, into Thomas's hand.

"This is too much. If I offer it, the informant might realize the significance of your knowing and try to arrange a better deal with your mark."

"You be the judge, then. Keep the rest for your trouble."

"Still too much," Thomas argued.

James rolled his eyes. "Then buy books, tuition or send your bairns to Cambridge! But for God's sake, get on to that inn, would you?"

"Done. I'll stop on the way down and arrange for your baths. Did you ride all the way here?"

"Thomas, go," he ordered, "and hurry back."

That accomplished, James closed the door and turned to find Susanna watching him.

"Well done of you, James," she said. "I had forgotten you knew where Durston stayed before. He will know Father's coming here, so I suppose we can expect him to turn up. What of Miranda and Fowler? They will have gone on to London, you think?"

"It's possible they telegraphed him from Beauly or Kinloss."

"And perhaps awaited his answer?" she asked, worrying her bottom lip with her teeth.

"Possibly. If so, we might have to deal with all three of them. But unless Durston is traveling *with* your father, I believe we have succeeded in our goal."

Susanna tossed her hat onto a chair and began unbuttoning her gloves. "He and Father never leave London at the same time. One of them always remains behind to see to the business."

"He was here for that attack," James reminded her.

"Ah, but they did not travel together. Father had no knowledge of Durston's following him here that time. If Father's gone to the Orkneys, he travels by ship and Durston could not have accompanied him without arousing suspicion. I'll wager he's either here or on his way to await Father's arrival."

James nodded thoughtfully and shrugged. "Well, then. I suppose the only thing we can do is wait."

"For two whole days," she said wearily, laying her gloves aside and sitting to remove her half boots. "Meanwhile, I am planning nothing more than a hot bath and a long sleep."

He smiled as he knelt to help her with the buttons at her ankles, wishing for all he was worth that he could join her in that bath and in that bed. But there was too much to do yet to indulge his own needs.

"You should visit the bank," she said, lifting her other foot to him for assistance. "We shall need things."

When he said nothing, she touched his shoulder. "James, you won't mind it, will you? Have we settled this between us?"

"I have money and we will use that first. Then I won't mind. It is for the common good, as you said. I'm not unreasonable."

She rewarded him with the sweetest smile and touched his face with her hand. "There's my good lad. I do hope our son is just like you."

His hands stilled on her ankle and his heart almost stopped. "Son?" he repeated.

She nodded and clasped both her hands to her middle, her smile a bit crooked now. "Well, I suppose it could be a daughter. If so, I hope she doesn't inherit your huge feet."

James sighed. "Suz, it's early days yet to suspect you're with child. We've only... Well, it was just once, you know."

With a sad shake of her head, she scoffed. "Ah, James, did your parents tell you nothing? I have it on best authority that it only takes the one time."

James backed away from her and stood, dropping the small boot beside its mate on the floor. "I see. Well."

"You're too tired to take it in, aren't you?" she asked, most likely concerned over his lack of enthusiasm. "I just assumed you knew."

"You said you had questions for me," he reminded her, wondering how he was to supply the facts she needed and also correct whatever misinformation she had been given without making her feel the fool.

She stood up and headed for the bedroom on her right. "I know what I said, but since this comes as news to you, I doubt you would know much about the other things."

"Other things?"

It took all the willpower he possessed not to follow her into that room and show her exactly what he did know. But these were lessons that would require plenty of time and also attention not clouded by exhaustion. Not to mention energy, which in her case, was probably in short supply at the moment. Besides, there was a lot to be said for the pleasure of anticipation.

She slept through the afternoon and night that followed. While he did not trust himself to go into her room, James peeked in now and again to see whether she was all right. He had begun to think about waking her when she emerged from her bedchamber, already dressed for the day.

He stood, shoving aside the newspapers Thomas had brought to him a half hour ago. "It's eight o'clock." Realizing how accusatory that had sounded, he smiled and shrugged. "I worried you might be ill."

"I'm hale as ever. Has any further word come from Father?"

James shook his head and went over to the occasional table to pour her a cup of coffee. "He'll probably arrive tomorrow or the next day. Thomas will be checking at the inn to which I followed Durston that night and inform us if he shows up." He took her coffee to her on the settee.

"Thank you, James," she said, taking the cup and sipping. "Are you going out?"

"Only for a short while." He sat at the other end of the settee so they were a scant three feet apart.

She said nothing until she had emptied the cup and set it aside. Then she faced him. "I need for you to do some errands. There is a list of things I wish to purchase. Would you mind?"

"I'm afraid you'll have to choose your own gowns and bonnets, Suz. I'd be a daft hand at it."

Her smile hardened and her eyes narrowed. "I thought perhaps you might see about more tools for building so the workmen needn't share. That should speed along the repairs. Plows and perhaps oxen would help enormously. Or mules if you prefer. We could grow extra barley if we clear more of the land."

"Land for grazing," he reminded her.

"Whisky export could make us more than the wool, unless I'm mistaken," she informed him. "As it is, we send out very little."

"Because of the excise tax," he replied. "No getting around it and believe me, we have tried. Wool's less trouble."

"I bow to your wisdom and experience," she said with a jerk of her chin and a haughty sniff. "I am rather new at this. You doubtless believe me a featherwit now, but I daresay it won't last for long."

James ducked his head, realizing how he had insulted her by thinking she was only concerned for herself. She had every right to suggest what she had since she was mistress of Drevers and he, her steward. But he also knew she was including Galioch of which he was master. She cared for both properties and the people who lived on both as much as he did.

"Then you may take me to buy bonnets," she added with a sly grin.

He smiled. "Aye, I will. Do not open the door to any-one other than Thomas or your father, should he arrive earlier than we expect."

"I shall be extremely careful," she promised.

James rose and went to get his hat. "Look for me back about midday," he told her. As if it were but an after-thought, he stopped while striding past the back of the settee and leaned down to kiss her.

Though his move obviously surprised her, James noted that she did nothing to avoid it. In fact, she turned her head so that his kiss landed on her lips instead of her cheek. He caressed her shoulder with his hand and let his mouth linger near her ear. "Until later," he said.

"Was that by any chance an apology for thinking me a hen-wit?" she asked with a saucy look.

"As close as I'll come to one," he admitted, tapping her nose with one finger. "Might have been more sincere if you hadn't mentioned the bonnets after all."

Her laughter followed him out. James was glad enough to have the excuse to go on his own this morning. He needed to go to his bank and make a withdrawal, and also to speak with his former employer to explain that he would no longer be available for special projects.

Another reason for his relief in going alone was that it would have been devilishly difficult to purchase the articles he needed to complete Susanna's education about *other things*. He couldn't very well do that if she had insisted on accompanying him.

He left the hotel, secure in the knowledge that Thomas would remain at the hotel and keep a sharp eye out for any trouble.

Susanna poured the tea while Thomas stood by, hands folded behind him, a silent sentinel and chaperon. "It was good of you to come and bring the statue with you, Monsieur Aubert. It is rather heavy, isn't it!''

The French gallery owner smiled and accepted the cup she offered him. "*Oui,* madame, but I dared not trust it to another's hand. It is too remarkable a piece to allow such a risk. Are you certain you will not reconsider selling it?''

"It is not mine to sell. You may ask Lord Garrow, of course, but I warn you I shall do everything within my power to dissuade him from letting it go. You see, I quite fell in love—'' Her words halted midsentence when the door opened.

Thomas blocked the entrance until he established it was James. "M'lord,'' he said, by way of greeting.

"Thomas. Why was this door not secured?''

"M'lady has a guest, sir.'' He stood aside and gestured toward the sitting room.

"Good afternoon, Garrow. Join us, please,'' Susanna said pleasantly. She smiled in response to James's questioning look, knowing that he would soon be very pleased by what they were about to impart to him. She stood, as did Aubert, the dapper little Frenchman who had brought the good news. "Lord Garrow, Monsieur Aubert, owner of Le Coeur d'Ecosse Galerie.''

"My lord.'' The little man bowed, grinning from ear to ear.

James nodded. "Monsieur Aubert.'' Then he looked to Susanna for an explanation of the man's presence. She saw the instant his eye caught on the object sitting within arm's reach on the tea table. Though his expression changed little to the uninitiated eye, she did mark a hint of displeasure. Odd.

"I asked Monsieur Aubert to examine your sculpture

when we were last here, and had no time to collect it before we left.''

Aubert spoke up. ''Ah, m'lord, if I could only express how much everyone has enjoyed viewing *Désespoir!* Having it on display vastly increased my patronage these past few weeks.''

''Désespoir,'' James repeated, his voice containing both anger and disbelief. He glanced again at the statue. *''Desperation?''*

''Mais, oui!'' Aubert exclaimed, oblivious to James's rising ire. ''She speaks to everyone who sees her,'' he gushed, gesturing toward the statue as if running a finger along the lines of it.

Susanna reached out and did precisely that, the stone cool beneath her fingertips as they grazed over the incredibly varied textures he had created. The piece invited touching, almost required it of the viewer. James had created it from a two-foot block of dark-rose marble. The woman he had depicted wore a look of fierce determination as her body twisted and struggled to free one foot which he had left imbedded in the rough-hewn base. A powerful statement, to be sure.

Susanna's gaze wandered back to James, trying to communicate without words how much she admired his work. He said nothing.

Aubert rambled on. ''I fear I created the title myself since Lady Garrow provided none. I had to print something on the card to identify it. The message you impart is so clear, my lord, so vivid I think you could call it nothing else. The woman embodies Scotland so perfectly, your beautiful country, bound fast in the clutch of England for so long.'' He sighed. ''A desperate and eternal struggle, to be sure, one my own country has historically attempted to aid.''

"To no avail," James said acerbically.

Aubert was not intimidated in the least. "Lord Abercrombie has offered to buy her, but your lady cannot seem to part with her." The man gave a small shrug. "Four thousand pounds sterling does seem low."

"Four thou… Sold," James said.

"James, no!" Susanna cried. He couldn't sell it. "Please!"

He shot her a look of astonishment. "You want th' thing?"

"Please," she repeated, reaching out to him, taking his hand.

Aubert interrupted. "I must tell you that Abercrombie has offered seven if you would create another that is life-size."

James swung to stare at him. "Seven thousand pounds?"

Aubert smiled. "I can get you at least nine, but I expect a healthy commission. Say fifteen percent?"

"Ten," James shot back.

"Two thousand to begin," Susanna announced. "We shall have to order the marble and have it shipped."

"Done." Aubert stood and stuck out his hand to set the bargain. James shook it and the little man hurried out.

Thomas broke the stunned silence that followed with a laugh. "Poor fellow. He missed the mark by half a league. Anyone can see that's not the meaning you had in mind when you carved that." He pointed to the statue. "It's so obvious that the woman is humanity itself, fighting to escape the sucking mire of poverty." He shrugged. "Still, the title fits well enough, doesn't it? *Desperation.*"

James inclined his head, looked at the statue for a moment. Then he waved Thomas out. "That will be all,

Thomas. Thank you.'' He followed and slipped the lock on the door.

Susanna returned her attention to the statue. ''Amazing how they both misconstrued your intent, isn't it?'' she asked when he returned and sat beside her. While he poured himself a cup of tea, she tried to find words to state her appreciation of what he had done. ''James, I knew the moment I saw her just how truly you understood the plight of all women.'' She looked again at the statue. Lovingly. ''Whenever I doubted that these past few weeks or suspected you of trying to order my life for me, I would remember how well you expressed your sympathy with our attempts to break free of oppression. You are nothing like so many other men who fear to see us come into our own.''

He stared at her. It was a full minute before he opened his mouth to speak. ''Well, I hate to disappoint you.''

''What do you mean?''

He flipped a hand toward the statue. ''It's just a woman with her foot stuck in the rocks.''

Chapter Nineteen

"Wait!" Susanna cried as James headed for the door. "Why are you leaving? Are you angry?"

In the open doorway, he turned, his face a study in barely controlled fury. "Have I ever tried to make you into something you're not, Suz? Have I?"

She stopped short, confused. "Why, no, but—"

"I am no artist, Susanna. I've never pretended to be. I never *want* to be!"

"But you are, James! You're a wonderful sculptor."

He flung a hand towards the statue. "Nay, I'm a stone carver. At least I *was* until I met you. If that daft Abercrombie wants to part with a fortune, I'll relieve him of it. God knows I'd be stupid to refuse seven thousand pounds under the circumstances. But it's just this once, Suz. I will not be pushed into the life my father led. Not by you or anyone, daft or no. Do you understand *that?*"

"No! What's wrong with producing beautiful things and being paid for it? What better occupation could anyone have? That's all you would need to do, James. Think how rewarding it would be, and not only financially!"

"I'll not be reduced to a dilettante, hacking away in the cellar, feeding delusions that I have some profound message to impart to humanity! I'll not be your eccentric pet to show off to your friends, Susanna. I cut stone for money and that's that!''

''James—''

He stopped, obviously in an attempt to regain control of his anger. When he spoke again, his voice was lower, tightly mastered. ''Well, I have *seen* a life lived that way, and I will not embrace it, not even to please you. *Especially* not to please you!''

''Oh, James, you must know I only meant to help. I thought you would be delighted to have your work recognized.''

She glanced at his sculpture and back at him. ''You have to love something to do it that well. You simply *have* to!''

''And you get to decide that, do you? You have the final word? I've news for you, Miss Vindication of Women's Rights. I have rights, too. And one of 'em is to—''

''Children, children!'' chided a voice from the open doorway.

''Father!'' Susanna cried. ''We did not expect you this soon!''

James turned, then moved aside. ''Sir,'' he said in a curt tone.

''You two should speak a bit louder,'' her father said calmly. ''I could barely hear you when I first entered the building.''

He closed the door and looked from one to the other. ''Actually, I saw your name on the register. So what are you doing in Edinburgh and what is all this fuss about?''

''We came to warn you,'' James said, yanking the door open again. ''Susanna will tell you. I shall return in an hour or so. At the moment, I have business to attend." He shot her a scathing look. "With my *patron.*"

Susanna blew out a breath of relief when he refrained from slamming the door.

"He's angry," she said, still shocked by James's response.

"Do tell."

Susanna huffed. "It seems I've overstepped the bounds of good wifery."

Her father laughed. "What have you done now?"

"The unthinkable, according to the high and mighty laird." She walked slowly back to the settee and plopped down. "See that?" she asked, nodding at the statue. "James did it."

He studied the sculpture for a moment. "Ah, a woman with her foot caught in the rocks."

Susanna pressed a palm over her eyes and sighed. "Yes. I suppose that's all it is."

"You have not yet told me what you and James are doing here in Edinburgh," her father said. "I had thought to travel on to Drevers and see you there."

"Good heavens, I forgot!" Susanna reached out and placed a hand over his. "Father, Mr. Durston was the one who ordered and probably participated in the attack on you and James when you were here before."

Her father was already shaking his head. "Not possible. Durston was himself attacked in London and nearly killed. He remains in serious condition. That is why I had to go to the Orkneys myself. As you know, he routinely handles the business there, but was not able."

"Did you see his wounds and bruises?"

He looked confused. "No. I called at his house. His housekeeper told me he was still abed and unable to receive visitors. Surely he could not—"

"Miranda had a miniature painting of him in her locket, Father. James recognized Mr. Durston immediately as the man who arranged the attack on your carriage that night. We have the inn where he stayed under watch and expect him to return at any time."

The betrayed look on her father's face saddened Susanna. Then anger replaced it. "What of that chit, Miranda? Did she threaten you in any way? God, I should never have agreed for her to come to you. Durston sent a message, delivered by her own hand, pleading with me for her protection. Scoundrels, both!"

Susanna scoffed. "Three if you count that wretched cousin of hers, Brodie Fowler. Both spent the entire visit attempting to seduce James and me into a tête-a-tête."

"James would not countenance any of that foolishness, I'd wager."

Susanna smiled. "Certainly not. Fowler shot him, you know."

Her father bolted upright, outraged. "He what?"

She fanned him back. "Merely a peppering with birdshot, but it could easily have been worse."

Susanna dared not mention the episode on the parapet at Galioch that could very well have ended with her death. Just as she had not confessed to James how Brodie had suggested twice that they meet at midnight outside the manor house. She was determined that no husband or father of hers would be hauled away, charged with murdering the man.

"You should hear how James finally convinced those two to leave!"

Her father laughed bitterly. "Not gently, I suspect. Ah, Suz, I do regret you and James have had all of this to deal with in addition to being newly wed, but it will soon be over, once I have Durston and his cohorts taken up.

If you do not mind my asking, how is your marriage going? Has Garrow been good to you?''

She shrugged. ''Very, all things considered. Though he is rather upset with me at the moment, as you saw. I suppose it was my fault. It had to do with the statue he created.''

Her father glanced at it again. ''That?''

''Yes. I sent it to Monsieur Aubert for appraisal. James is not pleased about that.''

''Not surprising. He does not strike me as an artistic sort.''

''Don't be absurd, Father. Of course he is. However, I must admit that I misconstrued his vision. He probably resents me for that, as well as my presumption at having his work valued.''

''Really? How badly did you misinterpret it?''

''I thought it represented his empathy for womankind and our inability to throw off our servitude.''

He laughed out loud. ''Ah, Susanna, Susanna.''

''Well, that was what I saw in it.''

''My dear girl,'' he said wryly as he sat beside her and took her hand in his.

''You think because I'm a female, my observations are too fanciful? Well, I wasn't the only one who mistook his meaning.'' She explained what Monsieur Aubert and Thomas Snively had thought.

Her father nodded. ''You do realize that our perception of everything we see and everyone we know is always affected by our own life experiences, Susanna.''

She grunted and shook her head. ''That must be why you and I seldom see eye to eye.''

''No doubt about that. For instance, your cause. You see women as downtrodden slaves at the mercy of whatever men happen to hold them in power. I can't think what might have happened to you to make you believe that.''

''Can't you really?'' she asked, her words mocking. ''What of the laws that say a man may beat his wife, that he may sell off or gamble away her property, even her earnings should she have any? What of taking a mother's children from her if she dares leave him to protect her own life? And then accuse her of desertion and leave her without a sou? Tell me you can ignore such injustice and pretend it does not exist!''

''No, of course I can't. The laws need changing, I agree. But not every household in Britain abides by those antiquated statutes, Suz. Mine certainly did not and unless I have lost the ability to judge men, neither does yours.''

Unable to sit still, Susanna jumped up and began to pace, wringing her hands with frustration. ''A husband can do whatever he will with a wife and you know it. He can work her until she drops. Treat her as a brood mare for his so-called champion line! She has no recourse but to submit until the day she dies! Well, I'll *never* submit to that sort of thing!''

He stretched out an arm along the back of the settee and sighed. ''I seriously doubt James has ever demanded that of you. No man with any conscience would. Having your mother for my wife and you for my daughter would have dissuaded me even if I had been so inclined. She always had the ability to twist me 'round her finger, just as you do.''

Susanna coughed with disbelief, astounded. ''A pity she didn't know that or she might be alive today!'' Realizing what she'd said and seeing the horrified shock on her father's face, Susanna clasped her hands over her mouth.

"What do you mean?" he asked, his voice soft with hurt and confusion.

Wishing she could retract her words, she simply shook her head and avoided his probing gaze.

"Tell me, Suz," he demanded. "You believe I caused your mother's death?"

"I know you never meant to, Father. I know that. But she—she died exhausted. All the responsibilities she assumed, duties required by you, combined with the stillborn children left her weakened and ill. She lived to please you in every way and died in that last attempt."

Unable to bear his anguish, she gentled her voice even more and placed a hand over his. "I know you would never have caused her any harm on purpose, Father. You were simply running true to course in what men are taught from the cradle. But I feel I must do whatever I can to change the way things are."

He closed his eyes and brushed a hand over his face. The grief-stricken sigh tore at her heart. Then he looked at her. "I loved her," he said simply. "Beyond all reason, I loved your mother. I never asked anything of her, Suz. She stayed incredibly busy, I grant you that. Charity work, organizing this soiree and that ball, not to mention the usual household affairs. But she was one to set her own duties and I swear she thrived on them."

"But it took so much out of her," Susanna argued. "You should have made her take care, go more slowly, give up some of her work and rest!"

He looked at her with sadness. "Ah, Suz. Would you listen to yourself? Think of your own activities. Would you allow James to schedule your days for you?"

"No," she admitted, feeling vaguely guilty. "But that was not what took her from us. There were the—"

"I know. The babes we lost. Infant deaths are all too

common, but somehow I never imagined that I should lose her as well. Had I had my way, you would never have been born, my dear.'' He softened the pronouncement with a smile. ''There was a lad who came before you. When he did not survive, I thought I could never bear such grief ever again. But your mother was much stronger than I in that respect. She wanted a houseful of children and meant to have them. I suffered each loss and pleaded with her to cease in her attempts to have more.''

''Well, it does take two to create them, so I'm told.''

He blushed and cleared his throat. ''So it does, but she could be...most persuasive.''

''I should not hear this,'' Susanna mumbled, discomfited by his unusual candor.

''No,'' he agreed, sounding defensive and a little angry. ''Perhaps I should not have said that much, but I do want you to know that your mother was not some poor wretch I kept chained to my bedpost unless she was slaving away and arranging parties to build my standing in society. I loved her, Suz. I did everything I could to make her happy and content because of it. She was every whit as demanding and opinionated as you, only she was much more subtle about it. And she was probably much more successful at getting her way, I might add.''

For a long time, neither of them spoke. Susanna sat beside him again, her hands clasped in her lap as she attempted to digest all he had said.

Memories flashed through her mind. Her mother's capability, her cajoling smile, the wily look in her eyes as she made a suggestion. Susanna remembered her quickened step as she hurried thither and yon always planning, delegating, arranging, rearranging. Never still for a moment. Then there were Father's concern and his warnings, his grumbling at attending this or that to-do. She had conveniently forgotten those things. As well as how dreadfully lost he had seemed for months after her mother succumbed.

Could it be that she had substituted anger for her own grief? That she had grasped desperately at this cause of hers because of that? Partly, she had to admit. Oh, she was not mistaken about those unfair laws. They did exist and must be altered, but she had no right to heap the injustices of the world on the head of every male who existed. Especially not this dear man who loved her so. Or even James who had shown her nothing but fairness and kindness. And passion, which she had readily accepted and would again. Soon, she hoped.

"I am so sorry, Father," Susanna said in a small voice. "I had no idea. Mother was always soft-spoken and seemed so meek."

He laughed, sounding bitter. "Well, I never said you inherited her manners, did I?"

"Will you forgive me?" she asked, brushing a tear from beneath her eye.

He shrugged. "What's done is done, and perhaps I am to blame for not standing fast against her wishes. But I do think you might take a page from Mother's book and speak a bit more softly to that husband of yours. Shouting won't gain you a thing."

Susanna smiled, fiddling idly with the ribbon on her gown. "Good advice and I shall take it."

"Many's the day I've wanted to turn you over my knee and swat your backside," he admitted. "At other times, I could hardly contain my pride. But you are no longer a child, Susanna. The time has come when you must accept that no one has all the answers or always does the wise thing. God knows I have erred and I daresay, so shall you."

She thought she might as well take advantage of all this plain speaking. "Father? Since we are being so forthright, may I ask you something regarding marriage?"

He tugged at his collar with one finger and cleared his throat again. "If you must."

"Is there a way to prevent getting with child and still…?"

His eyes flew wide and fixed on her. "Good God, Suz, you won't refuse him children!"

"No, no, of course not!" she assured him. "We've already begun one. I only want to know because a woman producing too many children too rapidly might—"

"Oh, no," he said vehemently. "Suz, it is against the law for women to speak of this in public forum. Others have been arrested and imprisoned for even suggesting…" His words trailed away as her other pronouncement registered. "You are having a child, Suz? I'm to be a grandfather?"

She nodded, then laughed with surprise when he embraced her. Patiently, she waited until he had done with exclaiming over her condition and preening as if she had already produced a baby. Then she returned to the topic he had abandoned. "Father, would you answer me? I need no improper details, just a yes or no. Is there a way other than abstinence?"

For a moment he looked confused, dismayed, then muttered, "Uh…yes."

"Thank you!" she said, hugging him back. "Thank you so very much!"

"Well, here now," he said, disentangling himself and slicking his hair back over one ear in a nervous gesture. "It's not as if I invented the damn things. And you'd best not ever mention them aloud."

Things? Now she would need those details, Susanna

thought with a sigh. But she knew she would not get them from him. Perhaps if James did not know about whatever they were, he could think of someone to ask. Providing he would even speak to her again, much less entertain such intimate conversation.

He was so angry when he had left. She looked over at the sculpture and tried to be objective about what she saw. The marble face contained a wealth of emotion, determination, frustration, fury. Smoothly burnished skin exuded sensuality. Where the roughness of the stone had been cut away so painstakingly and polished to reveal the unrivaled smoothness within revealed much about the man who had created it. No matter what James said, his art held great meaning. Perhaps his own perception of it was too clouded by his early experiences for him to even realize that.

Misconceptions of her own had certainly skewed her thinking for years. She still needed to come to terms with what she had just learned about her mother, to figure out what effect these truths would have on her long-held beliefs and future actions.

Her views of the unfair inequality of men and women and the issues of her marriage in particular, were inextricably tangled together in her mind. Unfairly so, she now thought. One thing she did know, that James had made very clear to her in their earlier, rather heated exchange. He had never once tried to change her. He had never imposed his will on her or made her do a thing she had not wanted to do.

Unfortunately, she could not say the same for herself. Until this business with his sculpture, Susanna had to admit James had been remarkably patient and accommodating. He had provided the freedom she required. He listened to her ideas and gave them credence. She had his trust and trusted him. Even if she had not begun to love him in addition to that, she should be perfectly satisfied with such an arrangement. What more could a wife ask? She owed him a heartfelt apology for her interference in the matter of his art. One delivered in soft-spoken tones and with a kiss of peace.

Though she felt she was right in urging him to use his talent as it was intended, she should leave off now. James must make that decision for himself. Someone must have strongly discouraged him in the past. Oh, how hard it would be not to rail at him, to push at him, to insist that he should welcome the joy that must live in creating wonderful things with his own hands. How could he be happy doing otherwise?

She recalled her mother's manner whenever she had dealt with Father. Susanna obviously had mistaken that gentleness for meekness. She realized now that her mother had always had her say and generally got her way in most matters. She simply had not shouted her demands loudly and caused a ruckus. There was surely a lesson in that.

Her father had no defense against sweetness. What man did? All that quality had fostered in him was a genuine desire to please her, even when what his beloved wife had wanted had gone against his better judgment and eventually proved disastrous. He could not have known that it would.

Outrage and forthright argument might be called for to obtain results when trying to right a moral dilemma such as the laws concerning women or the treatment of them in general. But in private with a husband, Susanna suspected that she would get more results with her mother's methods.

If one approached a man with a smile, wasn't he more

likely to pay closer attention than if one came at him shaking a fist? What a revelation. Who knew? It might even be effective on a larger scale. Reason as opposed to accusation. Yes, that made a great deal of sense.

The epiphany calmed Susanna immeasurably. Somehow it was very freeing not to feel she must ever play the fiery revolutionary, the voice of gloom, the insistent implementer of new rules. Of course, she still believed very strongly that change was needed in the world with regard to women. She also believed James should decide to live up to his God-given talent. But she needed to change as well, and she would. Now she could calmly implore, gently teach and show by quiet example.

The relief of it was nearly overwhelming.

A hesitant knock on the door distracted her. "That must be Thomas with our supper. Have you eaten, Father?"

He shook his head, still contemplating all she had told him about Durston. Susanna went to answer the door.

"Thomas?" she asked, listening before she admitted anyone.

"Yes, my lady," came the muffled voice.

She turned the handle to pull the door open, berating herself because she had forgotten to set the lock after James had left.

Suddenly, the heavy panel pushed inward almost slamming her against the wall. Strong arms banded around her before she could recover her balance and a hand clasped over her mouth. Someone else closed the door.

"Well, well," Frank Colin said to Susanna with a sneer. "We meet again. I thought you and the Scot would never leave the protection of the blessed *clan*."

He pointed a pistol toward the settee. "Sit back down, Lord Eastonby. And remain quiet, or I shall have to kill you now."

Chapter Twenty

Susanna knew, looking into Miranda's gloating eyes, what the plan was. "You are waiting for my husband."

"Precisely," Miranda said with a nod. She smiled at Frank Colin, then at Susanna again. "And this time we aren't playing any games. Brodie was a squeamish, weak-minded fool."

"I suppose that means he hadn't the proper fortitude for murder," Susanna guessed. "So you've done away with him? Did you think to warn Mr. Colin here that intimacy with you is no guarantee of survival?"

Miranda's eyes narrowed and her lips tightened. It was Colin who spoke. "Sit down and be quiet unless you want a bullet right now."

Susanna spread her arms wide. "Shoot me where I stand, then. Bring the entire hotel staff down on your head. I can think of no better way to save my husband's life."

Suddenly her father leaped in front of her. "No! Don't!"

Miranda swung the pistol she was holding and it cracked against his head. Immediately, even before he fell backwards onto the settee, she leveled the barrel at Susanna. "Stay where you are. I *will* shoot."

No idle threat. Hate fairly rolled off the woman in waves.

Susanna watched her father for any sign of movement. His chest rose and fell, so she knew he was still alive. The blow had left a nasty bruise at his temple.

James would save them when he returned. She had to believe that. If he returned in time and was not caught unawares. Perhaps her father would regain consciousness by then and it would be three against two. At least one of them might survive.

She noted that Colin carried a repeating pistol while Miranda's held but one shot. And Colin's right hand was still bandaged where Susanna had shot him at Drevers. Therefore his aim might be off a bit. She needed to keep them engaged, distracted.

"You had your own father attacked in London, didn't you?" she asked. "How could you have done that?"

Miranda smirked. "A neat ploy to throw off suspicion, wasn't it? No doubt he'll succumb from his injuries soon after you three are dead and gone. Until then, he's well dosed with laudanum and won't suffer."

Susanna nodded. "Ah, patricide." She threw Colin a speculative look. "You actually trust a woman who would do away with her lover and her father?"

Colin laughed bitterly. "I trust no one. But she has concocted a way for me to have Drevers and that's all I care about."

Miranda's surprised gaze swung his way. "But you said—"

"Leave off. You'll have the business, Miranda, and whatever else comes with it."

"Oh, now I see," Susanna said, leaning against the

arm of the settee and crossing her arms over her chest. "Get rid of the three of us and your father assumes control of Childers Shipping. Then he dies and you inherit." She clicked her tongue and shook her head.

"It was Father who gave me the idea," Miranda said. "But he would have stopped with the earl's death. He had borrowed heavily from company funds, you see, and feared he might be discovered."

Susanna shook her head. "It would not have worked in any case. Mr. Durston obviously knew nothing of what my father put in his will. A distant cousin in Wales is heir to the title, the estates and all of the holdings, including Drevers and the company. So you see, you'll get nothing for your trouble."

"You lie!" Miranda cried, looking from Susanna to Colin and back again. Her hand holding the pistol trembled and she tried to steady it by grasping it with the other. "She is lying, Frank! There is no cousin. Father looked into that!"

"Did he?" Susanna smiled and raised her brows. "You'll see, but then it will be too late." She noted Colin's face darkening with fury. He believed the tale she'd made up about the cousin. "So it has all been for nothing," she added. "There's no point in following through with this."

"Don't listen to her," Miranda warned Colin. "She's only trying to save herself."

"Killing a peer of the realm will get you hanged in short order," Susanna warned Colin. "Add to that a baron and his wife! I doubt you'll even merit a trial the outrage will be so great."

"They'll never know who did it," Miranda assured her. She laughed nervously, shifting her gaze back and forth between Colin and Susanna. "We have rooms just down the corridor. Once we eliminate all of you, we retreat there. As Mr. and Mrs. Smythe, we have no connection to Earl Eastonby or you and Garrow. The person who shot you will be thought to have escaped out the windows, which we shall leave open.''

Susanna shook her head again and fixed Miranda with a look of fake sympathy as if her logic were faulty. In fact, it was not. What they intended to do might very well work.

''Enough talk,'' Colin declared, his voice menacing. His gun hand looked very steady indeed. ''Keep your mouth shut or we won't wait for your husband.''

Oh, God. They would kill James the moment he entered the room. ''Then shoot!'' Susanna challenged. ''I dare you. Kill us and James Garrow will hunt you down like the mad dogs you are!''

''Lord Garrow! Wait!'' Thomas Snively called, running across the lobby of the Royal Arms, his long legs eating up the distance.

James halted and turned at the bottom of the wide staircase.

Thomas gasped, out of breath. ''Someone asked at the desk which rooms you occupy. Not more than an hour ago.''

''Was it the man in the miniature?''

''No, it was a couple. I was out at the time, checking whether this Durston fellow had arrived at that inn. I took the liberty of enlisting several of the staff here to assist in keeping watch. Harrison told me about these people just now. I showed him the picture. It's not Durston.''

''It has to be Fowler and Miranda,'' James said. ''Were they informed?'' James asked, glancing up the stairs.

"I fear so. They took rooms on the same floor just down the corridor from yours. Room 206. He signed the register as Mr. and Mrs. Smythe."

"Thank you, Thomas. You've been a great help."

James felt no sense of urgency. Fowler and Miranda were probably here to keep watch on his, Susanna's and the earl's activities until Durston arrived. That meant he would probably show up soon.

For now, James decided, a confrontation with Fowler was just what was needed. He marched directly past his and Susanna's rooms and headed for 206.

He rapped on the door, but there was no answer. Angrily he gave it a push. To his surprise, it opened.

"Fowler?" he called. No answer. They could not have gone downstairs after they arrived or they would have been seen. Where the devil were they? After departing Drevers under the circumstances they had, he could not imagine they would attempt any contact with Susanna or himself.

Still, he wasted no time finding out. Eastonby was there with Susanna. Nothing would have happened, he assured himself. But he still felt a niggle of unease as he approached the door to the suite. James tried to open the door, but found it locked. He banged on it with his fist. "Susanna!"

He heard the rasp of the key and the door swung open. James could see inside the sitting room. The earl was on the settee, lying against the arm of it as if asleep. Miranda Durston stood beside Susanna. Too close, he realized. Then James saw Susanna's wide-eyed warning glance shift to the area behind the open door. *Fowler?*

Without further pause, James slammed the door hard against whoever was behind it. But it wasn't Fowler.

Frank Colin, surprised off balance, threw up the pistol he was holding and fired.

James grasped Colin's arm, pushing it upward. They struggled for control of the gun, both falling hard when James landed a kick to the man's knee and it buckled. James dug his fingers into Colin's wrist and shook it until the weapon dropped free.

Both women were screaming. Another shot rang out, this one not from Colin's weapon which lay on the floor. Concerned for Susanna, James risked a glance at her. Colin's fist connected with his jaw. With a roar, James struck back. Again and once more. Colin collapsed beneath him.

"Suz?" he shouted, his ears still ringing from the report of the gunshot. "Are you hurt?"

"See to Father, James!" She was sitting on Miranda's back, both hands fisted in the woman's hair, pulling her head backward while Miranda screeched. Her gun lay next to Susanna's foot.

James picked up both weapons, keeping the repeater at the ready while he hurried over to see about the earl.

"A nasty bruise on his head," James reported as he checked for other injuries. "I think he's only knocked out. Colin did it?"

"No, *she* did!" Susanna hissed, giving her prisoner's hair a hard tug. Miranda screamed an obscenity.

"There, that's enough now," James ordered. "Let her up. If she moves from that position, I'll shoot." He said it strictly for Miranda's benefit. He had no intention of shooting her or anyone else if he could help it.

"Shoot her anyway!" Susanna exclaimed. "She might have killed Father! They meant to murder us all!"

"Aye, but he'll be fine and so will we, Suz. Get up now."

Thomas ran through the open door with several men behind him. "We heard shots! What hap—?" He stopped, gawking at the sight. Susanna—red curls tumbling over one eye, her bodice torn and skirts hiked to her knees—still pinned Miranda to the floor while Colin sprawled unconscious nearby.

"Thomas, see to his lordship's injury, if you will. And someone go for the constable."

The next hour passed in a flurry of questions and explanations. They had repaired to the earl's suite so that he could be put to bed and his injury doctored by Snively. Susanna and James were being interviewed in the sitting room by Constable Jenkins.

Jenkins had seen to it that Colin and Miranda were taken away and jailed immediately until they could be brought before a magistrate to answer the charges James intended to bring.

Susanna provided most of the answers the constable needed since Miranda and Colin had boasted about their plans before James had arrived. The explanation was as much for him as for the constable, however.

Though James had already guessed at most of it, she did provide a few surprises. One of those was how she clung to his hands as if afraid to let go of him. For one formerly critical of public displays of affection, she was giving the good constable the impression that she and her husband were inseparable. James took full advantage and slipped his arm around her shoulders. For all her strength and courage, she felt frail as a bird right now.

"Please continue, Lady Garrow," Jenkins prompted.

"Miranda hired someone to attack Mr. Durston in London. Then she arranged for her and Fowler to come to us," Susanna related with a sigh. "After that, she ordered that her father be kept abed and well dosed with laudanum. They planned to get rid of him later.'' James watched her grimace. "He would supposedly die as a result of his injuries."

"But he was the one who came here last month and ordered Earl Eastonby killed," James declared.

She shifted closer to him. "Definitely. And Colin was a part of that plot, most likely the man you never saw who got away the night they attacked you on the road. Fowler was probably enlisted at the last when Miranda decided to come to Drevers to get rid of us. Colin would have needed to be elsewhere since he would have been the obvious suspect."

"Indeed. I had him followed to Fearn. He remained there, but I suppose he was having us watched in turn, waiting for Miranda and Fowler to see to the deed, eh? So when Durston died as a result of his injuries and all of that unnecessary medication, everything would fall to Miranda," James concluded.

"Well, to her and Fowler, as her nearest male relative," Susanna said. "You know very well a woman cannot have control of anything at all."

James scoffed. "Tell that to Miranda. I believe you were well in control there for a while."

She managed a small smile. "Yes, an exceptional moment."

"For an exceptional woman," James said, giving her a hug.

To his surprise, she leaned her head against his shoulder. Most wonderfully improper, he thought with a smile.

"I wonder what became of Fowler."

"I believe I can answer that, m'lady," Jenkins told her. "I was summoned to an inn on Dundas Street last evening where a body was discovered. Papers on his person and in his bags identified him as Broderick Fowler, late of London.''

Susanna snugged closer to James's side. ''How did he die?''

''Poisoned,'' the constable said.

James had had enough of this. All he wanted to do was take Susanna back to the privacy of their suite and hold her, make her feel safe again. The excitement which had kept her buoyant throughout the entire episode had faded completely now. He could feel her wilting with exhaustion.

Reluctantly he released her for a moment and rose, holding out his hand. The constable had no recourse but follow suit, shake hands and accept that he was now dismissed. ''Thank you for coming, Constable Jenkins. If you need us for anything else, we shall be in Edinburgh for the next few days.''

''And back for the trial, I expect?'' Jenkins asked.

''Of course. Goodbye.''

''Come,'' he ordered Susanna the moment the man was gone. ''We'll say good evening to the earl and then we're off.''

He fully expected her to protest, to insist she must stay with the earl, but she went meekly as a lamb. She wished her father good sleep, nodded to Thomas and left willingly.

''Are you all right, lass?'' he asked when they entered their own suite a few moments later. This ready capitulation was so unlike her.

She turned and frowned up at him. ''I am changed, James,'' she said. ''All this has changed me.''

''Ah, lass, I hope not,'' he replied, touching her brow, her cheek and the edge of her trembling lips. ''For I love you just the way you are.''

Suddenly as that she burst into tears and threw herself against him, her hands clutching the back of his coat. Her words muffled in the fabric of his waistcoat. "...love you, too."

He set her away so that he could lift her in his arms and carry her into her room. "You're safe now, hinny," he promised. "No need to weep." He laid her down on the bed, stretched out beside her and blotted away her tears with his handkerchief. "There now. See? You're fine."

"No, oh, no," she argued, shaking her head and sniffing. "I am not fine at all."

"The danger's over," he told her, smoothing back her hair.

She waved that away and sniffed again. "That's nothing compared to how I've almost ruined my life. And Father's. And yours. Most especially yours. I thought I knew so much, but I knew nothing. *Nothing*," she cried, wiping her eyes with the back of her hand.

James tried to soothe her. "What is it, sweeting? You weren't wrong to worry about the laws you object to. They are unfair and no one should disagree they need to be addressed."

"I am sure enough of that," she said, her voice angry. "But I spoke out against having one child after another and had no notion it was preventable in...other ways. I still have no idea how...that is accomplished."

He hid a smile. "I can help you there."

"You can?" Her interest sparked, then suddenly dimmed. "Oh, but I practically accused Father of killing my mother with hard work and too many confinements. I hurt him abominably, James."

"And he'll forgive you if he hasn't already. I trust you had words while I was out sulking?"

She lowered her lashes and sniffed. "Yes. It was not his fault. Or at least, not entirely. Apparently Mother would have her way and he could not bear to say no to her."

"Ah. Well, such happens." James lay back, his head propped on one arm. "My father gave in to my mother's every whim and fancy, too. If he had not, they might still be alive." He recounted the useless trip, the carelessness of drink that had caused the accident. "I can't blame him for it. I tried to do the same thing for years. Almost everything I did was to please her, to make her aware that I existed. I would have done anything to make her care for me and love me as much as I loved her. Unfortunately, nothing was sufficient to that end."

"Oh, James." She lay her head on his shoulder. "I am sorry."

He pulled her close. "So you see why I fought loving you as hard as I did? I was determined not to grant you that power over me." He laughed at himself. "But I've given in after all and that's that. I'm bound to live with it. So you may do what you will."

"Don't be absurd. I would never be unreasonable."

He grimaced, knowing she couldn't see his face. "Nay, I'm sure you wouldn't."

"I mean it. I will listen and try to do as you ask."

"Unless, of course, it goes against your principles."

"Well, that goes without saying. But I told you I've changed and I have. Today's events have made me realize there are things much more important than which of us has the final word, James. We could have lost one another today. I admit I can behave selfishly. But no more. I am reformed."

"You're not selfish, Susanna. Everything you do is

done for the sake of others. If you would reform someone, I would look further afield if I were you.''

She shrugged off his praise. ''Well then, let us say I mean to amend my faulty tactics. Haranguing lawmakers and every male I meet gains nothing in the way of progress. At least not for me. From here on I intend to use sound reasoning and persuasion, a gentler and hopefully more effective ploy.'' She shook her head and uttered a small sad laugh. ''You see, I have to believe there are other men in the world like you, James. Men with honor and a sense of fairness who will be receptive to a woman's views.''

''No more speeches then?'' he asked, careful not to sound as if he cared one way or the other. In the Highlands—at least at Galioch and Drevers—it would not matter much since most of the women had equal say. If not granted by law, they usually took it. However, if she insisted on public meetings farther south, say in London, she would encounter another scandal or worse yet, danger.

''No more speeches,'' she declared. ''And no further accusations. I shall be quiet, reserved and exhibit the height of diplomacy in all matters.''

James smiled to himself, wondering how long that bit of foolishness would last. Susanna was Susanna and he wanted her just the way she was, the way she had always been, strong in her beliefs and unafraid to speak her mind.

How could any man tolerate some namby-pamby little goose who cowered in the face of criticism, not to mention life-threatening danger? The boredom would drive him mad in a month if she were like that. His Suz had spirit and courage to spare and he could not imagine her not using it to advantage.

James felt compelled to touch her, to trail his finger down the side of her cheek. "I wouldn't change a hair on your pretty red head, I swear it."

She leaned into his hand as if seeking comfort. "It is possible I might slip in my resolve on occasion and I hope you'll forgive it if I should. There are times when I feel so powerless, James. I feel I must do something to right matters, even if it is wrong. Can you understand that?"

"Believe it or not, I can and do," he admitted. His mother had worn the same expression of near desperation he had seen on Susanna's face occasionally, he remembered now. Why had he never realized that before? He certainly had spent enough time comparing the two women. But always unfavorably.

His English mother had married a Scot and come from London to the Highlands to live, the same as Susanna had done. Only Christine Williamson had been little more than a child, barely eighteen when she'd married his father. How lonely she must have been, given his father's reticent nature and the then current attitude of the Scots towards any outsider.

Small wonder she had lost no time in surrounding herself with people who would fawn over her. Anyone would have done, James suspected, and she had not been very particular. He had long believed she had thrown out invitations to anyone who wished to rusticate in the quaint setting of Galioch and provide her some entertainment. Many had taken advantage of her generosity, some of them unsavory and hard to be rid of.

When she had borne a son at nineteen, he must have represented a chain that would hold her in place forever. So she had tugged against it, tried to ignore it, traveled as much as Father would let her in a frantic attempt to remain who she was.

Like Susanna, she must have craved at least a few choices in her life after her parents had married her off to a then wealthy Scots baron. She probably felt betrayed by them, separated from all that was familiar to her and cast into a rather rough existence despite the new and available riches. So she had used that. In fact, used it up. His father's love for her had not been enough, but in retribution, she had used that, too.

Thank God, he was a bit more perceptive than his father had been. James resolved to see to it that Susanna never regretted her lot. She was not Christine. In the first place, Susanna was older, more compassionate and possessed some direction in her life. At least, she cared about him. He must foster that at all cost, even if it meant compromising.

At the moment she looked so sincere, so willing to give and so lovely in her distress, he was moved. "I'll do whatever it takes to ease your mind, Suz. You have but to ask it."

"So, you would agree to fill the gaps in my knowledge?" she asked hesitantly. "I despise being uninformed. Would you tell me about those...things that prevent child bearing?"

The best course was to keep the facts simple and straightforward, James decided. "Very well, there are devices called French letters—"

"A good joke, that," Susanna said, interrupting with a soft laugh. "If you're away writing to me from France, I could hardly get with child by you, now could I? But answer me seriously, James, and be specific. This is important."

He rolled his eyes and groaned. "Then be quiet and

let me finish! It is made to fit over the…male member to…contain the seed.''

"Good heavens! Never say it!" She colored bright red.

"Well, there you are. You did ask."

"Why do they call it a French letter, do you suppose?"

James sighed. "Earlier on it was named an envelope, I think, and from that came the obvious term, letter. Medical fellows call it a condom. Another name is the *redingote anglaise*."

"An English riding coat?" Her brow creased with confusion.

He fished in his pocket, drew out a small package and plunked it in her hand. "Here, see for yourself."

Slyly, out the side of his eye he watched her open it gingerly and examine the thing. It was the newest invention of its kind, made of the substance rubber. She looked fascinated. Then she bit her lips together and cut her gaze towards him. "And it truly works?"

He shrugged. "So I'm told."

"I see. So you've never used it and cannot be certain," she said. It was not a question.

Prudence seemed called for. James was not about to enter into a discussion about former women in his life. She obviously believed there had been none. Assuring her that he had vast experience would hardly endear him to her at this point. "I've been told it is better than relying on herbs that might be dangerous to a woman's health."

"Ah," she said, nodding in agreement as she returned the apparatus to its wrapping and handed it back to him. "I suppose you should save this for after the child is born."

Drat his luck, she still believed she was increasing. Though he was beginning to feel more like tutor than husband, he really should set her straight. How appalling that women were told nothing practical before becoming wives. There was a cause she should take up. But for now, he would tend to the lessons.

"Suz, one coupling does not necessarily make a babe. Some people are wed for years before it happens. I understand that the first time is not as likely as those following to produce one."

She had gasped and covered her mouth with her hand and was looking at him with widened eyes.

"But you weren't entirely wrong. It might," he qualified with a shrug. "If your...uh, courses stop, then you probably are with child."

"That's what you meant when you said it was too soon for me to know?" She thought for a moment, then frowned. "Then it's quite possible I am not."

"That must be something of a relief to you," he commented, watching her reactions carefully.

She pressed a hand to her abdomen and looked at him. "No. No, it isn't, actually. I had sort of gotten used to the idea and quite looked forward to it. I even told Father. He was overjoyed, of course." For a while she said nothing, then suddenly asked, "Would you be, James? Would it make you happy?"

He had to nod. "Aye, but only if you were glad of it."

She reached for his hand and held it between hers. "I want children very much. I only fear to have them one after the other, year after year."

"I'll see you won't," he promised. "If I have to travel to France and write to you until you recover."

She laughed merrily, then turned shy again. "Must we wait until I have my courses to try again? I mean, if I am already with child, could it be hurt?"

James grinned with anticipation. "Not at all, I promise."

Suddenly she reached over, grasped his lapel and pulled him into a kiss so forceful he almost jerked away for fear he would hurt her. But then her soft tongue traced his lips and she made a sound of need so intense, he groaned in response. The kiss deepened further, his mind whirling in a maelstrom of desire. All thought of the gentle comfort he had intended blew away like leaves in a gale-force wind.

She urged him on with frantic hands, tugging at his neckcloth, pushing at his coat. He stripped off both, then kissed her again, hating every instant their mouths must part, their hands must deal with buttons, their bodies must writhe together hampered by so much cloth between them.

"Hurry," she whispered, yanking free the shirtwaist beneath her open jacket.

He buried his face between her breasts, tasting her skin, seeking her breasts, first one, then the other, while he tugged up skirt and petticoats and undid the flap of his trousers.

"Now!" she demanded and pulled him to her, surrounding him with her heat, enveloping him within her fervor and welcoming him into her with a cry.

"Ah, Suz." His breath rushed in on a wave of keenest pleasure, then exhaled on the words, "I love you." A brief spate of sheer contentment did nothing to foster control. She rose beneath him, seating him more deeply and he was lost to reason, to sensation and to any but the most primal need to mate.

The scent of her skin, hair, the feel of her fingers sliding frantically through his hair and along his neck, the rasp of her nails raking his shoulders drove him like velvet whips. Faster and faster they moved, racing toward a finish. He reached it with a burst of power matched only by her own. Her throaty cry of surprise mingled with his own groan of release and they tumbled together through a thousand silken ribbons of pleasure that tickled along his skin and made him shudder. She shivered, too, creating little aftershocks of ecstasy that seemed as endless as they were sweet.

James slid his arms beneath her and cradled her close as he rolled to one side. Sleep and exhaustion pulled insistently, but he fought it. Somehow he knew she would not yet be able to surrender to sleep and couldn't bear to leave her awake. She would feel alone then no matter how close he held her.

"I love you," he whispered again, unable not to.

Her lips moved, a soft kiss against his bare shoulder. "And I love you, James. I do."

"I wish you were happier about it. It won't be so bad," he assured her. "I'll not use it against you, Suz. Ever."

Her laugh was soft and a bit wry. "I was wrong to suspect you ever would." She heaved a long, weary sigh. "How puffed up with pride I've been, thinking I was so different from other women. But I'm not. There's no defense. I want nothing more than to please you, to do whatever you wish, so that you'll be happy. It is almost as if what I want counts for nothing to me."

"There's a conflict here?" he asked.

She shook her head and smiled. "Certainly not at the moment."

James kissed her long and thoroughly. He knew fully what her admission of love had cost her. He owed her no less, so he drew away and looked into her eyes. "You have defined it so clearly. That's what love is, lass. And it is exactly the same for me. 'Tis only when the love's one-sided that things go awry. If I always strive to see you happy and you always do the same for me, how can it be a sad thing? How can we ever be less than we were meant to be because we love one another?''

Her eyes brightened. ''I had not thought of it that way.'' She pushed up on one elbow to look down at him. ''But what if it doesn't last? What if it becomes unequal, *one-sided*, as you say? It is bound to do that. We shan't always agree, surely.''

He smiled up at her. ''Well, that's what keeps love interesting, I expect. I think the trick is to hold fast to our *wish* to keep it even as possible. No doubt that will take a bit of work on my part and on yours.''

She snuggled against him, nestling until they fit perfectly. ''But for now, we are measure for measure, you think?''

''Seems so to me. It feels grand.''

''Definitely *grand*,'' she quipped. ''You wish to please me right this moment, aye?'' she asked, a smile and that borrowed lilt in her voice. Her knee teased him unmercifully.

He laughed. ''Aye, 'tis obvious enough I do. More than anything.''

''More than I wish to please you? Oh dear, the love seems to be shifting to one side already.'' She moved over him in a sinuous glide filled with promise. ''I suppose 'tis time I went to work.''

''Ah, lass, yer nothin' if not dedicated.''

He loved a woman who embraced a cause with everything she had.

Epilogue

Edinburgh, December, 1859

Susanna grabbed the bottle of ink and set it aside before little Jamie could topple it. At two years old, he was dreadfully curious about everything, a trait he had inherited from her, she supposed. In looks and humor, he was James all over again. She bounced the boy on her knee to quiet his protest at having a potential plaything taken away.

"Shall I mind him until you've finished there?" his father asked, scooping the boy up and holding him high in the air. The giggles and squeals were enough to deafen the guests in the lobby. "Time for a lie down, m'lad. Your granda will be here in a few hours' time and we'll want you rested."

Susanna smiled as they left the sitting room of their suite in the Royal Arms. This was the first holiday they had taken since Jamie's birth, though they did have business in Edinburgh as well as pleasure.

James pretended tomorrow's exhibit of his sculptures at Monsieur Aubert's gallery meant no more than the annual sale of wool, but she knew better. His spirits were high and doing constant battle with the worry that no one would come to look or buy. She knew better than that, too, for his work was wonderful.

The only creation she thought better was the son he had fathered.

She paused in her writing to listen to his lullaby for Jamie. His voice rang deep and true, almost moving her to tears, though the words of the old tongue would always remain a mystery to her. He was the essence of their beloved Highlands, the rock upon which both Galioch and Drevers stood. He was *her* rock, her calmer of fears, her staunchest ally and the best of friends.

Both estates were profitable now, their wealth augmented nicely by the commissions James received for his "little people" as he called his sculptures. He steadfastly refused to explain the inspiration behind any of them. They were what they were, he declared. But hearts responded to what he did, no question about it.

When he returned, she put away her paper and pen and stoppered the ink. "There," she said, rising from the writing desk and moving into his outstretched arms. "That is enough for today."

He kissed her deeply and hugged her close. "You labor too hard, lass. I thought you'd rest from all that correspondence if I brought you on holiday."

"Not correspondence," she replied, nipping playfully at his lips, wondering if she should tell him what she had begun.

"Another speech?" he questioned, manfully attempting to sound cheerful about it.

She knew he feared the time when she might take her stand for the better treatment of women back to London.

So many had come to grief there of late over their out-spokenness. But her work was in Scotland now and tak-ing a different turn altogether. Women already *knew* that change was needed, so speaking to them did little good. The men were the ones who must be convinced. James shared her beliefs and gave her his full support. But he still worried for her safety.

"No more speeches," Susanna assured him. "I am writing a book now. A very thought-provoking, con-science-tweaking, persuasive thing that should set all the males who read it on their collective ear."

He tensed. "A book? About what, or should I ask?"

"How to be the perfect husband," she replied. "Yes, I think that would prove an excellent title for it. Everyone will read it, too. I can almost guarantee that."

James sighed and looked heavenward. "Ah, Suz, are you writing this under your own name?"

She brushed suggestively against his chest and smiled up at him, batting her eyelashes. "Of course not, darling. I'm writing it under *yours*."

Instead of the shocked protest she expected, James leered down at her. "If I'm to take the blame for this masterful bit of instruction, surely I can have a hand in the research."

Susanna shrugged and shot him a coy look, eager an-ticipation warming her heart and other parts considerably. "I suppose I *could* use a spectacular example for the ending if you have something unique in mind."

He scooped her up and headed for the bedroom. "Ah, lass, you're goin' to love my bein' coauthor," he de-clared, nuzzling the curve of her neck.

"Coauthor?" She drew back and glared with a mock frown. "Let's not get carried away there, *laddie*."

"Aye, let's do," he argued, grinning. "I've devilish fine input to offer and ye may do with it what ye will." A fair-minded man for all that, was her Scot.

* * * * *

Can't get enough of
our riveting Regencies
and evocative Victorians?
Then check out these enchanting
tales from Harlequin Historicals®

On sale May 2003

BEAUTY AND THE BARON by Deborah Hale

Will a former ugly duckling and an embittered
Waterloo war hero defy the odds in the name of love?

SCOUNDREL'S DAUGHTER by Margo Maguire

A feisty beauty encounters a ruggedly handsome
archaeologist who is intent on whisking her away
on the adventure of a lifetime!

On sale June 2003

THE NOTORIOUS MARRIAGE by Nicola Cornick
(sequel to LADY ALLERTON'S WAGER)

Eleanor Trevithick's hasty marriage to Kit Mostyn
is scandalous in itself. But then her husband
mysteriously disappears the next day....

SAVING SARAH by Gail Ranstrom

Can a jaded hero accused of treason and a
privileged lady hiding a dark secret save
each other—and discover everlasting love?

Visit us at www.eHarlequin.com

HARLEQUIN HISTORICALS®

HHMED30

eHARLEQUIN.com

Sit back, relax and enhance your romance with our great magazine reading!

- **Sex and Romance!** Like your romance *hot?* Then you'll *love* the sensual reading in this area.

- **Quizzes!** Curious about your lovestyle? His commitment to you? Get the answers here!

- **Romantic Guides and Features!** Unravel the mysteries of love with informative articles and advice!

- **Fun Games!** Play to your heart's content....

Plus...romantic recipes, top ten lists, Lovescopes...and more!

Enjoy our online magazine today— visit www.eHarlequin.com!

COMING NEXT MONTH FROM

HARLEQUIN HISTORICALS®

- **TEMPTING A TEXAN**
  by **Carolyn Davidson,** author of THE TEXAN
  When beautiful nanny Carlinda Donnelly suddenly shows up and
  tells the ambitious and wealthy Nicholas Garvey that he has custody
  of his five-year-old niece, he couldn't be more shocked. But before
  it's too late, will Nicholas realize that love and family are more
  important than financial success?

  HH #647 ISBN# 29247-3 $5.25 U.S./$6.25 CAN.

- **THE SILVER LORD**
  by **Miranda Jarrett,** book one in *The Lordly Claremonts* trilogy
  Behind a facade of propriety as a housekeeper, Fan Winslow leads
  an outlaw life as the leader of a notorious smuggling gang. Captain
  Lord George Claremont is an aristocratic navy hero who lives by his
  honor and loyalty to the king. Can love and passion join such dis-
  parate lovers?

  HH #648 ISBN# 29248 1 $5.25 U.S./$6.25 CAN.

- **THE ANGEL OF DEVIL'S CAMP**
  by **Lynna Banning,** author of THE COURTSHIP
  Southern belle Meggy Hampton goes to an Oregon logging camp
  to marry a man she has never met, but her future is turned upside
  down when her fiancé dies in an accident. Without enough money
  to travel home, Meggy has no choice but to stay in Devil's Camp,
  even if it means contending with Tom Randall—the stubborn and
  unwelcoming log camp boss who's too handsome for his own good!

  HH #649 ISBN# 29249-X $5.25 U.S./$6.25 CAN.

- **BRIDE OF THE TOWER**
  by **Sharon Schulze,** the latest in the *l'Eau Clair* series
  On his way to deliver a missive, Sir William Bowman is attacked by
  brigands. More warrior than woman, Lady Julianna d'Arcy rescues
  him and nurses him back to health. Julianna suspects the handsome
  knight may be allied with her enemy, but she can't deny the attrac-
  tion between them....

  HH #650 ISBN# 29250-3 $5.25 U.S./$6.25 CAN.

KEEP AN EYE OUT FOR ALL FOUR OF THESE TERRIFIC NEW TITLES

HHCNM0203

LYN STONE

A painter of historical events, Lyn decided to write about them. A canvas, however detailed, limits characters to only one moment in time. "If a picture's worth a thousand words, the other ninety thousand have to show up somewhere!"

An avid reader, she admits, "At thirteen, I fell in love with Brontë's Heathcliff and became Catherine. Next year, I fell for Rhett and became Scarlett. Then I fell for the hero I'd known most of my life and finally became myself."

After living for four years in Europe, Lyn and her husband, Allen, settled into a log house in north Alabama that is crammed to the rafters with antiques, artifacts and the stuff of future tales.